D1927844

New Beginnings

Johanna Nield

CRANTHORPE
MILLNER
PUBLISHERS

A CIP catalogue record for this title is available from the British Library.

ISBN 978-1-9164400-8-1 (Paperback)

www.cranthorpemillner.com

First Published (2019)

Cranthorpe Millner Publishers
18 Soho Square
London
W1D 3QL

About the Author

I began writing at the age of 10, purely for my own entertainment, and only began to share my stories when I discovered online fanfic communities about twenty years ago. Feedback gave me the courage to start sharing my own creations and in 2008 I began to write 'New Beginnings', sharing extracts online and utilising constructive criticism from fellow authors. The completed version underwent several subsequent changes thanks to input from family, friends and anonymous reviewers, until Kirsty-Ellen worked her editing magic and transformed it into the novel I always wanted it to be.

I am deeply indebted to everyone who cared enough to provide honest input into the development of 'New Beginnings', and to family and friends for their unswerving faith and support.

Friday 4 January

New Year, new blog!

I'm not sure who I'm writing this for, but Hayley said on Facebook that everyone's doing it so I thought I'd give it a go. Plus, given how things ended with Gavin, and seeing as I've actually made NY resolutions this year, it might be a good idea to give myself somewhere to record my feelings and then I can look back later and see how I'm doing.

I'll keep it private, I think. I just need somewhere to put down my thoughts and feelings without anyone reading them or trying to offer advice or anything like that. I need to just get things out of my head, and hopefully seeing my thoughts in black and white in front of me might make it easier to work out what I'm doing and where I'm going. I need to get on with my life, and hopefully this blog will help me work out some plans for the future.

I've finally written my letter to Gavin's mum and told her the truth about what happened, rather than Gavin's edited version of it. I only posted it on Monday so with the usual seasonal backlog and the Bank Holiday she probably hasn't got it yet, but I feel so much better about it all now - writing it all down was very cathartic. I think I can even forgive him now, too, which is new. Hopefully this means that I'm moving on.

I still fancy Jamie like mad. I know he's married and it's obvious he adores his wife and their little girl, but a girl can look, can't she? I wish I didn't find him so attractive - I get all flustered when he's around, and I know it's never going to go anywhere, so it's a complete waste of time - but he's just so bloody gorgeous. He came into work wearing a new red jumper yesterday and I couldn't take my eyes off him - had to take myself off to the kitchen to clear my head. Lisa said he'd had it for Xmas, and she said he had a lovely new aftershave on too but I didn't let myself get close enough to get a whiff ... might have lost control if I had.

Christmas and New Year seem to have flown by in a flash, even with the two weeks I had off. Coming back to work yesterday I felt like I hadn't been away! The Xmas party was good, but I was gutted that J wasn't there. I know he doesn't do those things, but I'd hoped he might have had a change of heart. He said yesterday that his little girl had been poorly on New Year's Eve so I don't suppose he got to do much then either, even at home. Darren snatched a kiss under the mistletoe; nice kisser, nice looker, but he's not J. [sigh] I wish this thing had emojis!

Work at the Home is going fine. The kids we've got at the moment are a rowdy bunch but they're no trouble really and we're all working really well together, especially now we have J for a manager. The only downside is that Vinnie now thinks he should be Deputy Manager and he's a bit grumpy that that's not happened, but I'm sure J and the Area Director will be doing something about that. Not sure I want V as DM, to be honest - he's too bossy as it is - but hey ho it's not for me to decide.

With it being Friday I worked the late shift today, so no drinks night for me tonight. I'm not that bothered, if I'm honest. All they do is talk about work stuff and I'm usually just sitting there wishing that J would join us. The fact that he's a devoted family man does nothing to distract me from lusting over him. I am a bad, bad woman.

I'm off to bed now. I bought a new duvet and cover at lunch time, and it's all soft and snuggly. I will NOT think about snuggling under there with J...

Wednesday 16 January

I've been resisting the urge to write about Jamie every day. Every time I've sat down to write something new here, the only thing that's come to mind has been some thought or 'news' of him, and I really need to not go there. But ... I've been booked on a training course on 31st January ... and J will be going too! He's offered to drive, and Lisa, Ben and I will go with him. It's a full day training course (9 - 4.30) so including the drive there and back I'll get nearly nine hours with him. Will I be able to concentrate??

Gavin's mum rang me on Sunday. She was lovely, and she said she'd suspected that G had been glossing over things. Bastard. We talked for ages, not just about him, and she said I sounded so much happier now. Bless her.

Hayley says I should be nice to Darren and go out with him. She doesn't know about my feelings for J. I think Lisa suspects, but she has no idea how bad it is.

Sunday 27 January

The Burns Night do at the Pig and Whistle on Friday was brilliant. We'd tried to persuade J to come, him being Scottish and all, but he said no. I was going to say 'declined graciously' because he did, as always, but how bloody besotted does that make me sound? I'm rolling my eyes at myself. We had a great time, though, and I've even discovered a liking for haggis!

I can't remember how it came up, but Ben said that J's family still live in Scotland, and his dad's got Alzheimer's. It made me think of Mum, and I got a bit tearful, and Ben was so sweet and apologetic, bless him. Why are all the nice ones unavailable? Or, as in Ben's case, gay!

Tuesday 29 January

Lucy rang from the airport while I was at work this morning, reminding me that all her hotel and excursion details are on that email she sent me last week. She sounded so excited, and I just wish I was going with her. Roll on August and the trip to New York :). We got a bit tearful when she was saying goodbye though - four weeks is a long time for her to be away on her own and even if she is older than me, I still worry about her travelling alone. I made her promise to ring me every time she changes hotel.

Saturday 2 February

OMG! Training day on Thursday was fantastic! The training was actually quite interesting as it covered legislation around cared-for children and not just the processes for what we can and can't do for them. I also learned a lot about the history of our children's home and it made me feel really proud of what we do, and what I've learned today can be included towards the Duty of Care module of my NVQ. But more importantly I got to talk with J outside of our normal work environment and it was lovely. Not just me, obviously - we were quite a big group and at lunchtime we all ate together - but there were a couple of times when it was just me and him talking and I didn't get all flustered like I normally do, so that's progress.

This is what I've learned about the very delicious Jamie MacDougall.

- He grew up near Glasgow and went to Glasgow Uni. That's where he met his wife.

- He was a Social Worker before he came to work for our charity. He started as a project co-ordinator and in three years worked his way up to manager.

- He was promoted to manager at our project last May, so he'd only been here for three months before I started. I thought it was longer.

- He likes music and dancing and cycling and low-budget films and reading (swoon).

- His favourite meal is chicken arrabiatta which he can make from scratch (another swoon).

- His middle name is Alasdair (swanky!) and he's 36 (37 in April but I don't know the date).

- He smells bloody lovely - Obsession for Men, I think (guuuuuh).

- He has absolutely no idea how gorgeous he is.

- He trained as a teacher (and he'd have made a brilliant one, I reckon), but he went into social work after volunteering in his last year at Uni. Their loss, our gain.

- He's very, very passionate about his work, and the work that we do at the Children's Home. I knew that already, but it really shone out during the training. He had us all really motivated and energised - it was fantastic.

- He worships his wife and daughter. He didn't give much away about them - never does - but it's obvious. I overheard him saying that his daughter has communication problems due to brain damage at birth, but he didn't mention her multiple physical disabilities.

All of these things - even the fact that he's a devoted family man, damn him - have made me fall for him even harder. I don't know what to do - I'm getting really obsessed. Lisa calls it a crush but it's much deeper than that - I absolutely adore and respect and idolise him. Yes, I lust after him too, but who wouldn't?

I need to find a boyfriend.

Sunday 10 February

I went out last night with Darren. He's been asking me for weeks, ever since the Xmas party, and I finally caved and we arranged to go to the pictures and then for a drink. The film was good and we had a lovely long chat afterwards and seem to have a lot in common but he doesn't push my buttons. We got into a fairly hefty snog at one point, which was nice, but I'm just not attracted to him in the way that I want to be attracted to him. I like him a lot, and I'm fairly sure that if I wasn't so hung up on Jamie then I'd probably fancy him quite a bit, but all I'm doing is comparing Darren to J and Darren just comes out lacking. He's asked me out to dinner on Thursday - Valentine's Day - and I've said yes so that I won't spend the day and night mooning over J. I really need to get over him before I fall any deeper.

Lucy rang from Las Vegas. She's having a whale of a time and I wish I was there :(

Friday 15 February

Well I've had 24 hours to think about it, and I'm still thinking... *SHIT!*

We went out to dinner, and Darren was lovely, very attentive and wouldn't let me even buy a drink. It felt a bit weird at first, it being only our second date, but he's so sweet that he didn't come across as overbearing or desperate or anything like that, just really genuine and nice. I ended up inviting him in and we had sex. He stayed the night and when he got up, he was all happy and excited, full of energy like a fucking puppy. SHIT. I shouldn't have slept with him. I guess it didn't occur to me how much he likes me.

While we were shagging, I was thinking of J and I had the most intense orgasm ever. I feel awful. I am a very, very bad woman :(

When we were having a coffee break this morning, Lisa asked J if he'd had a nice evening last night (he'd let slip that the wife was planning something) and he did that sweet little shy smile that he does and I felt so-very-jealous. It's ridiculous. He's been married for at least 12 years and he loves his wife. I've no right to be jealous.

Monday 18 February

7.50 p.m.

Lucy's in bloody San Francisco, having the time of her life, and I'm sitting here on my own, fantasising that I'm J's wife because it's her birthday and he left work early to make a special dinner for her. I should be at the gym, and I said I'd meet Darren afterwards, but I can't be bothered. I need to stop wishing my life away like this and get on with it but I'm so miserable and so bloody obsessed with this gorgeous, gorgeous man.

11.05 p.m.

Hayley talked me into going to meet Darren. She still doesn't know about J - she just thinks I'm feeling low - and I let her talk me into it. We had a few drinks and now he's in my bathroom and I daresay he'll stay the night again because I need to take my mind off HIM.

Wednesday 20 February

Oh god. Where do I start?

I don't even know how to say this. I don't know what to do.

Jamie's wife died. Helen is dead.

She was in an accident yesterday morning. She was hit by one of those big oil tanker truck things while driving their little girl to school. From what I can gather she was killed outright. The little girl, Beth, she's in hospital. I've heard she's not too badly hurt but things are complicated because of her disabilities. J has been there with her since it happened.

The police came to work yesterday morning. I was in the hall with Ben when they arrived but we didn't hear what they said. Then I heard J say, "No that can't be right…' He just kept saying, "No, no, no," his face white with disbelief, his eyes closed like if he didn't look at the police then it couldn't be true.

Ben and I cautiously approached them. J turned to me, his face a picture of anguish. "They said Helen is dead," he told us. "Helen can't be dead."

He went with the police to the hospital and as far as I know he's been there ever since. We all feel so useless, but we're doing what we can. No one's expecting him back at work for a long time. How do you ever return to normality after something like this? I can't even imagine it.

I want more than anything to go over to the hospital and keep him company, but I don't think it would be right. I want to be near him but it's not my place. I've heard he has a small family, just one brother and sister, and both his parents are still around. I hope they're with him. I hope he's not alone. When Mum died, I was surrounded by people and it really helped - I couldn't have coped without them, especially Lucy. I hope Jamie has that kind of support. I think tomorrow I'll talk to Ben and see if he thinks there's anything we can do to help.

The kids did something really sweet this afternoon - they all clubbed together and got a really lovely card for J. Lisa and I were crying when we read what they'd written in there. They may be unruly little sods and right little tearaways - that's why they're in residential care after all - but they've got big hearts, bless them.

Now I feel like crying again so I'm going to have a bath and go to bed.

Thursday 21 February

I can't stop thinking about J, all alone in that house, with everything ahead of him that still has to be organised. The funeral, the flowers, choosing the coffin, deciding on burial or cremation and what hymns to have. I could hardly face all that stuff when Mum died. How can he possibly be feeling? How can he make it through the day? And he has to be strong for his daughter.

I want more than anything in the world to be with him and to be able to help but it just feels inappropriate.

Friday 22 February

J phoned work today and I ended up talking to him. He said he was phoning for Ben, I think they're quite close actually, they've certainly known each other the longest, but Ben had just gone for lunch so I spoke to him. We've never spoken much about personal things before obviously but he just seemed so grateful to have someone to talk to. He told me it was easy to talk to me. He sounded surprised but...pleasantly so.

He talked a bit about his family and I get the impression they're very close. I'm glad he has someone.

The funeral will be next Wednesday at 11am at St. Jude's.

I've just realised that it's five months today that Mum died.

Sunday 24 February

I've been fantasising today about Jamie coming to me, asking me to help him through this whole thing, being the person who picks him up…and I can't decide how I should feel about that. Part of me just thinks, obviously it's because I'm a good person and I want to help a friend in need, but there's another part of me that thinks otherwise. I'm trying to push it down and ignore it but…is it possible I want to be the person to help him because I hope he'll fall for me if I do? That's awful isn't it. Does that make me a bad person?

Monday 25 February

Lucy rang last night from LA, just as I was going to bed. She'll be home sometime today I think (time zones do my head in) but I told her we can catch up when she's slept and got over the jet lag.

Jamie called into work this morning. It's the first time I've seen him since the accident, and goddam he was looking good. Oh god why am I thinking like that! He actually came to find me though and talked to me for a bit which was nice. I wasn't expecting it. He told me he's taken his little girl out of school and he's changing his hours. He said he'll be back at work next week though, which surprised me. I thought he'd need a lot longer.

'I need to keep busy,' he told me. 'It's too quiet at home. Everything makes me think of her. But here…' he trailed off then met my eye and I swear he blushed. Why would he blush? Then he sort of fumbled over a sentence about needing to go and nearly ran from the room. It was weird.

Went to the gym after work and had a bloody good work-out. Darren met me outside and we went for a drink but I really wasn't in the mood. He's got an early shift tomorrow so we didn't stay long. He came in for coffee but when he started kissing me, I told him I've got my period, and lo and behold he went home half an hour later. Why are single men bastards and married men not? Or... ugh, I'm being unfair. Is it just that I want what I can't have??

Tuesday 26 February

Lucy rang while I was at work this morning. She got back from the states last night and she's already desperate to go back. She asked if I'd started saving for the New York trip and I half-lied and said yes (there's £5 in the kitty) and she said she's going in August whether I come or not. Love you too, sis.

Wednesday 27 February

God what a day. Why can't these people just have a little compassion and keep their bloody mouths shut instead of lashing out and causing so much hurt? It was a funeral and still people only think about themselves.

Ben and I got to the church just after 10 this morning and we were one of the first people there. I could see J standing on the opposite side of the road, having a row with a woman I didn't recognise. He seemed very upset.

There was a small group of people gathered in the churchyard, so we approached them and they turned out to be J's family. We introduced ourselves and it turned out they knew who we were. J's sister, Elspeth, said J had talked about me a lot. I thought that was strange, what had I done to warrant him telling his family about me? Then I felt like they were all staring at me, waiting for me to say something, but I didn't know what.

Not long after, the woman J was rowing with came over into the churchyard and joined the group of family, and Ben and me. She just stopped and stared at me like I was a Martian or something. Elspeth introduced us, and I realised this was Muriel, Helen's mother. I said hello but she just looked daggers at me and said, "You might have waited until my daughter's in the ground before making a move!"

I was speechless. I tried to tell myself she was just grieving, that she didn't mean to be so hurtful, but something in the way Elspeth was awkwardly shifting her feet and avoiding the conversation, not to mention the shouting I had just heard between her and J, suggested otherwise. This woman truly believed I was moving in on her dead daughter's husband, and she was perfectly ready to accuse me of it at the funeral. What was I meant to say?

Then I remembered my fantasy of being his saviour and him falling for me through it all, and I felt sick. Was I trying to make a move on him? What on earth was I doing?

J came over shortly after Muriel, pushing his little girl in her pushchair. He hardly said a word to me. I tried to break the tension by saying hello to Beth but I seemed to just upset her. J told me she's not used to strangers, then bent down to her level and said, 'This is Tasha. Tasha is one of daddy's very good friends.' I suddenly felt my face flush hot, and I was aware everyone was staring at me again. Beth looked up at me and I focused on her instead and said hello again. This time, she smiled.

The church was packed, with people standing at the back. The service was lovely. Jamie got up and talked about Helen and their life together and how much they loved each other and Beth - he was emotional but he managed to keep it together and it was absolutely beautiful. It made me wish I had known her.

At the end, during the worst bit – where you have to shake everyone's hand and thank them for coming - Helen's mother said something awful about Jamie being all calm and cool, like he'd already got over Helen and was ready to move on. Helen's sister (Angela) told her off and tried to take her out of the way, but Muriel was having none of it. I decided to just get out of the way and went with Ben to the hotel for the reception. We were there before anyone else and were the only ones there when J and Beth arrived on their own. J apologised to me for what Muriel had said, making excuses for her having lost her daughter and being out of her mind with grief and all that. I just told him not to worry about it.

The reception was lovely, but I could tell it was hard on J. People kept coming over to him and telling him how much they thought of Helen, and sharing memories of her - he'd said that's what he wanted, during the service - and it was really sweet but I've no idea how he didn't break down because if people had done that about Mum at her funeral I would have lost it.

Elspeth rang me a little while ago, just as I was getting ready for bed. I guess she got my number off J, I don't know. It was weird though. She and her mum will be going home tomorrow so she wanted to say goodbye and to say thank you for helping out with J and stuff. But then she said, "He's really vulnerable at the moment and he could so easily get hurt." I told her I wouldn't hurt him for the world and she said, "Just be careful."

What should I make of that? She's clearly picked up on the fact I like J. Does she think I'm only helping him because I fancy him? Oh god, am I only helping him because I fancy him?

I bit the bullet and asked her why she was saying these things to me, had he said something? And she said he's not said anything in particular, but she could tell there's something there and he feels guilty about it. Oh my god!

Thursday 28 February

I called in on Jamie this afternoon, on my way to work. I told myself I was just being a friend; I was just checking in on a friend the day after his wife's funeral. I told myself I definitely wasn't doing it because I had dreamt about him all night and I couldn't think about anything but him.

We went through to the kitchen, and I could see he was in the middle of opening a pile of mail. He said it had been piling up for days, and most of it was cards. We were sitting down and talking about work as he opened another envelope and went all still. His freckles stand out really dark when he goes pale - I hadn't noticed that before today. I asked him if he was okay and he said, "It's an insurance claim," and it took me a minute to realise he meant life insurance. I was going to offer to help him fill the form in but he looked like he didn't want to face it just then so I didn't say anything. I asked if everyone had got off okay and he said Elspeth had taken Muriel and Angela to the airport and then she was driving home with their mum. He said he hadn't seen his brother, Dougal, since the reception after the funeral, but he'd probably be back in London by now. I get the impression there's a bit of friction between him and Dougal, but he didn't say anything about that. Dougal looks a lot like J and he's nice enough - a bit older than J, I think, and not as tall or as thin, and his hair's a bit lighter - but I don't think they have much in common.

I didn't stay long, I had to get to work. I didn't want to leave…

Lucy rang tonight - she said she's coming up tomorrow for a weekend visit. I've hardly had time to talk to her since she got back from the states, but tonight she asked me if I'm still lusting over J or if I've found a proper boyfriend and I just changed the subject. I'm really scared that I've fallen in love with him and I don't know whether to tell her or not.

Friday 29 February

Well, for a Friday it's been fairly quiet. None of the kids got sent home from school - a first! - and everyone turned up for their shifts (not so unusual, but it certainly made the day easier), and I got a lift home off Jamie :)

I was walking to the bus stop (car's in for its MOT, I'm picking it up in the morning) and he pulled up and offered me a lift. He said he had to pick Beth up from school on the way and asked if that was ok. I said of course it was, and off we went. I waited in the car while he went in for her, and when he came out he was looked deathly pale, and I know now that that means he's upset, so when he'd settled Beth into her seat and then got in behind the wheel I asked him if everything's okay. He just nodded and started driving, but he seemed really off with me, like he didn't want to look at me. I didn't know what to do so I turned around and said hello to Beth. She seemed really pleased to see me! She said my name and everything. J looked really surprised. "She never remembers people like that," he told me. "She seems really comfortable with you."

After he dropped me off, I picked up some stuff for dinner and made spag bol because it's Lucy's favourite. She'll be here in an hour or so, if the traffic is okay. Still don't know what to tell her about J. I mean, big sisters are there to listen and advise, aren't they? She's always been good at that, and I know I can trust her to not say anything to anyone if I ask her not to, but ... I don't know what I'm scared of. I don't know what she's going to say, but I don't want her telling me to step back because I know I can't do that. I don't think I can, anyway.

God I'm in a mess.

Sunday 2 March

Fuck fuck fuckity fuck fuck. I am such an idiot and I don't know if I can face him tomorrow. He's said we're fine, but are we? Oh god I don't know. And Lucy's not rung me so I don't know if she's talking to me or not.

I ended up telling Lucy everything about J - she has that big sister knack of getting stuff out of me even when I'm fairly sure that I don't want to tell her. She said straight off that I should stop and think about what I'm doing. She said the fact that he was married had made him off limits to start with, and I should have just stopped mooning over him (her stupid words) as soon as I found out he was married, but now he's widowed he's even more off limits because it would be taking advantage in the worst possible way. I told her I wouldn't do that and I've no intention of making a move on him but she just said, "If you had the chance to kiss him, would you?" and she just knew I couldn't say 'No' to that and she got into an almighty huff about being on dangerous ground and I'd end up hurting him and myself. I'm beginning to wonder if there's something she's not telling me.

Anyway, she was only here for Friday night because she had a party to go to last night, but we spent half the day together yesterday and she came with me to pick my car up from the garage, and she left after our late lunch at Cafe Nero. We got into a bit of a row, though - she's insisting I either tell J how I feel about him so he knows what he's getting into, or I just take a massive step back and stay away from him altogether - but I can't do either. No way am I going to tell him that I've fancied him all along - what the hell will he think of me? So Lucy ended up leaving in a huff and saying she doesn't want to hear about it when it all blows up in my face, and that left me on a real downer. I couldn't ring her while she was driving, and then her phone was off last night and isn't back on yet. I've left her a message on voicemail though, so hopefully she'll get back to me tonight.

After Lucy left, J called me. I mean, on my mobile (!). He didn't talk for a while, he said he didn't know why he was calling. He didn't sound ok, so after we got off the 'phone I went to his to check on him.

He had visitors when I got there, but they were on the point of leaving so J invited me in and introduced us. When they'd gone, he told me that they were old friends from Uni and they'd heard about Helen and had come to see J because they'd lost touch years ago. I suppose they just wanted to give him their condolences in person. He said it was nice to see them, but it had been a bit awkward because they hadn't been in touch with each other for years and he quickly realised that they had little in common now, and neither of them knew about Beth and he hates when people get uncomfortable around her, so he said I'd arrived just at the right time because it gave them all a good excuse for them to leave.

I could tell straight away he wasn't ok, so for some reason I offered to cook him dinner, thinking maybe he needed help after a long day entertaining people. He said ok. Now I think about it, he said, "Um, yeah, ok, if you're sure" which wasn't very enthusiastic. If only I'd been sharp enough to pick up on it - he was probably only agreeing to be polite.

After he had put Beth to bed (she seemed really happy to see me again. I'm really starting to adore this little girl. I know some people feel uncomfortable around her, but she's so kind-hearted and gentle and sweet. My heart breaks for her. Imagine growing up without your mum), I made him some tea and we ate it together. Then he asked if I wanted a drink and I (stupidly!) asked for a glass of wine. He said he had a bottle leftover from when his mum and sister were staying, and he went to get it. Before we knew it – the bottle was empty.

He told me he wanted to explain what had upset him yesterday when he picked Beth up from school. I said there was no need but he was adamant.

It's Mother's Day today, and the kids had made their own cards in school. Obviously Beth hadn't been discouraged from joining in, so she'd been waving her card at J when he arrived to pick her up. What had upset him, was that she'd signed it herself and this is the first time she's managed to do that on her own, and he said Helen would have been so proud and delighted because she'd spent such a long time with Beth teaching her how to do it, and now she'd finally mastered it but Helen would never know.

"Then, I guess I was thinking about how Helen's gone and she'll never experience these things, she'll never experience so many things, and that just made me feel even more guilty..."

"Guilty?" I said, putting my glass down. "What do you mean?"

He just turned and stared at me. "Surely you know what I mean?"

My head was racing! My throat went dry, my hands started to shake. What was happening??

He continued, "I've been asking you to help, I've been calling and making up reasons to talk to you, I'm a bad person, I can't believe she's barely gone and..." then he put his face in his hands and started to cry.

I didn't know what to do, I just put a hand on his shoulder, shifting closer to him to do so, then he looked up and... oh, I don't know. Did I kiss him or did he kiss me? I have no idea but suddenly we were kissing. Then he pulled back a bit and murmured, "*Helen...*"

Then he really broke down. He just cried and cried and cried. To be honest I think he probably hasn't cried enough since Helen died and he's got a lot to get out of his system, so I just put my arms round his shoulders and let him cry. We sat there like that for ages before I realized he'd cried himself to sleep – god knows I know how that feels – so I stayed where I was rather than disturb him and eventually I dozed off as well. It was about 3 o'clock when we both woke up - I hope to God I wasn't snoring, cos I don't know what woke us - and it was so awkward. He didn't know where to look, I didn't know where to look, and we were still both apologising, so I told him to go to bed and I'd go home.

He nodded like it was a really good idea, and said thanks for the dinner, and then he went upstairs so I let myself out and drove home. It took me ages to get to sleep because I couldn't stop thinking about that kiss, and his face when he realised what we were doing. What the hell was I thinking?? I'm fairly sure I didn't plan on kissing him. God he's a good kisser - I'm getting horny just thinking about it. The thing is that I enjoyed it, but he was absolutely mortified and so upset that it breaks my heart to think of it. Talk about being torn in two - half of me gets turned on just thinking about that kiss, while the other half is hurting for him because of it.

So I finally got to sleep sometime after 5 this morning and slept in until 11. I tried ringing Lucy, I even tried ringing Darren, though I don't know why because I keep blowing him off so I can't imagine he's talking to me, but both their phones were off. I was going to ring Ben but couldn't think of a decent way of telling him what had happened, so I'll leave that until I see him at work tomorrow. I went out for a walk after lunch and ended up in the park, sitting on Mum's bench and having a bloody good cry. I just kept thinking that I've caused J so much pain - and I realised that Lucy was right, and I need to get away from the situation before I make it worse. And then when I got home there was a message on my answering machine and a missed call on my mobile and they were both from J.

I was in two minds about ringing him back but I was too scared, so I waited and, in the end,, he rang this evening, just after he'd put Beth to bed, and I really wish he hadn't because I think I love him more than ever now. He's got no idea what he's doing to me, and I'm too scared to tell him.

He said he'd rung his sister this morning and told her about last night. OMG! I could have died when he said that, and I think he could tell that I was shocked because he said he hoped I didn't mind but he knows he can rely on Elspeth to make him think straight. I just said okay. He said he was sorry, and I did too, and then he said he hopes it won't spoil our friendship because he really appreciates everything I've done, especially with Beth, and he said he honestly doesn't think he could cope without me and Ben chipping in. And he asked me if we're okay and I could have cried, because it's totally not his fault - it's mine - and I said, "I am if you are" and he said "Oh that's so good to know" and he thanked me and I don't think I could feel any guiltier than if I'd stuck a knife through his heart and killed him.

So I guess we're fine and we'll just forget about last night and carry on as we were, just friends. I really am okay with that, even though in a perfect world I'd want much more. Then he asked me if I'd been okay today, with it being Mother's Day, and I told him I'd been up to the park for a bit of a wallow, and he said he'd have to try that. He said he'd taken Beth to Helen's grave to put some flowers there, and Beth had been quiet afterwards, so he's wondering if she's beginning to understand what's happened. I said we'll just have to keep taking tiny steps, and he said that's what Elspeth had said.

He'll be back at work tomorrow, and I'll have to face him and try not to think about that kiss and the fallout from it. I need to focus on the hurt it caused him, rather than the yumminess of it. Why, oh why couldn't he be a shite kisser?!

Tuesday 4 March

Lucy rang me late on Sunday night and she was fine. She said she's worried about what I'm getting into, and just doesn't want me to get hurt, but of course she'll always be there for me. She'd had a great time at the party and had ended up staying over and going home at tea time, which was why she didn't answer her phone. I haven't told her about the kiss.

I finally got hold of Darren on Sunday night too. He was a bit off with me, which I guess is fair enough. He asks me out all the time and I just never make the time for him. I had a really long talk with him and told him I like him and I like going out with him but I'm just not ready for a relationship yet. He said he's not either, but he just wants to know where he stands so I said that's up to him but I'm not doing the boyfriend/girlfriend thing. He said we should just see where it goes, and I said okay. He met me from the gym last night and we went for a few drinks, and it was nice. He's really sweet. He deserves someone much nicer than me.

Spoke to Ben yesterday at work. We were in the laundry room and I just came right out and told him what had happened on Saturday. He said he'd gone round there with his boyfriend, Adam, on Sunday evening and Adam had said afterwards that he thought Jamie had said something odd about me but couldn't quite remember what it was. I wanted to know what it was, and B said he'd ask but he didn't think it was anything to worry about. He was really concerned for both of us and asked me what happened after the kiss so I told him it all, even about me fancying J, right up to Jamie's phone call on Sunday night, and I said I was going to start looking for another job so that I could get away. He just shook his head, pulled me into a hug, and said, "Don't rush into things." I said I don't want to risk doing something stupid again and he said, "You won't, it's not like you're in love with him," and I just went red and he said, "Oh dear," and rubbed my back in that lovely way that he does.

And then, of course, it was only a few minutes after that that I saw Jamie coming out of his office, and we both smiled awkwardly at first but then he just slipped into manager mode and started talking about the inspections due next week and we were fine. I'm struggling more than ever to not get flustered when he talks to me at work. When we're in his house I'm relaxed and able to talk with him about anything as if it's the most natural thing in the world. Which it is, because we're friends. So why does it feel different when we're at work, and I come over like a stupid besotted teenager with a crush?

I haven't been to Jamie's since Saturday. When I was leaving work this afternoon, I told J to ring if he wanted help with anything, and he just said thanks and let it go. So now I'm thinking that I've scared him off and he won't want me going round there anymore, and if that's true then I really will move away because otherwise it will break my heart.

Friday 7 March

That man is going to be the undoing of me.

This morning, J made a speech to everyone, apologising for being so stressed and unavailable. We all told him not to worry – we're all here to help him. Afterwards, Ben and I spoke to J to reiterate that, and J said if he wasn't so frazzled about the home side of things he probably wouldn't fret about work at all, so Ben asked him what he meant and J said it's all the household things that need doing, and fitting in with Beth's school schedule (it was easier for Helen, she worked there and her hours were the same as Beth's - he didn't say that, I'm just thinking it), and paperwork and bills and stuff - all the normal things they did together or between them that he now has to get done on his own. So Ben said (again) let us help him and J said he couldn't see how we could, so I said, just for an example, that it would be easy for me - or Ben - to pick up J's groceries while we're at the supermarket if that would help, and we could both help with any paperwork that needed looking at, especially since I'd already offered to do that last week. He was damn near blushing with gratitude - it's as if he feels a burden for even needing the help, let alone asking for it - and Ben had to tell him that we both really do want to help.

Some other people came in at that point so we changed the subject, but Ben talked with Jamie again later and arranged to do the supermarket run with him over the weekend. It never occurred to me before, but it must be quite difficult for him to do that with Beth as she's a bit too big to sit in the trolleys, so he'd need someone to push her pushchair or look after her while he does the shopping. No wonder he's so grateful for the odd pint of milk and the like! When he was leaving work this afternoon, I made him tell me what he was short of as I was going home via the Co-op and could easily drop off some bits and pieces for him, and he asked me to get tea, sugar, milk and bread so God knows what state his cupboards are in. I dropped them off when he was giving Beth her tea, but I wouldn't let him pay for the grapes and bananas I'd bought - I said they're a treat for Beth, so he was okay with that. He said he's going to take Beth to the park tomorrow and asked if I'd like to go with them. There's no way I could say no to that man, even if I wanted to, so I said I'd go to his house and we could walk from there.

Lucy asked me tonight how things are going. I didn't tell her much - said it's all okay - but I asked her if she'd ever been out with a married man, and she told me then that Max had been married with three children! I was shocked, and a bit hurt that she'd felt unable to confide in me about it at the time but she explained that Max was terrified of anyone finding out (well he would be, wouldn't he?) so she couldn't tell anyone, not even me. She said she'd tried to end it when she found out he was married, but Max persisted and ... well it all ended in tears, didn't it? I knew they'd broken up quite badly, but now she tells me his wife divorced him and moved away so he only sees his kids once a month, and she'll never stop feeling guilty about that. So now I understand where she was coming from last weekend, but that's not going to happen with me and Jamie, is it? It's a totally different situation, there's no wife to divorce him. And I can't believe I'm even thinking like that, after all that's happened.

Saturday 8 March

Our walk in the park this afternoon was lovely. We went to the swings first and Beth had a whale of a time, then we went to feed the ducks - I'd brought some crusts and a couple of stale slices - and she absolutely loved that. She fell asleep in her pushchair while we were walking round the gardens, and while we were there, I showed J my mum's bench. He got a bit choked and said it was a lovely idea, and he asked me if that's where I'd gone for my wallow last Sunday, and I told him I often go there to sit and think and stuff, and he said it's good to have somewhere like that. He said he goes off on his bike when he needs to think, and then he changed that to "I used to" and I thought well that was when Helen was alive, but now of course he can't leave Beth on her own, so what does he do now? So I said if ever he wants a sitter for Beth, I'd be very happy to do that, and he did that shy little smile that makes my heart stop. God, if only he knew the effect he has on me.

We were on our way back to the house when Beth woke up and she was quite agitated, pulling at her hair, so Jamie picked her up out of the pushchair and carried her the rest of the way home. There's nothing of him, he's so thin, so I don't know where he gets the strength. Beth's tiny for her age but it still can't be easy to carry her for very long. I suppose he's used to it, though. I stayed until he'd put her to bed, then got the hell out of there before either of us got any more nervous about a repeat performance happening. Well, to be honest, I don't think he'd even given it a second thought but I was very, very aware of what happened this time last week. I'm ashamed to say, knowing how much it hurt him did nothing to stop me fantasizing about it.

Sunday 9 March

I ended up going out with Darren last night for a couple of drinks. He asked me what I'm doing for my birthday and I said I hadn't thought about it, so he asked me out to dinner. I told him that Lucy might be coming up - it's not an out and out lie, because she has done that before and might decide to come at the last minute – and I said I'd let him know on the day, and he seemed okay with that. He's been very good at not pushing the dating thing, and I decided in the end not to bring him back to mine for the night. I don't want to give him the wrong idea and I'm not sure if I can broach the subject of fuck-buddies with him, more's the pity. The thing is that I fancy him enough to shag him, but I don't want to be with him in a relationship. And, since I really need to be honest with myself, if we were to shag again I just know that I'd be thinking of Jamie while we're at it and whilst it gave me a fantastic orgasm last time I don't think I can live with the guilt for using Darren in that way, it's just not fair to him.

J called earlier and took me up on my offer to look after Beth. He rang me around 2ish and asked if I was busy and I said I wasn't but let's face it, I'd have said that even if I was, and he asked if I'd mind sitting with Beth for half an hour while he went out to clear his head. He said he took her to the supermarket earlier, I think Ben went with them, and Beth really hadn't been happy at all, just like the other day. He's really worried about her and says he's going to take her to see her specialist during the week. Anyway, I went straight over, and he was all apologetic and I had to tell him off for that. He looked really knackered and frazzled, and I said he's not doing himself or Beth any favours by trying to do everything on his own all the time. That seemed to strike home.

I got Beth busy with glue and glitter – she really does seem so comfortable with me, it really warms my heart - and told him to take his time, and he went out. He was only gone about twenty minutes and I told him he could have stayed out longer. When he saw how happy Beth was, I think he relaxed. Maybe next time he will take more time for himself. Beth showed him the picture she'd made and he got glue and glitter all over his hands when he took it from her to look at it, and she just laughed and laughed like she'd heard the world's funniest joke, setting us both off.

I went home after that, but I said if he wants a hand with the paperwork, I'd come round one evening after work. Ben's good with bills and things, but J has a lot of stuff to do with Helen that needs sorting out, and Ben's as clueless as J about that sort of thing. Lucy and I sorted all the official paperwork after Mum died, so I at least know something about it.

I'm meeting Hayley in a bit - we're going to the cinema and maybe grab a takeaway on the way home.

Wednesday 12 March

Happy Birthday to me, Happy Birthday to me, Happy Birthday, dear Tasha, Happy Birthday to me :)

I've had some lovely cards from the guys at work (including J), some perfume (Lacoste) from Darren, a huge bouquet from Ben and Adam, a gorgeous card and a CD from Lucy, another CD from Hayley, and a big box of Roses from Lisa. Jamie's card is one of those hand-made ones they sell in the craft shop, with a cute little fairy sitting on a big box/present on the front, and inside he's written 'Happy Birthday and thank you, from Jamie and Beth x' and he'd posted it to my flat so I got it first thing this morning. It's ridiculous how over the moon I am about it, but I don't care.

We sorted through his mountain of paperwork last night. He'd asked me to pick Beth up from school because he was going to be late which I thought was pretty huge. He must really trust me. Beth was a bit puzzled to see me but she didn't say anything, but then when the teacher and I got her into her car seat she started saying, "Dada" so I told her we'd go home and draw some pictures and her daddy would be home soon, and she seemed fine with that. The teacher said she'd been pulling at her hair again, so I mentioned that to J when I rang him to tell him we were at his house. He's already made an appointment for her on Friday so hopefully they'll get to the bottom of that.

He got home not long afterwards and he insisted I stay for tea, and after Beth had gone to bed, I said we might as well get started on the papers while I was there. I remember how much there is to do from after Mum died, so he knew I was happy to help, and he seemed really grateful. It's a lot to take on for one person on their own. At least I had Lucy.

Jamie's sister rang while I was there. I popped up to the loo to give him some privacy but when I came back downstairs, he was still on the phone, and it sounded a bit serious so I went into the kitchen and made us some tea. I stayed in there to drink mine and by the time he came in his tea had gone cold so I made him a fresh one. He said their dad has finally been diagnosed with Alzheimer's, which they've suspected for some time, and their mum isn't taking it very well. Elspeth is worried that their mum can't cope with their dad for much longer, and that they'll have to start looking at nursing homes for him.

Jamie looked really upset, and what the hell do you say to something like that? "Sorry" just doesn't mean enough, especially not with what he's already going through. I told him about Aunty Emma and the home she was in, so at least he knows that there are some good ones out there, although I suppose it'll be down to Elspeth to find one near where they live. He said he felt he should go up there when the time comes, because he doesn't want Elspeth to carry the responsibility on her own and he's pretty sure that Dougal won't want to know anything about it. I just nodded - didn't know what to say. We'd pretty much finished with the paperwork by then, and J said he'd clear what was left, so I came home.

Lucy had phoned while I was out, so I rang her back and we had a lovely long chat. She said she'd planned to come up for my birthday but her boss has volunteered her for something at work that she can't get out of, and I know how hard she's working towards that promotion. She asked me what I had planned, and she sounded surprised when I mentioned that Darren had invited me to dinner and I said I'd probably go. She asked me if he knows how I feel about Jamie, and when I said I didn't know she said maybe he should, but she didn't push it. She asked how J was getting on and I told her about the paperwork and she was really concerned about it bringing back memories for me, but I said it was okay. She said she found that part more difficult than the funeral, and I know what she means. Anyway, we talked for a bit about the New York trip - she's already got an itinerary worked out and is researching hotels - and then I went to bed.

Today was lovely - fab cards and pressies this morning, and Lisa put candles on my carrot cake at lunch time - and then this evening I went out to dinner with Darren. He even picked me up, which made a nice change, and we went to the new Italian place on Kendal Street and we had a really nice time. The food there is so good, I didn't want to stop eating! I'd said this morning that I'd only go if he let me pay for myself but he sneaked off to pay the bill when he went to the loo and wouldn't take any money off me, said he'd be hurt if I kept insisting. Stubborn sod.

When we were leaving, he asked if I wanted to go back to his place or mine, and I said his to keep myself on my toes, and he made fresh coffee with one of those expensive Italian machines and it was really good. I could see where things were going and part of me really wanted to, but then I remembered what Lucy had said and I sat him down for a talk. I asked him to promise not to say anything at work (and he said, "What, again?") and then I told him that I really like him and fancy him, but I also fancy someone else and I'm finding it all very confusing and a bit awkward. He knew straight away that it was Jamie, said he'd thought as much for a while, and then he asked me what I wanted to do. So I just told him everything that I've been thinking about, the whole thing - I think I love Jamie, I really, really fancy him, but I know there's no way that anything is going to happen for a very long time, if ever. I knew when Helen was alive that he wouldn't have even thought of me in any way other than a work colleague, and I've no reason to think that we'll ever be more than friends. Talk about a hopeless case.

I kind of talked myself into admitting that I know I'll never get anywhere with Jamie, and then Darren was so sweet and understanding and he said I should live with what is, not what might never be, and we ended up snogging and things just went from there and it was nice. I didn't think about J at all. Actually, I haven't thought about him at all until just now when I started writing this and now I'm crying. If I'd stayed the night at Darren's I wouldn't be sitting here writing this and maybe I'd have been able to finally get myself out of this emotional mess, but no I had to come home, didn't I? I'm so stupid. Is this what they call self-sabotaging?

Maybe the answer is to stop writing this blog, stop dwelling on it and just get on with it. I'm thinking far too much about it all when I write, and even though my feelings for Jamie haven't changed - and might have even got stronger - when I'm actually with him I'm just thinking about what I'm doing to help him and Beth, and not about how much I want to kiss/snog/shag him (well, not all the time, anyway) whereas when I'm not with him my imagination goes into overdrive and it all comes out on these stupid pages.

So, yeah. No more blog.

Saturday 15 March

Seems I can't stay away from this thing!

It's just that there's so much going on and I can't talk with anyone about most of it, and at least when I write on here it makes me think clearly … most of the time … or at least sometimes.

The big news is that Ben and Adam are getting married! Ben told us all at work yesterday, and I'm so chuffed for both of them. They've set a date - 12th September - and it will be at the registry office with the reception at Dawlish Grange, that swanky country house hotel on the road out towards the airport. He said it will be quite a small wedding, family and friends only, but I hope that means we'll get to go the reception. Me and the girls have already decided that we'll go to the registry office and wait outside to take photos 😊

Also yesterday, during afternoon tea break, Jamie asked Lisa, Bridget and me if we knew anything about children's parties. Bridget said, "They're hell on earth" and me and Lisa just said we'd been to a few and asked why. Turns out it's Beth's birthday on Thursday, and Helen had been talking about giving her a party. Jamie had mentioned it to some of the parents at school and they'd said their kids would love to go if she had one, but then he's realised he doesn't know the first thing about organising a child's birthday party - Helen always did that kind of thing. We said that McDonalds and the play centres usually host birthday parties at a price, and he said he was thinking more of a 'proper' party at home, next Saturday. So I said that's much easier and I said I'd give him a hand. It's just cake and jelly and ice cream, and some games - easy peasy. I must be mad.

So today I took them to the supermarket and we had a look at all the party stuff to get some ideas. Beth likes pink, so that part's easy, and we bought paper plates and cups, a load of pretty girly bunting and stuff, party hats and the squeaky whistle things with the feathers on the end. I told J that on Monday he needs to find out how many of Beth's school friends will be coming, and if at all possible, get their names too, and then we can write invitations on Monday night so he can hand them out on Tuesday. Hopefully it won't be too short notice.

Jamie got extra house keys cut while we were out - one for me, and one for Ben. He said it gives him peace of mind to know we could get in, if there was an emergency.

J left work early yesterday to take Beth to see her specialist. He's worried about the hair-pulling habit she's started and he wants to have her checked over to make sure there's nothing physical bothering her. Apparently, her teacher reckons it's Beth's way of grieving and J understands that, but he wants to be sure she's physically okay while they start tackling the emotional side of things. He said this morning that the specialist was quite sure it's Beth's way of externalising her confusion over Helen's disappearance - it's quite common, apparently - but if it continues to be a worry then he'll run some extra tests.

I haven't seen Darren since Thursday - he's gone to Birmingham for a long weekend with his brothers, to see some exhibition at the NEC. He was a bit off with me at work, though - sulking a bit because I wouldn't stay the night on Wednesday, I suppose. Lisa asked me if he was okay and I'm sure she knows exactly what's going on, even though I haven't told her anything - she looks at me like she just knows, and I'd love to talk to her about it all but I don't want to put her in an awkward position. I've already told Darren too much, and it would only take a slip of the tongue to cause all sorts of embarrassment. I'm fairly sure I can trust him, but I wish I hadn't told him quite so much.

Hayley's coming round in a bit - she's bringing DVDs and I'm cooking lasagne - such is the exciting Saturday night prospect for two single women in the 21st century. Whoop-di-woo.

Thursday 20 March

Just got back from Jamie's house. I went round there after work to take Beth her card and present and some gifts from the guys at work. Beth was delighted with everything and Jamie was pleased to bits for her. He said he's had eight RSVPs about the party, and I said we'll cater for more in case others have just forgotten to confirm. We're doing all the food tomorrow afternoon but Ben's picking up the cake on Saturday morning - there's no way I was going to ruin the day by attempting to make a birthday cake! He went a bit quiet when I mentioned the cake this evening. I bet Helen was brilliant at that sort of thing :(

Lucy rang me just now - she's going away for the weekend with Will, the guy from work that she's been seeing since before Christmas. They're renting a cottage in Wales somewhere, and she said she'll try and ring when they get there but Will doesn't think there'll be much of a signal. I told her to find a phone box if that's the case and she said okay, if she can remember how to use one. It's funny how, since Mum died, we're both paranoid about knowing each other's travelling arrangements, as if that could possibly make any difference if something were to happen. I hope the weather picks up for her, cos it's bloody cold here. Mind you, stuck in a cosy cottage miles from nowhere … no, I will not go there.

Sunday 23 March, 12.35 p.m.

I've just got home from Jamie's house, but I'm worried about him and wondering if I should have stayed.

He got hammered last night and I ended up staying over, sleeping in the spare room. He's okay now but he was rough this morning and so very apologetic that I almost lost my rag with him.

We had a fantastic day yesterday. Beth loved her party, she had a whale of a time and her little friends were so sweet and funny, and their mums (and one dad) were really nice to talk to, and some of them were drinking wine so there was a little adult party vibe going on too, and it was lovely to see Jamie being 'Daddy of the Birthday Girl' and mingling with the other parents. I know he's not the shy and retiring type, but I've never really seen him with people outside work and it was great to see him playing host and just being a normal parent. He took loads of photos and some video, and he and Beth didn't stop smiling the whole afternoon except when everyone was singing 'Happy Birthday' - then I noticed that he looked really sad, and I assume he was thinking of Helen.

When everyone had gone, he opened another bottle of wine and poured me a glass and toasted me to say thank you, and then we started clearing up. We were on our second glass when Beth started pulling at her hair again - she'd only done it once all day - so I suggested he take her up for an early bath to distract her, and I carried on cleaning. He was up there for ages, and when he came back down to the kitchen, he said he'd read to her and she kept asking for her mum while he was reading. He's been trying to read her books that explain loss but he's not sure what she understands and what she doesn't. And then he started crying, so what could I do? I just pulled him into a hug and let him cry. He said he's just so desperately sad, and he misses Helen, and he hates that she won't see Beth growing up, and it's cutting him up inside to think how much Beth must be missing her mummy and that she might never fully understand where she's gone.

By this time he was on another glass of wine, and I started to wonder how many he'd had through the afternoon because he was getting drunk quite quickly, but then I suppose if you don't drink very often it will have that kind of effect. I tried to slow him down but he said he just wanted to forget, just for a little while, and I felt so sorry for him that I let him carry on and he ended up very, very drunk. He went all quiet, and then he said he was going to the loo, but he didn't come back. I waited for about half an hour - it was nearly 10 by then - then I went upstairs and saw that he'd gone to bed.

I didn't know what to do at first. I thought about coming home, but then I thought about Beth needing her daddy in the night, and would he hear her or be capable of getting up to go to her? So I went back down and locked up, wrote him a note to say I'd be staying in the spare room (because I didn't want to surprise him in the morning), and then I went to bed. It took me forever to fall asleep, and I feel like I barely slept at all to be honest.

This morning we both woke up at the same time because Beth was calling him. I met him on the landing and he was wearing pyjama pants and a Fratellis t-shirt and, oh - my - god, I had to look anywhere but at him for a bit, just to keep myself from wanting to jump his bones. He just looked at me, all confused and embarrassed, and I said I'd stayed the night, just in case, and he went redder than the carpet. I helped him get Beth dressed and made him sit with her at the table while I made breakfast, by which time he'd gone really white and looked like hell. I made him drink a few glasses of water and gave him some painkillers, but when Beth started eating her cereal he flew upstairs and I heard him throwing up.

I told him to go back to bed for a bit but he wouldn't have it. He came back down and tried to drink some more water but he couldn't keep anything down, and I lost count of how many times he was sick. He kept saying how sorry he was for putting me in this position. I'd already said earlier that I don't mind but he kept saying sorry and in the end I lost my temper with him a bit. I told him I was going to take Beth to the park, and I asked him to drink some more water and go back to bed, and he did. I honestly didn't think he would, so he must have been feeling awful.

There were loads of people at the park, even that early on a Sunday morning - I'd forgotten it was Easter - and Beth loved watching the other kids running around, and the people out walking their dogs, and we stopped for a while to watch some lads flying kites on the top of the hill. It was cold, though, so I took her to the cafe by the duck pond and we shared a mug of hot chocolate before feeding the ducks, and then we headed back to her house.

Jamie was still in bed when we got back and it was then that I realised how very difficult it is for him, being on his own with Beth - I was busting for the loo but was too scared to leave her on her own while I went to the bathroom. I'm still not sure what she can and can't do, but I wasn't going to risk leaving her for a couple of minutes in case she had an accident of some kind. I was trying to remember if Jamie had ever said what he does - leave her playing on her own, or strap her in her buggy, or take her with him? Anyway it got to the point where I was going to have an accident of my own, so I made a game of it for Beth and said, "Let's find Daddy" and after looking around the lounge for a bit I took her through the hall and helped her up the stairs, and then she seemed to know exactly where to find him and was laughing and went into his bedroom.

It's a lovely room, all cream and beige and red (same red as the hall/stairs carpet), and the bed is massive, at least a king-size, and we could just see his hair peeping out from the top of the duvet. Beth slapped at the duvet, still laughing and calling him, and he kind of darted out from under it, as if he'd had an electric shock. I was still at the door - didn't seem right, going in there - and I said we're playing hide and seek, and I really need the loo, and he nodded and lifted Beth into the bed with him. I could still hear her laughing from the bathroom.

By the time I'd finished he was coming out onto the landing, carrying Beth. He still looked pale but not as bad as he had earlier, and he'd got dressed. When we got down to the kitchen, I asked him how he manages when he's on his own, if he's cooking or he needs the loo, what does he do about Beth? He said when he's cooking he just brings her into the kitchen and keeps an eye on her, and when he goes to the bathroom he closes all the bedroom doors and shuts the stair gate and that makes a sort of play pen on the landing where Beth's quite happy to sit and play with whatever toys are to hand. She could reach the door handles if she wanted to, but up to now she hasn't bothered to try. I told him I wasn't sure what to do before, but I really needed the loo, otherwise I wouldn't have woken him. He went all quiet and I could tell he was really embarrassed about last night, and possibly by the fact that I'd stayed over. I didn't want to make him feel worse, though, so I didn't say anything about it, just asked him what I should make Beth for lunch. He said he'd do it so I could get off home, and he went to find my coat so I took that as a hint that he wanted me to go.

So now I'm home, and I should be getting a shower and brushing my teeth and changing my clothes but I can't help worrying about him. I need to find a way of telling him that he needn't be embarrassed when I do things to help him out. I want him to know that I really enjoy being with him and Beth, but how can I do that? He wants his wife back and if it wasn't for the fact that she's gone, I wouldn't be doing any of this and he certainly wouldn't be needing the help. How can I tell him that I love helping him, when he'd give the world to not need my help?

More than that, though, I'm worried because he's obviously on another downer today. Maybe it's just the hangover, but I wish there was something I could do. I think I'll ring him later, or maybe ring Ben and ask him to go over and see him.

4.20 p.m.

I rang Ben in the end, and just asked if he'd planned on calling round at Jamie's. He said he and Adam were thinking of calling in on their way home from Ikea so I told him about last night and said I was a bit worried, so he said he'd check in on him for sure. He rang me back just now and said that J seemed fine, a bit quiet but nothing too worrisome. He said J was probably just embarrassed that I'd felt I should stay there to keep an eye on things because he was so out of it, so I suppose I'll just have to leave it at that.

My period has arrived today. Maybe that's making me more anxious than necessary. Grrr.

Tuesday 25 March

Lucy rang me this morning, just as I was leaving for work. She said Will is hinting at getting engaged, so she wants me to go down for the weekend to meet him. I said that sounded nice.

Jamie was back in work today after his long weekend off. Beth goes to a play scheme during the school holidays, so he won't need to work strictly to term time, and it's a good job he came in because yesterday was a tense day and Vinnie didn't handle it very well.

Two of the boys were arguing all day yesterday, apparently it was something to do with a girl at school. Ben talked with both boys separately at lunch time and we thought it had all calmed down, but then later they kicked off again and Vinnie took their pocket money off them as punishment, which made them both even angrier. Mikey phoned his social worker, and she phoned the office and we heard Vinnie shouting at her over the phone, but then he ended up giving Mikey his pocket money back. He wouldn't give Jason his money, though, and that sparked another row, and Vinnie grounded him. Anyway this morning, Jamie took both lads into the lounge and they were talking in there for ages, and then afterwards J called Vinnie into the office and we heard V growling something but he wasn't shouting, so we couldn't tell what he was saying. He didn't half slam the door when he came out of there, though. He's such an idiot.

Darren came back yesterday, knackered but buzzing after his weekend. He met me from the gym and we went for a curry, which wipes out all my efforts but it was nice. He dropped me off at home and didn't seem to be waiting for an invitation to come in, he just kissed me and waved and off he went. I wonder if he's told his brothers what's going on? Maybe they've told him to play it cool, because that's what he was doing. I don't mind - it's much less confusing, that's for sure, when I'm not having to wonder what the hell I'm doing.

Friday 28 March

I can't believe this is happening - Ben says that Jamie has handed in his notice today.

Ben's still trying to talk him out of it, and he's talked to the AD and asked him not to accept it for the time being.

After Jamie had gone home on Tuesday, Jason and Mikey kicked off again. They were fighting in the hall, and Vinnie and Neil went to break it up between them. Vinnie threatened them with a week's worth of no pocket money, no outings, and no mobile phone and they calmed down okay. Then on Wednesday as they were getting ready to go out, they kicked off again and this time Jamie and Vinnie went to sort them out. They were upstairs, by the fire door at the top of the stairs, and Vinnie was holding the door open with his foot so they could get at them where they were fighting on the other side, and he made a grab for Jason and there was a scuffle. None of them seem sure of exactly what happened but somehow Jamie got knocked or pushed against the door frame where he hit the side of his face, and then he fell backwards down the stairs to the first turn and whacked his head against the wall. It knocked him out and we had to call an ambulance.

To their credit, both boys were really upset and Lisa took them off to the kitchen to give them a good talking to. Ben went in the ambulance with Jamie and I spent the next hour feeling sick, I was so worried. Ben rang me around 3 and asked me to go and get Beth from the play scheme. He said Jamie hadn't been out for long but he'd completely lost it when he woke up and realised where he was - but he was fretting over Beth being stranded, not about himself. So I took Jamie's car and went to pick her up, and she was so pleased to see me, bless her, and I took her home because Ben said he'd take J there from the hospital once they'd released him.

He looked dreadful - he had a cut on his cheekbone and a lump on his forehead, and I expect he's got a nasty bump on the back of his head too - but he was so relieved that Beth was okay. He insisted that he felt fine, and Ben said they'd checked him for concussion earlier and said he was okay, but we were both still worried so we hung around for a bit. Jamie wasn't very chatty, though - he was very quiet and wasn't really putting much into the conversation - and Ben told me when we were outside that when Jamie was upset at the hospital, he kept going on about how he's all Beth's got. It's like it's suddenly hit him that if something happens to him, he doesn't know what will happen to Beth.

And that was that. This morning J handed in his notice. Ben says it's probably just that having the accident so soon after losing Helen has made J feel a bit sensitive to things, and he probably just needs a bit of time to settle into being a single dad.

When we were leaving work, Ben and I had a chat about it all and we've decided we'll just carry on as normal - J might still need a hand with stuff, even if he's not going to be in work, so we'll keep to our routines and hopefully that will help him get back on track. Ben said he's really worried, though - he thinks J might be heading for a bit of a breakdown. I said I'd ring Jenny, who used to work with us - she's working in mental health now and might be able to give us some advice. I rang Lucy tonight, too, and told her I wouldn't be going this weekend. She was okay about it and I promised that I'll go next weekend if I can.

Sunday 30 March

It was Ben's turn to do the supermarket run yesterday and he rang me when he got home. He said J had him on pins in the car cos he was driving really nervously, and J mentioned to him when they were back at the house that he's become really anxious about all the things that could happen, like crashing the car or the brakes failing and that kind of thing. Ben said he tried to talk sense to him, but he's not sure if he got through - he said Jamie seems to be magnifying every little worry and getting really jumpy about things. I told him what Jenny had said - that he's more likely depressed and possibly that's warping his sense of perspective, but we should help him nip it in the bud if we can - and Ben said he hopes so.

I rang J this morning and said I was going for a walk down to the river because there's a charity plastic duck race, and I asked him if he thought Beth might like to see that. There was a bit of a pause and then he said yes.

We talked quite a bit on the way down to the river. I asked him how he was feeling after the fall the other day and he said he's ok but he's got a huge bruise all up the side of his face and a bit of a black eye, so he must be sore. I let it drop though, because I don't want him focusing on things like that.

We were at the river by then and there was quite a crowd there, but we managed to squeeze Beth into the front so that she got a good view. Jamie crouched down beside her and was pointing out all sorts of things for her to look at and she laughed like mad when the little plastic ducks went past, but then she started crying and pulling at her hair again.

We moved away from the crowd and tried to distract her. We followed the path down to the weir, where the swans are but she kept pulling at her hair and after a few minutes of that Jamie stopped and picked her up. She fell asleep while we were walking so he put her back into her pushchair, but he said he's still worried about this hair-pulling business and is thinking of talking with one of the therapists at her school. I said that's a good idea - anything to put his mind at rest.

We walked back through the park, and he asked me where I'd got Mum's bench from and how long it had taken to get it, so I told him all about that and warned him that the council take forever to sort out permission for them to be placed anywhere on public land. He didn't say where he had in mind, and I didn't ask, but I said to give me a shout if he wanted more information as I still have all the paperwork from when I ordered Mum's.

Darren had phoned while I was out, so I phoned him back but he didn't answer. I rang Lucy and she said they're coming up here next weekend if that's okay, so I said yes. She knows that Ben and I are taking it in turns to pop in on Jamie and go to the shops and the like, so I just said that next Saturday I'll be doing the supermarket run with him but otherwise I'll be free until Sunday afternoon when I have to be in work for 4 o'clock. She and Will are coming up after work on Friday, and they'll go home after lunch on Sunday.

Wednesday 2 April

Darren had gone to the pub on Sunday night. He'd phoned to ask me if I wanted to go to the cinema - he didn't say what film he'd wanted to see. He met me after gym on Monday and we went to the pub. Darren said he's organising a trip to the bowling alley either next weekend or the weekend after, if I fancied going, so I said yes. I haven't been bowling for ages, and it'll be a laugh. He walked me home and we had a bit of a snog but he didn't come in (I didn't ask him). I wonder how long he'll stay interested? I really need to make up my mind what I'm doing with him.

I haven't been round to Jamie's since Sunday but Ben has, and I've phoned him a couple of times. He sounds fine on the phone but Ben's said a couple of times that he looks rough and apparently he's not taking Beth to school in the car any more, he's walking with her in the pushchair, even in the rain. Ben said he and Adam are going to the cinema on Friday and he's asked Jamie if he'd like to go too - and kindly volunteered me to babysit! - but Jamie said no. He said if it's okay with me, he'll ask J again tomorrow and see if he can get him to change his mind. I said okay - I should still be home before Lucy and Will get here.

Monday 7 April

I've just got home after an all-nighter at work and a visit with Jamie, and I'm knackered but I haven't had time to update this thing for days, and I know if I don't write this down now I'll forget half of it so here goes.

On Thursday I called round to Jamie's after work and dropped off some milk and fruit. It was the middle of the afternoon - I'd been on an early shift - and he was in his pyjamas. He looked like he hadn't shaved all week, either. I'm not complaining cos the beardy look suits him, but it's worrying. He was really embarrassed, though. He told me he'd felt rough earlier so he'd gone back to bed, and he said he was just about to get ready to go and collect Beth from school when I got there. He ran upstairs to get dressed, and I walked with him part of the way.

Ben had tried to get him to go to the pictures with him and Adam, but Jamie wouldn't go. We both know it's not a trust thing so either he doesn't like the cinema or he's just not ready. Me and Ben decided not to push it for now.

Friday I went out for tea with Darren after work, and he came home with me and was here when Lucy and Will arrived, but he didn't stay the night. Will's nice -

very handsome! They hadn't eaten, so I made them some bacon butties and we sat up late, talking.

Then on Saturday I went round to Jamie's for 10, leaving the other two in bed. We went to Asda and now I know what Ben had meant about Jamie suddenly being a nervous driver - I was a bag of nerves myself by the time we got there. I kept trying to calm him down, telling him it was okay, but he looked like he was terrified. Beth was grizzling, too, which I'm sure didn't help him concentrate. I made him let me drive home, but he wasn't much better. I made us some tea while he was getting Beth's lunch ready, and I tried to casually suggest that he might want to see his GP or someone to help him sort out his anxieties. He just snapped at me, saying he wasn't being irrational because if anything happens to him then Beth will be on her own, and he's perfectly justified in being worried about that. I said we all worry about things like that but it's important to not let it overtake our lives, and he just shook his head and rubbed his nose like he does at work when he's trying to keep his patience, so I let it drop.

Lucy, Will, Darren and I went out for dinner on Saturday night. We went to that nice Italian that Darren took me to on my birthday, and it was yummy again. I really like Will and it's obvious that he adores Lucy, so that's good. Darren didn't come back to mine afterwards - he said he needed to be up early on Sunday for a footy match, but I think he was just being polite, wanting me and Lucy to have the time together with Will.

There was a message on my answering machine when we got in - Jamie had phoned, and he just said "Tasha it's me, I'm sorry I railed at you earlier." and Lucy asked me what that was about so I told her, and Will was listening and he said that Jamie should see a bereavement counsellor. He said his sister had a hard time after she lost her husband a couple of years ago, and she'd been helped a lot by going to see a counsellor. Sounds like a good idea to me.

On Sunday we got up late and Lucy and Will headed off. I rang Jamie after they'd gone and said I'd got his message. He didn't say much, and I didn't mention any more about it.

Today I got the chance to talk with Ben a bit at breakfast this morning, and he's just as worried about Jamie as I am, and he said that Adam thinks Beth is picking up on Jamie's anxieties. I haven't noticed anything different in her, but maybe the hair-pulling is part of it? I said I'll keep an eye on her this week, to see if I notice anything.

I got home just before 10 this morning and gave Jamie a ring but his line was engaged, and his mobile was going straight through to voicemail, so I left it and went to have a shower. The phone was ringing as I was getting out and I got there just as it finished, but there wasn't a message. I didn't recognise the number but I could tell it was in the Glasgow area, so I rang right back in case it was Elspeth and it was. She said she'd been trying to ring Jamie all morning but couldn't get an answer either at home or on his mobile, and she wanted to know if I'd heard from him recently so I told her I'd spoken with him yesterday afternoon.

We got into a nice little chat, and it turns out that she's worried about him, too. She says he's not himself and all this business with the car and other things he's worrying about is just not like him. So I told her about bereavement counselling and she agreed that it's a good idea, if he'll listen; she said she'll try and suggest it too.

I called him again and this time he answered it. He said he was in the park, and when I said I'd walk over to meet him there he said he was sitting on Mum's bench which threw me a bit.

When I got there he was leaning back with his arms stretched out against the back of the bench, and his head was tilted back a bit and his eyes were closed - he looked like he was soaking up the sun. I called out "Hiya!" as I walked up the hill and he sat up properly and did a little wave, and then when I got to him he stood up and said he hoped I didn't mind him sitting there. I told him it's a public bench, and why would I mind, but he looked like he didn't quite believe me and only sat down again after I did.

I told him straight away that Elspeth had phoned me because she'd been trying to ring him, and he nodded but he didn't say anything so I asked him what was wrong and he kind of laughed. Not a 'Oh that's funny' kind of laugh but the kind that means it's not funny at all. He didn't say anything for a while, so I just waited, and then he told me he's thinking of moving back to Scotland. He said he needs help with Beth, and Elspeth's going to need help with their parents, so it makes sense to move back there. Plus, apparently, Elspeth's eldest daughter is nearly 18 and is going into nursing and she's already offered to move down here and live with Jamie to help out, but he knows she'd really prefer to study and train up there. He's just worried about unsettling Beth with the move - new home, new school, new paediatrician, etc - and he said he doesn't know if he's just running away or if it's a good idea, or what.

I was nearly crying by that point - I don't want him to move away! - so I said he'd be best talking it over with Elspeth, and I reminded him that she'd like him to ring her sometime today. He said she doesn't know anything about it, it's just something he's been thinking about in the last day or two, and he's struggling with it because if Helen was still around then moving back to Scotland would be the last thing he'd ever want to do, but he feels like it would be the sensible thing to do. I said not to rush into it, wait until he feels 100% sure about it, and he said he'd never get to that stage but he needs to do what's right for his family. I said he needs to do what's right for him too, and he said, "Nothing's right any more" and that just made me cry. I wiped my face quickly so he wouldn't see it - he was looking over towards the lake - but I think I must have sniffed or something because he looked at me and I could tell he knew, and he looked surprised and sort of confused, so I said I'd be sorry to see him go.

And then he just got up really quickly and said he should probably get home. He hesitated for a moment, but he invited me to come with him. He said we could have a coffee. I felt a little silly for getting so weepy at the thought of him leaving and thought maybe I shouldn't, but let's face it – no way was I going to refuse. So of course I said yes.

We got back to his and he went upstairs to call Elspeth while I made coffees. He wasn't on the phone for too long, and I was still in the kitchen when he came back down. Straight off, he said sorry for rushing away from the park and when I said it didn't matter he said it did, and then he said he's having a hard time with his emotions and it had upset him to see me upset. I honestly didn't know what to say. I mean, of course he's having a hard time with his emotions - he's just lost his wife - but why would me being upset, upset him? So then I said sorry for upsetting him, and he was like, "No, no, don't you say sorry" and it just seemed so daft that I couldn't help smiling, and he did too (which, god help me, still makes my heart stop) and he did that cute thing where he scratches his eyebrow with his little finger (yes, I'm obsessed - I find everything he does cute) and shook his head, and then we sat down to drink our coffee.

He said Elspeth wanted to talk to him about nursing homes, because the situation with their Dad is becoming more difficult for their Mum. He said he should go up there and look at the places she's found, rather than leave it all up to her, and I, like an idiot, said I'd go with him to help with Beth if he really wanted to go. He just looked at me for a bit, like he was thinking about it, then he said his niece would do that so there was no need, but he thanked me for offering. So I asked will he drive or go on the train, and I could tell he hadn't thought about that part because he came over all anxious, so I just said it might be more comfortable on the train, just to keep him from going through all the worst case scenarios of driving up there, and he nodded.

And then I could see he was thinking again, and then he said he probably would need help on the train, with Beth and the buggy and their luggage, so I offered to take them to the station and help him on with everything if someone else could meet him the other end, and he smiled so gratefully it made me shiver. So he rang Elspeth and made arrangements with her and it was all settled: he's going up there next Saturday and I'll take them to the station and pick them up on Sunday. It'll be a hectic trip for him, especially since they want to go and view 3 or 4 nursing homes on the Sunday morning before his train home, but it's something he feels strongly about doing and I'm sure Elspeth will be grateful.

So we got that sorted, and he poured us some more coffee, and I asked him how he's doing, and he said Ben had asked him the same question yesterday and it bothered him that we were that worried about him. I jumped in and said that I had thought about mentioning bereavement counselling and Jamie nodded, and said that Elspeth had mentioned it too, and he was thinking about it, and then he asked me what I thought about it! So I said it had helped people I know, and that it might help him handle things with Beth, and how it's important that she doesn't pick up on his worries and stuff, and he nodded again and said it was that that was making him think he should give it a try, because he'd talked himself out of taking her to the park yesterday due to his over-active imagination (his words) and she was very unhappy by bedtime, and he'd been kicking himself over it, so now he realises he's got to do something about it, and that's why he was in the park today.

So then I asked him how he's doing, really, because he hadn't answered, and he just made a face and shook his head and said he didn't know. He said it's okay - not 'okay' okay, but not so bad - when he doesn't think about it, but there are so many reminders of Helen and what's happened, and sometimes all he wants to do is sit down and cry. So I said he should let himself do that, to get it out of his system, rather than bottle it up, and he shook his head but I could see he was close to tears and I felt like kicking myself for making him think about it. He said he does, sometimes, when Beth is in bed - he just sits down here and cries - but it never feels any better, so I said, "Maybe you're not done crying yet." (because I remember it took me ages to get through the crying stage, and people said to just go with it because one day I wouldn't feel like crying so much anymore) and he nodded and put his face in his hands.

And it was only when I noticed a drip on the table that I realised he was crying behind his hands, because he was so quiet about it, so I touched his arm and asked him if he wanted to be alone and he shook his head and said,

"No." really quietly. So I sat there and he cried, and I didn't know what to do because I know he doesn't like to cry in front of anyone and this was a huge trust thing for him to sit there like that.

After a few minutes his shoulders started to move, like the crying was getting harder, and he put his arms on the table and rested his head on them, just letting himself sob, so I put my hand on his shoulder because I was fighting the urge to hug him and I just had to touch him somehow. I rubbed and patted his shoulder for a bit, hoping it felt comforting, then just left my hand there until he sat up again and wiped his face with his sleeve. I thought he was going to launch into a big apologising thing again but he didn't, he just said, "Thank you." and sat there looking at his hands. I could tell he was embarrassed and I didn't want to say anything to make him feel worse, so I just got up and poured us some fresh coffee.

He asked me then if I knew of any counsellors locally, and I said we've got someone's contact details at work - the one that the AD had mentioned last week - so he rang Ben and got the number off him. He was talking with him for quite a bit, but I couldn't tell what about - I didn't want to eavesdrop so I washed the breakfast pots while he was on the phone. Then I heard him saying he wanted to make an appointment, so he must have rung the counselling service straight away, and he got up and wrote on the calendar that's on the pantry door, and when he'd finished the call he told me he's going on Thursday after he's dropped Beth off at school. I smiled and said I'm sure it will help, and he just shrugged and nodded.

My stomach rumbled then - talk about embarrassing! - and I remembered I had food shopping to do, so I said I was going into town and asked if he wanted anything, and he said he'd come with me! I told him I was going in the car, because I needed to get potatoes and other heavy stuff, and I could see him hesitating so I made him check his cupboards and work out what he needed from town, to get him thinking properly - it's like when we're teaching Life Skills to the kids, something I never thought I'd ever use with another adult (kind of sad, really). He wrote some things down on the back of an envelope and then we went.

I parked on the High Street and he couldn't get out of the car fast enough. He was shaking and pale and I tried to make a joke of how I'm not that bad a driver, but he just sighed and said sorry, which I'm starting to hate hearing. I needed to get a birthday card for Lucy so we went to the Card Cabin first, and he got a funny look on his face when we went in there but he didn't say anything. By the time I got to the till, though, he looked ill - even paler, if that's possible, and a bit sweaty - so I said let's go for a cuppa and we went into Greggs next door.

I got a cheese pasty and he said he'd have one too, and I wondered then if he'd had breakfast but I'm not going that far in checking up on him. We sat down at the window table and I told him he looked like shit and asked him if he was feeling okay, and he kind of smiled and said he really appreciates my bluntness (not sure whether to take that as a compliment or not). He said he thinks he's started to have panic attacks - that would explain the paleness and the sweating in the Card Cabin - but he fights them and didn't realise it was that obvious. I said it wasn't really, he just looked kind of ill, and he nodded. I said I can understand it happening in the car, but why a card shop? He said there's no logic to it, they happen anywhere, but then he stopped and took a big breath and said it's their wedding anniversary on Saturday and the card shop reminded him of that. I felt like he'd kicked me in the stomach, because there's no way I'd have gone in there if I'd known, and I was about to say sorry when he looked at me and shook his head and said, "Not your fault" - what do you say to that?

We finished our lunch and went back out to the shops, then walked back to the car to go to Asda. When we got to the car he said he didn't need much, so he'd get his things from town and walk back home. I'm fairly sure it was an excuse to avoid going in the car again, but I didn't say anything except "Okay." and he said, "Thanks for today." and squeezed my arm, which was nice of him.

So here I am - knackered, emotionally drained, trying not to think lusty thoughts (even a pastry crumb in the stubble on his chin got me going earlier .. what am I like??) - and it's only 3 o'clock in the afternoon. I really need to go to the gym tonight and work off this restless antsy feeling I've got, which is all due to unrequited lust, I'm sure. Darren might be in luck tonight. And I can't believe I'm even thinking like that, but I am. I don't like it, but if I'm going to use this blog honestly then I need to be bloody honest about how I feel!

Wednesday 9 April

I feel fucking sick with myself. I knew I'd do it, too, and I knew I'd hate myself if I did, but I still went ahead. I feel so guilty it's making me feel physically ill, and I can't tell anyone. I really should tell Darren what I'm doing, and I should finish with him because it's horrendously unfair to him and he doesn't deserve it. I could hardly look him in the eye yesterday morning and I could tell he was puzzled but he probably went home thinking he'd done something wrong when he couldn't be further from the truth. It's me who's wrong. I'm using him, and I'm not even thinking about him when we're doing it, and I'm having the best sex of my life but it isn't with him. Well, it is - he's the one who's there, and in fairness he's very good - but in my head it's Jamie who's shagging me, and it's fantastic while it's happening but when it's over and I open my eyes I feel so sick and I just want to cry, but I have to pretend that it was Darren who did that to me and let him think he's the one who's making me go wild. I hate it. I hate myself.

Thursday 10 April

I rang Jamie at tea-time, like I said I would, so he could tell me how it went with the bereavement counsellor this morning. He said he'd found it really difficult, but by the end of the hour he'd realised it was going to help, so he's made another appointment for next Tuesday. I asked after

Beth - haven't seen her since Saturday - and he said she's fine, but she's pulling at her hair a lot more and he and her teachers are trying to break her of the habit but it's really difficult. I suggested he make a note of when she's doing it, keep a kind of diary, and he said that's a good idea so he'll start that today, since she has her annual check-up next week and it will help to have notes.

Saturday 12 April

I got to Jamie's house for 8 this morning and it took him ages to come to the door. He looked awful and I could tell he'd either had or was having a panic attack, and I could hear Beth crying in the lounge. He said he was having second thoughts about going to Scotland. We went into the lounge and Beth stopped crying as soon as she saw me, and gave me a lovely smile, so I went over and gave her a hug. Jamie said she'd been crying non-stop for over half an hour, and he had no idea why. I asked him how long he'd been having second thoughts about the trip and he looked at me like he was wondering what that had to do with it, but he was obviously thinking it through, and then his shoulders sagged so I think I was right - Beth had picked up on her dad's panic attack, and that was why she was upset.

He lifted her up then and said, "Sorry darling" in that lovely way that he talks to her, and she was fine. Jamie said he'd started worrying about what could go wrong on the train, and he said he finds it really difficult to think rationally once he gets in that frame of mind but now he realises he was over thinking things. He's already arranged with the train people for someone to meet him at Warrington for the change of trains - they'll help with his luggage onto the train up to Glasgow - so he knows there isn't much to worry about anyway. I wonder what sort of disasters he imagines, but I'm not about to ask him about it. I also thought it might have something to do with today being his wedding anniversary, but I didn't mention that either.

Anyway, I suggested he get their luggage in the car while I finished dressing Beth - she still had her nightie on over her jeans - so we got organised that way and then headed for the station. Considering they're only going for one night he didn't half take a lot with him - a suitcase the same size as my pink one, the one I take for a week's holiday, and a huge backpack, and a hold-all, plus the buggy. I didn't say anything, because I suspect it was a case of panic packing and we've all done that. He looked a bit grey when we got to the station, and he had to take a huge breath before getting on the train, but I helped him with Beth and the luggage and stayed on the train until they were seated, then waved them off from the platform. He didn't wave back - he was busy talking with Beth.

I rang him from work at 11, just to check that the change of trains had gone smoothly, and it had. He sounded okay, and he said thank you again for this morning. Ben said he'd pick them up tomorrow, but I said I had nothing else planned, so he suggested I take them round for tea with him and Adam, which was nice of him. He's going to ring Jamie about it tomorrow, so he doesn't have too long to think up an excuse for not going!

Darren wanted to go out tonight but I said no. I'm trying to think of what to say to him, because I want to finish with him but I don't want to hurt his feelings. I'm not going to see him again until I've worked out what to say.

Sunday 13 April

Jamie's train was a bit late getting in this afternoon, and he was obviously very relieved to get off it - he was shaking and rushing, dropping things and bumping into people. I just concentrated on helping Beth down the steps and into her buggy, and then when I straightened up from strapping her in, he just pulled me into a hug and said, "Thank you for coming." as if he'd forgotten we'd arranged it all. I knew Ben had phoned him just after the change at Warrington, and I knew he'd talked Jamie into going to theirs for tea, so I just said we'd best get a move on or we'd be late.

Tea was lovely - Adam had made something like a carbonara with loads of salad, and a little pasta bake for Beth, and there was apple crumble and custard, and some of Ben's mum's chocolate fudge cake. Ben and Adam got Jamie talking about the Scotland trip and he said it had been hard going but he's glad he went: his Dad is much worse now, and his Mum is worn out with it all, so it's important that they get organised sooner rather than later. He and Elspeth went to view five nursing homes while he was there, and they've picked one and made arrangements for their Dad to be admitted later in the week. He even said that they had a good cry together in the car outside the home, which is not something I'd have expected him to admit but I'm glad he did. Oh, and Elspeth made him shave off his beard while he was there!

On the way back to his house after tea, Jamie said he'd talked with Elspeth about moving up to Scotland. Apparently she doesn't think it's a good idea - she said it's too soon - and she suggested he waits six months and see if he still feels the same then. I'd have kissed Elspeth if she'd been here. Beth was getting tired, so I said I'd see to the luggage while he got her bathed and ready for bed, so he went straight upstairs with her and I lugged his stuff into the house. I picked up the mail from yesterday and took it through to the kitchen and put the kettle on, then called up the stairs to say I was going home. All I could hear was Beth giggling, so I left.

Jamie rang me about an hour later. He said thank you again for 'all the running around' (his words). I love that he's so polite but I wish he'd get it into his head that it's no trouble, and that I actually enjoy doing it.

Tuesday 15 April

I didn't go to gym last night. Darren rang and said he'd meet me afterwards, so I said I wasn't going and said I had a bad stomach. He didn't question it, just said, "Get better soon." and said he'll see me later in the week. I've got to get myself sorted and work out how to finish with him.

I got a call from Ben as I was leaving work this afternoon, asking me to meet him at Jamie's house, so of course I flew round there wondering what was wrong - Ben didn't want to say over the phone. He answered the door and we went through to the kitchen, and Jamie was there with some letters on the table and I recognised the logo thing on one of the envelopes, it was one of the ones that had arrived on Saturday. Ben said they'd been having a discussion and thought a third view would be a good idea because the insurance company had sent Jamie a cheque (Helen's life insurance policy) and J didn't want to accept it. Ben said he'd already suggested that Jamie should pay it into his account and use it to supplement his income cos that's what it's intended for. Apparently there'll be another one coming soon, paying off Helen's half of the mortgage, so that's going to be taken care of, seeing as he's already negotiated a lower repayment. Jamie said the thought of it makes him feel sick (Ben told me later that J had actually thrown up when he opened the envelope and saw what was inside).

So I'm standing there listening to them both and thinking, 'Thanks guys - you're putting it on me to decide what to do with it' and wondering what the hell to say. And then it just dawned on me – J always puts Beth first - so I just said the money will mean he won't have any worries about Beth's future, because he'll always be able to provide for her. They both looked at me and I thought maybe I'd said the wrong thing, but then Jamie took in a big breath and looked at the cheque, and Ben did a little thumbs up out of Jamie's sight.

Wednesday 16 April

Lucy and Will have got engaged! He popped the question this morning while she was opening her birthday cards, and when she said yes he gave her a ring - solitaire, on a platinum band - and she rang me straight away to tell me :) She's sent me a photo of the ring and it looks gorgeous. They're not setting a date yet, not until they've told everyone, and she said they probably won't have a big wedding which I think is her way of saying I may not get to be bridesmaid but I'm not bothered about that, I'm just happy for her.

Work's been busy today. We've taken in a new girl, Erin, who arrived this morning with her social worker. She's not happy, bless her, and we could hardly get a word out of her - not that that's new for teenagers, but we still like to try - but when the other girls got in from school they got her chatting and she seemed like a different kid. I suppose she has that inherent mistrust of adults, and obviously she doesn't want to be in residential care, but hopefully the girls will help her settle in. We also had the dreaded Regulations inspection, which took ages, but everything went okay. And then, just as I was getting ready to go home, we had a fire alarm and ended up spending 40 minutes outside while the fire brigade went over the building. They think it's a faulty alarm, which is a relief but annoying - why couldn't it have happened after I'd gone?? The kids thought it was fun, though, and Lisa and I got Erin talking a bit while we were outside, so I'll put that down to a good thing.

I called at Jamie's on the way home – Ben and I make sure one of us calls in at least once a day, and I'd said I'd pick up bread and milk for him today - and he was making Beth's tea when I got there. Beth was at the table in the kitchen, drawing with her favourite glitter pens, and she gave me one so I could do some too. Jamie asked me if Ben had mentioned helping with a hospital appointment for Beth tomorrow and I said yes. Of course I would help him with anything he needed. He said I do too much and so I told him I love spending time with Beth and that he needs to stop thinking about it like that because if me and Ben didn't want to help we wouldn't have offered and we wouldn't still be offering. He leaned over to Beth and said, "That's me in my place again, Bethy" and she laughed.

I stayed until Beth had had her tea, and I'm glad I did because when Jamie took her through to the lounge to play with her dolls, she started the hair pulling again and once we'd distracted her from that we had a bit of a chat about it, and it turns out that school have told him she's been doing it a lot more lately, and her teacher commented that it's always the same side of her head that Beth pulls at and we'd noticed that too, so it's the first thing Jamie's going to mention tomorrow.

Thursday 17 April 9.10 p.m.

God, what a day. I really wanted to stay at Jamie's this evening but he didn't want me to, and I didn't want to insist, so I've come home. I hope he's okay. I told him to ring me or Ben if he wants to talk or anything. I don't suppose he will - he'll be too worried about disturbing us. I think I might text him before I go to bed, just to check.

We got to the hospital this morning with about five minutes to spare - Jamie had had a bad night and had slept in, so neither he nor Beth were ready when I got to his house, and that put him in a bit of a panic. Well, not so much a panic but he was flustered, and then Beth got upset, so I sent him upstairs to get himself sorted and I carried on getting Beth dressed. Traffic was awful and he was a bag of nerves, and I'm really glad I'd said we could go in my car because I think if he'd been driving we'd have had an accident.

We'd only just got to the waiting room and sat down when Beth started to pull at her hair, and I said that wasn't such a bad thing because at least the paediatrician would see it for himself, but it upsets Jamie when she does it and he did his best to distract her and ended up walking her around the waiting room and letting her talk to the other kids. It's so heart-breaking, watching her try to communicate and watching the other kids look at her like she's a freak - the older ones, I mean, because the tots tend to just babble back at her - I don't know how Jamie copes with it.

When Beth's name was called, I said I'd wait in the waiting room but Jamie asked me to go in with them, so I did. Beth's paediatrician is lovely - he's a big bloke, and very jolly, I think his name is Burgess or something like that, and I'm fairly sure I'd seen him at the funeral - and they've obviously got to know each other quite well (I think he's been looking after Beth since she was born). Jamie introduced me as a friend, which was nice. They chatted a bit about Helen and how Jamie was doing, and then Dr Burgess asked about Beth and Jamie told him about the hair pulling and Dr B was surprised it had got worse, so he said they'd do a thorough check today to rule out anything physical.

I sat near the door and felt a bit of a spare part, really, but I suppose Jamie just wanted to know he wasn't on his own. Beth had the usual medical check-up - height, weight, reflexes, etc - and a couple of other tests that I couldn't quite figure out but seemed routine. Dr B had a good look at her head too but Beth didn't like that and tried pulling away and started to cry, so Dr B said he wanted her to have a scan as that would give them a better idea without having to prod and poke at Beth too much, which I thought was sweet. It meant sedating her a bit, though, because there's no way they'd be able to get her into the scanner or to keep her still in there. Jamie wasn't too happy but he agreed.

We had to wait in the waiting room for a bit while it was organised, then Dr B called Beth back in to give her the sedative. We were then sent down to the x-ray department as that's where the scanner is - practically on the other side of the hospital! Jamie carried her, and I pushed the buggy. We were both glad that the staff were ready and waiting when we got there - I was gobsmacked, to be honest, because whenever I've been there I've had to wait for ages - and it was all over quite quickly. Beth was very groggy by then, but she was obviously a bit upset and one of the nurses had to hold her hand all the way through, which I don't think they're supposed to do (they wouldn't let J stay with her). Then we went back to the paediatrician's waiting room and sat down to wait. Beth had dozed off on the way back, with Jamie carrying her, so he sat there with her on his knee and I went to get us some tea.

We weren't waiting long - I think we'd not long finished our drinks when Dr B called Jamie into his room. Beth was still mostly asleep, bless her. Dr B said it would probably make her dozy for an hour or so before it wore off, so J just carried her in and settled her on his knee again. I knew straight away that something was up from Dr B's face cos he wasn't smiling like he had been before. I think he chose his words very carefully - he said it looks like there's a little shadow on the scan that might mean some slight pressure on Beth's brain, in the region where she's tugging at her hair. He said she could be in pain from it, or it could be no more than a dull ache, or it could be absolutely nothing, but either way something was clearly uncomfortable for Beth so they need to look into it and he'll schedule some further tests. Dr B offered to prescribe something to alleviate any discomfort and he was quite persuasive about it in a gentle way, and he assured J that he doesn't think it's serious and there's nothing to worry about, he's just taking precautions by setting up further tests.

He asked if Beth had been hurt in the crash and I think it threw Jamie because he didn't answer, and Dr B looked at me and I said I didn't think so, and then J said, "No there wasn't a mark on her" so there were more questions about whether she might have bumped herself somewhere, but Jamie couldn't think of anything. They talked a bit more, then Dr B said that Jamie could ring him any time if he had concerns about Beth - I got the impression that that's something he always says at these things - and then we were on our way. Jamie carried Beth to the car and she started waking up a bit as he put her in her car seat, but then she closed her eyes again and didn't really wake up properly until we got back to their house.

Jamie was quiet all the way there, and I didn't know what to say, and when I was parking outside his house I noticed he'd gone all pale and sweaty like he did the other day. It was raining by then so I said I'd open the front door so he could leg it inside with Beth, and we'd get the buggy later. So we did that, and ended up not getting too wet, and Beth thought the run up the path was funny, which put a smile on Jamie's face. She was still a bit woozy so he asked me to sit with her while he made some lunch, but then he went upstairs and - bless him - I heard him throwing up. When he came back down he looked at me and said, "I never used to be such a wuss" and I said, "You're not a wuss, you're a very caring Daddy" and he looked like he was going to cry.

He went to make a cup of tea. I could hear a lot of clattering and banging and things dropping on the floor but I left him to it, mostly because I'd said I'd sit with Beth but also because if he was having a cry in there I didn't want to get in the way of that. He brought me a cup of tea eventually and he looked okay, still white but better than he'd looked in the car. It was nearly half twelve by then and I had to be in work by 1, so I asked him if he'd be okay and he nodded but he didn't look too sure about it. I said he could ring me or Ben this afternoon if he wanted to, and I'd call in again on the way home from work.

So I got to work and all hell had broken loose because Erin and Carly had been fighting on the school bus and then got sent home from school, but Erin had run off so Vinnie and Gemma had gone looking for her and Lisa had spent the morning trying to get to the bottom of it with Carly, while trying to liaise with the police and the social worker about Erin, because the other three were with their NVQ assessor who'd made it quite clear she wasn't prepared to postpone again (she travels up from Norwich somewhere, so you can't blame her). Talk about all hell breaking loose!

They'd all missed lunch, which was good for me as I hadn't had any, so I cracked on with that and took them all some tea and sandwiches and answered the phone and made myself useful. Ben finally got free of the NVQ woman around 2 o'clock and I told him what had happened at the hospital, and he went straight off to the office to ring Jamie. He's so sweet, such a caring man. I did wonder for a while if he fancied Jamie but I honestly don't think he does, and anyway he's so much in love with Adam that I doubt he even sees anyone else in that way.

The NVQ assessor wanted to see me then, because apart from the Duty of Care training in February, I haven't done any work for months and she asked me if I wanted a break from it. We had a chat and went over my portfolio, and I decided to plod on with it since I'm so close to finishing it, and she said she'll come back next month but if I haven't been able to get any work done on it then I've to let her know (I knew that already - she says it every time she comes). By that time it was nearly 3 and I hadn't done a jot of casework so I got on with that. As I was doing it, Ben came and told me he was going to call at Jamie's on the way home. He said J had said he was okay but his voice sounded shaky so he was just going to pop in and check he really is okay. Bless him. I expected him to ring when he got home, but he didn't, so I assumed everything was okay.

I nipped into town after work to get a card for Jamie - took me ages to find a nice one - and I got some fruit and chocolate for Beth and then headed over to J's house, and Ben was still there. He was actually just about to leave - he opened the door, with his coat on - and he said he'd stayed because Jamie'd been on the phone a bit, talking with Dr B and Beth's GP and someone else, and he'd been trying to get Jamie to stop panicking about Beth. Jamie was in the kitchen, and Ben whispered to me to not mention the hospital or anything related to it, and try and keep J talking about other things, and he said he'd ring me later.

So I went through to the kitchen and put the fruit and chocolate away, and Jamie made me a cup of tea, and I sat with Beth while J was cooking, and I told him about Erin and my NVQ and he got chatty about work, asking after people and the kids so I brought him up to speed on everyone. I never really noticed until half-way through, but he dished up three plates and we just sat there eating and talking with Beth and he hadn't even asked if I wanted to stay for tea, which was a bit odd when I thought about it but I didn't say anything because it was so nice and because it just happened so naturally.

When I was getting ready to go home, J said he was expecting a phone call and he asked me to hang on while he took Beth for her bath, and to answer the phone for him. So I did, and the phone call was from a woman in Blackpool about a weekend reservation for the Bank Holiday. When he came back downstairs after Beth had gone to sleep, he explained that he and Helen used to take Beth to Blackpool every year and stay at the same place. When Elspeth had asked him about it last weekend he'd been about to cancel it but his niece had offered to go with him.

We talked a bit then about Blackpool, and he said how much he's dreading it but he really doesn't want to not let Beth have that little holiday because she loves it and the people there make such a lovely fuss of her. We had another cup of tea and then I was just thinking I should get going, when Beth yelled really loudly and we both flew up the stairs to see what was wrong, and she was having a bad dream or something because she was thrashing about in her bed and sort of crying/shouting, and nodding her head in a very odd way.

Jamie sat on the bed and picked her up and held her to him closely until she calmed down, but then she was crying and it took ages for her to stop. He tried everything - stroking her hair, whispering to her, rocking her, even singing a bit - and I sat next to him and held her hand, and for a while I think we were both worried that she wasn't going to stop but she did eventually, and she fell asleep again. We stayed there for about ten minutes, just to be sure, then he put her back into bed and we went back downstairs. He looked awful - white and sweaty and kind of wild eyed - and he said that's the third time in the last week that she's done that, and he'd forgotten to tell Dr B and now he was fretting that it could be connected to the hair pulling and it might be really important.

I sat him down and got him to talk through what he was feeling - trying out that technique that Gemma had told us about for getting the kids to handle their anger - and he resisted at first but then I think he realised what I was trying to do and he went along with it. And then it was like verbal diarrhoea: he's lost Helen, he feels like he's lost his dad (he went into the nursing home today), his brother's hardly spoken to him for a year because of some stupid row over something he can't even remember, he feels like he's lost control of his life and he's going to lose his job and then the house, and he's absolutely terrified of anything happening to Beth.

I think there was other stuff, too, but by then I realised I'd bitten off more than I could chew and I was trying desperately to think of what to say to help him calm down. So of course I had to ask him if he'd mentioned any of this to the counsellor and he said he's only really talked about Helen up to now, so I said maybe he could mention the other stuff next time since it's all having an effect on him. And then he said he feels such a failure, and he can't understand how he's ended up like this because this is not who he is, and I said grief does strange things to people but you'll get through it and he looked like he didn't believe me. So I changed the subject a bit and asked him why on earth he thinks he'll lose his job, and he said it's because the AD rings him every week to ask how he is and if he's ready to come back yet, and he knows what the procedures are, and he's glad the AD didn't accept his resignation but he doesn't think this can go on for much longer.

So I just asked him straight out why he didn't come back to work then, and he said "Because" about three times but nothing else, and then he just shook his head and said "I can't" so I said maybe being at home on his own so much isn't doing him any good, and work could take his mind off things and help him get back on track, and he nodded and said he knows that but it's not that simple. So I suggested that perhaps he could discuss that with his counsellor too, and that's when he totally lost it. He threw his mug across the room and stood up, saying the counsellor wasn't going to wave a magic wand and fix everything and he wasn't so sure that the sessions would do any good anyway - there was a lot of effing and shouting and I missed a lot of it because his accent gets a lot stronger when he's angry - and he just stood there in the middle of the kitchen, ranting on about all sorts of stuff, and I just sat there and let him get it off his chest.

I was listening out for Beth in case he woke her up, and trying to follow what he was saying, and I just sat there and watched him. And then he just stopped and I'm not even sure what he was saying, but he stopped right in the middle of something and looked at me with his mouth open like he was absolutely horrified. He was about to say sorry but I just said, "Don't you dare" and he said, "I wasn't shouting at you" and I told him I know that and I'm just glad he's got it out of his system.

I let him pick up the pieces of his mug and clean up the mess - good job there wasn't much tea left in it - and I made us another cuppa, but instead of sitting back at the table he went through to the lounge so I followed him, and we sat there for a bit without saying anything. I was too scared to say anything in case it set him off again - not because he frightens me, but because I can't stand seeing him get so upset - and he looked like he was thinking so I didn't want to disturb his thoughts. Then he said, "It's my birthday tomorrow" and before I could say anything he said, "And it'll be two months to the day..." and I just filled up because no wonder he's so edgy - on top of everything else, this will be his first birthday without her, and it's an anniversary of her death.

It's obvious from what he's said before now that

they've always made a big deal of birthdays - mostly for Beth, I suppose - and he made such a fantastic effort for Beth on her birthday, and that's probably why, but he's going to be spending his remembering what happened two months ago. What can you say to that? I couldn't think of anything that would have sounded right, so I just made a sympathetic face and he nodded. Then he said he doesn't like being so out of control, and he said he didn't mean to lash out at me, and I said I didn't take it that way, and that it'll be a while before his emotions settle down. But then I thought it's been two months already and it will probably take him a lot longer than it took me, after Mum died (but I didn't say that to him). I suppose it makes a bit of a difference when you're expecting it, like me and Lucy were, but Jamie's got the sudden shock of it to get over too.

He'd gone a bit quiet again, so I asked him if he wanted to go out or something for his birthday, and I offered to babysit if he did, but he shook his head. Then I remembered that he and Helen didn't do much going out so that's probably not what they did on birthdays, and he'd made a special dinner for her birthday, the day before she died, and I was thinking about doing that but I think it will be too big a reminder. Then I wondered if anyone at school had thought to help Beth make or write on a card for him, and I nearly filled up thinking of that because I don't suppose it would occur to anyone. I thought about ringing Elspeth, but it's not really my place to go asking her if she'd thought about that. I just don't want him hurting on his birthday, but I don't suppose there's much I can do about that.

It was gone 8 by then and I was knackered, but he still looked so pale and shaky that I didn't want to leave him alone. I've no idea what I thought I could do for him, but sometimes company's enough, isn't it? He must have read my mind or something because he said he's not good company, and he said how I must have loads of things to do, so I took that as a hint but I said I was just going to have a bath and an early night, but I'd stay if he wanted the company. He said, "No you've done more than enough today" and he thanked me again for going with him this morning, and for putting up with him (his words) this evening, so I came home. I've had a lovely bath and I'm dead tired, but I'm not going to bed yet - I texted Jamie a minute ago, and I'm going to hang on a bit in case he answers.

11.05 p.m.

He hasn't answered, so hopefully he's okay or maybe he's gone to bed. I rang Ben just now, to tell him that I'd told Jamie he could ring him or me if he wants to. I had to tell Ben a bit about tonight, so he'd know what to expect, but I tried to gloss over it a bit. Ben said he'll call in on him on the way to work in the morning.

Friday 18 April

I half expected to see Ben's car at Jamie's this morning, but he wasn't there. I didn't go in, just pushed J's birthday card through the letterbox without knocking, because he'd have been getting Beth ready for school and also I didn't want to embarrass him by giving him a card face to face. He texted me later and it just said, 'Thank you.'

Ben got to work just before lunchtime. He told me he'd popped in to see Jamie on the way to the dentist and he'd been fine - he'd taken Beth to school, and he was opening cards he'd received (Ben said he had 6 or 7, including the one that he and Adam had sent, so I was pleased about that), and he told Ben he's going to see the AD at work next week. Ben said he thinks J might be planning to come back to work, so then I told him about last night in a bit more detail. He said it sounds like Jamie still has a lot to get out of his system, and he (B) is not so sure that I should be putting myself in that position. I said I'm not worried about that, I just don't like it when something I say sets Jamie off and gets him upset, and Ben just looked at me and said, "You know what it's like." and I do. It took me months before I stopped being hyper-sensitive to stuff, and even now I still get a bit tearful if someone mentions something that reminds me of Mum - so I suppose Jamie's going to go through the same thing.

Gemma came in at 3 and showed me the chocolate cake that she and the girls had made last night for Jamie - it had been Carly's idea, and she and Simone did most of the work on it, even the icing on top, and it looked great. The girls had made cards, too. Gemma asked me to take the cake and cards round to Jamie's after work, and I said she and the girls could go with me if they liked but she didn't think that would be a good idea.

When I finished, I went to Jamie's. I got just there as they were coming down the street. They'd been to the park, and Beth looked all rosy-cheeked and happy, bless her. I took the cake straight down to the kitchen and when I told him the girls had made it, Jamie looked really touched. He rang the Home and spoke to both of them, and I can just bet that the two of them were squealing about it afterwards as they both have the hots for him. He, of course, is oblivious to that.

He made us some tea, and we all had some of the cake which was scrummy. Beth made a bit of a mess with hers but she enjoyed it, little chocoholic that she is. He told me he'd spoken to Dr B this morning about her little outbursts at night, and Dr B had said not to worry as it's probably just discomfort triggering a bad dream, but he could prescribe something to help her sleep better (J doesn't want to go that route just yet). I got a sneak look at his birthday cards while he was giving Beth her bath (they're on the mantel piece), and someone has helped Beth make one for him so I'm really chuffed about that.

I wasn't going to stay long but he asked me to hang on until he'd put Beth to bed. When he came down he made some more tea, we had another piece of cake, and he said, "Thank you for the lovely card." Then he said he'd been doing a lot of thinking since last night and when he sees his counsellor on Tuesday he's going to discuss everything, then see if he feels any better about the idea of coming back to work. He said he misses it - misses us - and he feels like he's let us all down by being off for so long, but he knows he's got to get past some stuff first. He didn't say what, but I know it's all tied up with his fear of something happening to him that would leave Beth with no-one to look after her. It's irrational but at the same time it isn't completely irrational, and he knows it.

I don't know why he felt the need to tell me all this, and not Ben, but I'm glad that he did. I just said it sounds like a good idea, and we'd all be glad to see him back but he shouldn't go rushing into it (tried to tell him he's not letting us down, but he wouldn't have it). Then he said "Thank you for listening last night." and before I could say anything he said, "And I am very sorry for losing it like that when you were only trying to help" so I just told him to not feel sorry if it's helping, and he nodded.

And then he said he didn't answer my text last night because he wanted to talk to me about it, and I'm sitting there trying desperately to remember what I'd said in it, and all I could remember was something like 'Hope u feeling ok, ring if u need anything' and he said he really appreciates everything I do but he's worried about getting too dependent on me and Ben to bail him out all the time. I said it's not bailing him out, it's helping with what needs doing, and anyway we both like doing it and wouldn't offer if we didn't, and I said we'd talked about this before and we'd all agreed that me and Ben would tell him if we thought he was getting to rely too heavily on us, as if that's ever going to happen. I said it looks to me like he feels he doesn't need or deserve any help, and he did that little staring thing he does when he's caught out, and then he looked away and I'm positive that that's it - he thinks he doesn't deserve any help. So I just said, "You'd do the same." and he shrugged, but I'm sure he would - we all would, especially when there's a kid involved.

And then it dawned on me how he must see himself - he thinks he's letting us down by being off work, he thinks he doesn't deserve any help even though most of it is helping with Beth, so he must have quite a low opinion of himself - and yet we all think the world of him and think he's brilliant at his job (he really is) and he's also a brilliant dad, so how come he doesn't see all that in himself? It was on the tip of my tongue to suggest he talk about all that with his counsellor, but I didn't want to bring that up again so I just said we'd both stop coming over if it was making him uncomfortable and he looked up really quickly and said that that wasn't it at all, he just didn't want to be encroaching on our personal time and all that. So I just gave him my 'You're talking shite' look and he smiled and said, "I'll shut up then" and just the way he said it with that smile gave me a hot flush. It's been a while since I thought of him in that way (a few days, at least) and I thought I was getting over him, but he only has to do something daft like that and I'm all aflutter again.

Darren was standing on my doorstep when I got home. I've hardly spoken to him since Monday - he's been on nights - and I wasn't expecting him. He must have seen my surprise because when I got out of the car he said, "Hope you don't mind me just turning up?" and I said no but it made me nervous. I'd only had cake at Jamie's, so I said I was going to make something to eat and he said he'd have some too, so he hovered in the kitchen while I was cooking. We just chatted about work and general stuff, and then he just came out with, "I don't think this is working, is it?" which threw me a bit because I thought he must have been reading my mind. So I said we'd agreed we weren't going to be boyfriend/girlfriend, and he said he's not sure he agrees with that anymore because he wants to see more of me. So I told him I'm not ready for a relationship and he said I might be if I stopped wasting my time with Jamie! He's right, of course, but I don't need him telling me that.

We ate our pasta and really just skirted around it all, but then when I'd had a glass of wine I kind of found the courage to be honest with him and I just told him how I feel. I said first that I really didn't want to hurt him, and then I said that I feel like I'm cheating on him because when I'm with him I'm thinking of Jamie, and he said, "What? All the time?" and I couldn't actually say, "No, just when we're shagging" but he must have seen that in my face because he looked gutted. I felt awful, and I kept apologising but I also said I didn't think it was fair on him if I kept seeing him and using him that way.

I thought he might have got angry - Gavin would have gone berserk - but he didn't, he just looked sad and disappointed, and he said he needed some time to think this over. I thought he'd have ended it there and then, and when he didn't, I suggested that we should, but he said he wanted to think about it first, and then he left. So now I'm wondering what on earth he's thinking, and why he needs to think it over. If he's thinking about carrying on seeing me, even now that he knows what's going on with me, what do I do? It'd be too embarrassing to have sex, because we'd both know where my head would be … or maybe it wouldn't, now that I know that he knows? Oh god, I don't know! I think I might have to talk about this with Lucy because I'm getting too confused now.

Sunday 20 April

I went to Asda with Jamie and Beth yesterday morning, and it was loads better than last time. He's still jumpy in the car but it's obvious that he's trying really hard to relax. He didn't need much as he's been picking up bits and bobs through the week (which is a big change for him, and I hope it means he's getting over the daft idea that he'll get himself killed if he goes out) so we weren't there long. He and Beth were going out for the rest of the day with Ben and Adam - they were going to the zoo - and I spent the afternoon catching up on housework and even did a bit on my NVQ. Hayley dragged me out to bingo after tea, and we had a good laugh (didn't win anything though). Ben rang me not long after I got in and said they'd all had a lovely day and he's got the sweetest photo of the two of them feeding rabbits in the Petting Zoo.

I had a lovely long lie-in this morning - I love weekends off! Darren rang me at lunch time. He said he's going to his brother's and will ring me when he gets back tonight, but he hasn't so far. I spent the day mooching around the flat, tidying up and just doing stuff that I've been ignoring for the last few weeks or so. Jamie rang around 1 and asked if I wanted to go with them to the park again. I met them there, and we had a nice wander around and took Beth to the play park, then we stopped at the cafe for a bit, then went back to the play park before heading home. I didn't go back to his house - he didn't ask, and I couldn't think of an excuse for going, more's the pity.

I had a lovely long bath after tea, and I've just got off the phone with Lucy. I told her about my conversation with Darren and she was shocked but then she laughed and called me an idiot! She said we all do that, and she asked me why on earth I'd told Darren because now he'll just feel inadequate. She said I should have talked to her first, and she'd have talked me out of it. So now I feel stupid, and I feel even worse about hurting Darren's feelings over it. I just didn't feel that I could go on like that; it was like lying to him every time. Lucy said if it stays in your head then it's not hurting anyone, and she has a point I suppose, but I don't know - it just doesn't seem right.

Tuesday 22 April

Darren met me from the gym last night and we went to the pub afterwards and had a good long chat. He said he's still not sure how he feels about what I said, but he's really glad that I told him, and he appreciates me being that honest with him because he doesn't think many women would be (which is what Lucy said). He still wants to see me but he said, "Can we see how things go about the sex?" which is fair enough. Talking about it made me feel nervous and I think that's how I'll feel if we ever do get to that stage again, but we'll just have to see. I'm fairly sure that I AM in love with Jamie, but realistically I doubt I'm ever going to get anywhere with him.

The money came through today, from the sale of Mum's house. I got a phone call from my solicitor to tell me it would be in my account this afternoon. It made me cry a bit because that's the end of that era, now – it's someone else's home from now on.

Wednesday 23 April   2 pm

I'm at home, and I should be in work, but I've been put on sick leave for at least a week. It's my own fault, I wasn't looking what I was doing, but really who would expect a cat to be sitting on the step when it's never been there before? I was on my way to work this morning, running late, and flew out of the door and the next thing I knew I was on the path, in agony. That fat ginger cat from round the corner ran past me, yowling, and I think I must have trodden on it and then sort of fallen awkwardly on the step. No idea what the daft thing was doing there - I've never seen it there before - but I hope it's okay.

I don't remember, but I must have screamed or shouted or something because Mr Benyon from next door came running round, and he said he thought I'd broken my ankle so he rang for an ambulance. They didn't think it was broken but they took me to A&E anyway, and I was there for ages but the nurses and staff were very nice, kept bringing me drinks and checking on me. I rang Ben while I was waiting for the ambulance, and he said Gemma's phoned in sick so they're really stretched, otherwise he'd have organised for someone to sit with me at the hospital, bless him. I asked him to ring Jamie because I'd said I'd call round there after work and I wasn't sure if I'd be able to make it. Anyway, I eventually got x-rayed and I've cracked a tiny bone in my foot and sprained my ankle, and I've also badly bruised my elbow, so I'm not in plaster but my ankle is strapped up and I've got crutches and I have to keep the weight off my foot for a week, I think, then go back to Out-Patients sometime next week.

I'd had to switch my phone off when I got to hospital, but when I was ready to leave I switched it back on again and there were two missed calls from Jamie and one from Ben, so I rang them both. Ben said he'd pop out from work and pick me up and take me home, so while I was waiting for him I rang Jamie. He was very concerned, and he took a bit of convincing that I'm okay, just hurting in a few places but mostly feeling a bit of a nit. He said he'll call round when he picks Beth up from school, and he asked if I wanted anything fetching but I couldn't think of anything.

I've had a quick tidy up, but I'm so glad I did a big clean over the weekend! Ben was so sweet when he came to get me, carrying my bag and holding doors and I swear he'd have carried me to the car if I'd let him. I'm so glad I live on the ground floor - walking with crutches doesn't half make your arms tired, and I've no idea how I'd have got up the stairs if I lived higher up, so that's another plus for the garden flat choice! Ben made me a sandwich and stayed for a cup of tea, but he had to get back to work. He took the sick note that the hospital had given me and said to ring if I need anything. Lisa rang me a bit later and said the same thing. I have such lovely friends :)

7.30 p.m.

Jamie and Beth came round after school. Beth was fascinated - she loves looking around new places - and she loved my fluffy red cushions and the bead lamp, kept stroking them. We had a cuppa, and Beth had some juice but she wasn't too keen on it (not her usual brand) and they didn't stay for long but it was nice of him to come. He'd had to ring me to get my address, and he said he hadn't been down this end of town before even though it's not far from Beth's school, and he was very complimentary about the area. It's quieter than where they live, and we've got more trees - part of the reason why I moved here.

He told me that Beth has an appointment on Friday, he thinks for a more detailed scan. I said I'll go with him, but he'll have to drive, and he seems okay with that. I didn't say anything, but I'm surprised that the appointment has come through so quickly. I suppose they do things differently when it's kids.

I rang Lucy when I knew she'd be home from work. She was upset and talked about coming here to stay with me for a bit, but I told her I'm fine and will be up and about in a week, and there's no point in her losing time off work to just sit here with me all day, much as it would be nice. She said she'll come at the weekend then, so she'll be here on Saturday and will probably stay overnight.

Thursday 24 April

11 am

I'm bored already and it's only my second day off sick. It would be okay if I could get out or even move around without hurting myself, but I haven't quite got used to the crutches yet and I can't get very far on them, and the consultant at the hospital yesterday said that I probably won't be driving for a month or so! I'm reading a lot, which is nice, and I suppose I could take advantage of the time off and get my NVQ up to date, but I don't feel in the mood for that.

Darren called round last night, and Ben popped in after work. Neither of them stayed very long – is it me, or do men in general get antsy around people who are injured or ill?

5.30 pm

Jamie called around with Beth again after school, and he brought me some magazines and chocolate. He said he'd go on his own tomorrow if I didn't feel up to it, but I said I'd be glad to get out even if it is only to the hospital, so he's picking me up at 10. I'm not sure what help I'm going to be, cos I can't carry anything heavy, but

I suspect he wants the company more than anything.

Beth's started to say my name! She says it kind of like 'Tashshshh' but she definitely means me :)

9 pm

Darren's just left. He's been here a few hours, and he was ever so sweet, making me dinner and fetching cups of tea and cushions. We didn't mention the talk we had the other day, just talked about work and people and films and stuff, like we usually do, and it was nice.

Friday 25 April

Beth had a horrible time of it this morning, poor thing. She started getting upset when we arrived at the hospital, and she was fidgety and crying a bit through the first few tests – no idea what they were, because Jamie went in with her while I sat with the buggy and stuff – but she screamed when one of the nurses tried to give her the sedative medicine that she had last week, so she must have remembered it and known what was coming. After a few goes, Jamie took the medicine from the nurse and we went down to the café near the main entrance and between us we managed to get it down her without too much upset.

She was in the scanner machine much longer this time. As she was quite drowsy there were no tears, but when Jamie took her from the nurse afterwards she clung to him and cried for a bit. He took her for a walk down to the garden area – it's under glass, like a greenhouse –

and she dozed off properly then, so he came back for me and we went back to the car. Pushing a buggy when you're on crutches is not as hard as I'd thought it would be, but I'm glad Beth wasn't in it. I'd thought we'd be going back to see Dr Burgess for the scan results, but Jamie said he's got to wait for all the test results to be reported back to Dr B and then he'll get another appointment to discuss them.

I went back to his house with them and sat with Beth in the lounge while Jamie made us some lunch. She was still very dozy, but she was talking about something and seemed quite happy. I sometimes have trouble catching what she's saying. When she's drowsy like that it sounds like Russian, but she didn't seem bothered that I couldn't understand her. I stayed there for the afternoon – Jamie was talking a lot about the different tests and worrying about what they meant, but trying to reassure Beth and help her wake up properly, and all I could do really was sit there and talk to them both and just hope I was saying the right thing to not make him worry more.

I had a bit of an embarrassing moment when I needed the loo and he offered to help me up the stairs. I ended up going on my own because it would have taken too long and he needed to stay with Beth, plus I was getting all flustered having him put his hands under my arms and stuff to make sure I didn't fall. God love him, he means well but he's got no bloody clue what he's doing to me.

He brought me home after tea – he'd made enough pasta for me, without even asking – but he didn't come in, he just helped me out of the car and waited till I'd got inside. I got a lovely wave off Beth, the little sweetheart. I'm so chuffed that Jamie's been driving today – he wasn't brilliant and he's obviously still over-reacting in traffic, but he's much better than he was, and I didn't feel half as tense as I did last time.

Lisa called round this evening, bringing Get Well cards from work and some lemon drizzle cake that the girls had made. She said that Gemma thinks she's pregnant but won't know for sure until she's been to the doctor – she doesn't trust the shop-bought tests – and Vinnie's already whingeing about having to find agency staff to take her place if she goes on maternity leave. He's such a ball of sunshine, that Vinnie.

Lisa and I had a lovely long talk and I've told her about my mixed up feelings over Jamie and Darren (but not about the shagging thing) and she said she's known for a long time that I've got a crush on J, which made me feel a bit nervous about who else might have noticed but she reckons that no-one else has, or at least no-one's said anything to suggest that they have. She's positive that Jamie's 100% clueless because he just doesn't notice things like that – she said that she'd had to tell him that Simone and Carly have the hots for him, so he doesn't get himself into any awkward situations with them, and she said he was embarrassed as hell. Is it wrong that that just makes him more attractive?

Sunday 27 April

Lu got here about 3 o'clock yesterday. She said she just wanted to see for herself that I wasn't too badly injured and that things were set up for me to cope on my own, and she was here when Jamie phoned and when Ben and Adam called round, so she's satisfied that I've got back-up. We ordered a takeaway for tea, and spent the evening watching DVDs and talking. She said I should forget all about the Jamie fantasy thing with Darren and just see how the relationship with him goes, because we do still like each other and he's pretty good boyfriend material really. She thinks I'll get over Jamie, but I think that's because she doesn't believe I love him – she thinks I'm just lusting after what I can't have. I don't think it's that at all, but I wasn't going to get into an argument over it, so I just kind of shrugged and we went back to watching the film.

Lucy took me to Asda this morning and helped me get stocked up on food etc, then after lunch she went home. Jamie rang not long afterwards and invited me for tea – I was so chuffed that I got all flustered again – and he and Beth came to pick me up on their way home from the park. He made chicken risotto and it was lovely. He said he knows it's not easy to do much in the kitchen when you're on crutches – apparently he broke his leg some years ago, and remembers it well – and he said, if I wanted to, I could go round there to eat every day until I'm off the crutches or at least more steady with them. I said no (and thank you), because I'm not putting on him like that, no matter how much I love spending time with him, but he said I could change my mind any time, it's no bother. I love the way he says that, it's so Scottish, it makes me shiver. He brought me home almost straight after we'd eaten, because he doesn't like to disrupt Beth's evening routine if he can help it, but I'm just so happy that he did that for me :)

I've spent the evening working on my NVQ and now I feel all smug and accomplished. Hopefully at this rate I'll get it finished by the start of the summer.

Monday 28 April

I've been hobbling about without my crutches today and I'm aching everywhere. I should have started on Friday or Saturday, really - the nurse at A&E told me to give it a few days before I tried it - and I had a couple of goes when Lucy was here, but she was fussing so much that I gave up. Today I've moved all around the flat without crutches, kind of hopping but putting my foot lightly on the floor and trying not to put too much weight on it. I'm not even sure if I'm doing it right, but it's much quicker than with the crutches. I've got an appointment at Outpatients tomorrow - Ben's taking me - so hopefully they can show me what I should be doing.

Jamie and Beth picked me up after school this afternoon, and I went to theirs for tea again. He was a bit quiet - not that he's loud and bouncy normally - but I could tell something was bothering him. He said his niece rang this afternoon to tell him that she's been selected to do some special training or something to do with her college course and she was going to turn it down because it's this weekend, when they're going to Blackpool, but he told her not to turn it down, so now she's not going to Blackpool and he doesn't know if he's up to going on his own. Elspeth talked him out of cancelling the holiday, but he doesn't really see any other option: he wasn't going to go in the first place until his niece said she'd go with him, so now he might as well just forget about it.

He looked really down, so like an idiot I jumped in and said if there was no-one else to go with them, then I'd go. He looked surprised and a little embarrassed. I said I'll find somewhere to stay, hopefully not too far from where they are, and I can just be on hand to help out with Beth. Somehow I've managed to convince him (and me) that it could work, and up to now he hasn't cancelled. He rang the hotel and asked if there were any single room cancellations since last time he rang, but there aren't, so he asked if there were any nearby places with vacancies and she's promised to check and ring him back. I said if push comes to shove then I'll just take his niece's place and share with Beth, if he thinks Beth would be okay with that, and he said he didn't know.

I know he's only considering it because he doesn't want to let Beth down, but now I feel a bit like I've put him on the spot and I feel bad about it. He might not want me in the same room but is too polite to say it. I think if the landlady doesn't come up with a single room somewhere else, I'll not push it and let him cancel. I'd hate for him to feel obliged to go just because I've offered. Would he do that, just so Beth gets her holiday? I wish I knew. Maybe I should have a chat with Elspeth.

Darren came round this evening, and he brought a takeaway and a bottle of wine. We watched telly, and had a nice little snog, but that's all. He said he's applied for a job at the hospital, and it sounds perfect for him - it's more responsibility, and more in line with his qualifications, and no night shifts - so I'll keep my fingers crossed for him.

Tuesday 29 April

Well I've been doing it wrong, but now I know what I'm supposed to be doing. The little bone in my foot that was broken has started to knit, and I have to do little exercises and only walk so many steps at a time, but apparently everything is healing as it should. I asked about going to Blackpool at the weekend and the Orthopaedics guy said there's no reason why not, but I'll not be able to walk properly for a while, so that's something to talk to Jamie about and it might be the decider on whether or not we go. I can still use the crutches, but that limits what else I can do. I was at the hospital for ages, but most of that was waiting to be seen. Ben dropped me off there, then came back for me when I rang him. I haven't told him about Blackpool but he's obviously talked with Jamie about it because he (B) asked me if I'm sure about going and we had a bit of a chat about it. He's more worried about me being on crutches, I think. Anyway he brought me home and took my new sick note into work for me.

Jamie rang at lunch time. He said the AD had been round to see him, and they've agreed that he'll go back to work next week. He wasn't ringing about that, though - he'd heard from the Blackpool landlady this morning and she couldn't find anywhere within easy walking distance that had any vacancies at all, and I thought he was going to tell me he'd cancelled the holiday but he hasn't! So I said I'm still up for going if he's okay with the sleeping arrangements, and he sounded a bit unsure but he said he thinks Beth will be fine - he said she's seen more of me than she has of his niece just lately, so if anything she should be more relaxed about me being there, but we'll just have to see how it goes. I told him what the Ortho man said about walking etc., and he started saying maybe we shouldn't go but I said it'll be fine. So we're going to Blackpool on Saturday! Now that I think about it, I'm not sure I'll be able to sleep with him in the same room, but I've said it now so there's no going back.

He invited me to tea again but I said they could come to mine for a change, as I need to practise (I don't, but it was a good excuse) so they turned up after school - not in the car - and stayed for an hour or so. I made a tuna bake, a bit like the one he makes but less tomatoey, and they both ate it all so it couldn't have been that bad. For pudding, we finished off the white chocolate cheesecake that Lucy had bought on Sunday. Beth couldn't get enough of it, so I'll have to get that one again! I know Jamie went to see his counsellor this afternoon, but he didn't mention it. I suppose I'm just nosey, but I can't help wondering how it's going.

Wednesday 30 April

I went as far as the corner shop this morning on my crutches. It's the furthest I've been on them and there were no mishaps but I was knackered by the time I got back. I went the other way after lunch, as far as the traffic lights, just to see how far I can manage without needing to stop or sit down, and it's about half an hour so that's pretty good. I saw Gemma at the corner - she was on her way to work - and she's had confirmation that she's pregnant, so we had a little hug. I said I hope to be back in work next week and she said, "Oh yeah?" and then I realised she'd know that Jamie's due to start back next week, and it made me blush. So I said my sick note's only for another week so I should be right as rain by Wednesday, and I hope I am because it's boring being stuck at home.

Jamie rang me at tea-time. He said yesterday that he'd pick me up on the way home from school, but he didn't and I was wondering whether or not to ring him when he rang me. He said Beth hadn't been to school as she had a bad night - she woke up three times, screaming like last time, and it took him ages each time to get her back to sleep, so they were both knackered this morning and he rang school to say she wouldn't be in. He said the hospital phoned this afternoon with an appointment with Dr Burgess on Tuesday next week, for the test results. He said he asked if they could go earlier but that's the earliest they've got with it being a Bank Holiday weekend. I said that means it's not too serious, then, otherwise they'd have her in straight away, wouldn't they?

I think he feels a bit better about it now. Anyway he was ringing to apologise about tea - with having Beth home all day he'd completely forgotten until he was plating up, and he said he'd pay for a taxi if I wanted to get myself over there, but I said no because he doesn't have to do my tea every day and it'll be nice for him and Beth to just have each other's company. He had to go then because Beth was struggling with her food, so I said I'd ring him later.

I rang at 8 but there was no answer. I didn't let it ring for long, in case it woke Beth up, and Jamie rang me back a bit later. He said he'd given Beth some Calpol at bed-time to help her sleep, but he'd spent over an hour sitting on her bed in case she woke up or in case she had a reaction to the Calpol, and he said he hates being so anxious but it's really difficult to rationalise himself out of it. I love it when he talks to me like this – it's so personal and so sweet of him to share his feelings like that with me. I know he talks with Elspeth about the same stuff, but she's his sister and I'm just barely a friend, so it means a lot to me. I suggested he gets an early night, and I told him to ring me at any time if he wants me to go over there (I'll get a taxi) or if he just wants to talk himself out of his anxiety, and he said thank you in that way that makes me see him smiling all shyly. Oh boy.

Friday 2 May   11 am

Darling that he is, Ben took me into town yesterday so I could buy a few bits and pieces for the weekend. We had a nice wander around and a good long chat, and we stopped for coffee because I needed to rest, and he carried my bags for me. He and Adam are going to Brighton today for a long weekend, coming back on Tuesday, so we'll be back in work together on Wednesday, which will be Jamie's first day back :)

We saw Jamie on the way home - he was just coming out of the park when we were approaching the lights - and he invited us round to his for a cuppa so we met him there (he wanted to call at the newsagents on the way back). He said we should have gone in and put the kettle on rather than wait outside, which I thought was sweet of him. Anyway we had a cuppa with him and talked about the weekend - mostly about Brighton - and about work, and Jamie talked me into staying for tea, so Ben went home without me. I said I'd make tea while J went to pick Beth up from school, but he'd made it already so it only needed putting in the oven, so I ended up going to school with him in the car. Beth was chuffed to see me, bless her, and kept turning round to hold my hand on the way back to their house. J said he'll move her car seat back into the back, so she won't have to stretch so much, if she carries on wanting to do that.

Beth had one of her episodes after tea - nothing major, just a crying spell and that odd nodding thing she's started doing, but she didn't calm down for ages. Jamie carried her around the lounge and into the garden, talking so gently to her that I couldn't hear what he was saying, but he looked at me a couple of times and he looked like he wanted to scream. She stopped eventually and then carried on as if nothing had happened, playing with her dolls, but he looked exhausted. He said she'd only woken once on Wednesday night, but it was over an hour before she went back to sleep again, and he's starting to dread bedtime.

I asked him how much Calpol he gives her and it turns out he's only giving her a toddler's dose because he doesn't like the idea of drugging her, so I tried to convince him that millions of kids are given the suggested dose every day and it's very reliable. In the end I suggested he talk with Elspeth and see what she says about it, so I left him to phone her while I did the pots. He came off the phone looking all sheepish and said that Elspeth had backed me up, then he just came straight out and asked me if I'd mind staying over because Elspeth thinks it might be a good idea to have two of us there if Beth's waking up so much during the night. We're going to be sharing a room over the weekend anyway, so I said yes, and he nipped me home (with Beth, of course) so I could pick up some overnight stuff. After Beth had gone to bed we watched telly, but I went to bed not long after 9 because (a) it's too much bother to go up and down the stairs to the loo, and (b) I didn't want to crowd him in his own house. I heard him going to bed not long after, though, so maybe I should have stayed up and kept him company.

Beth woke up twice during the night, but Jamie said both times that she wasn't as agitated as she has been, so maybe the slightly higher dose of Calpol is helping. I got up with them this morning, but Jamie walked Beth to school and then came back to drive me home. I suppose he doesn't want anyone at school to see us together that early in the day and jump to the wrong conclusions. When he was dropping me off, I asked him if he wanted me to stay tonight but he said no. I'm pretty sure he does, but he doesn't want to impose - it's just the way he said it, like he wanted me to argue or something - but I didn't insist in case I was misreading him. They're coming to me for tea this afternoon, though, so I might ask him again then.

10 pm

J hasn't changed his mind about me staying tonight. I think it embarrasses him, and I'm getting a bit worried about how he's going to be over the weekend. They came for tea after school, and Beth was fine - very happy and giggly, like her usual self, which was lovely. When they were getting ready to leave, I asked Jamie if he'd like me to stay again and he said no, he'll be fine. He said it's more than enough that I'll have two nights of it this weekend, and I didn't want to push it.

Tuesday 6 May

I'm not even sure that I want to be writing this down; I just feel that I owe it to Jamie and his family to try and set down an accurate record of what happened. Some things are a blur, so I hope that by writing them down I'll remember more details. It's not something I ever thought I'd be writing about and it's not something I want to write about but I think I should.

I need to start at the beginning and try and keep my

head straight so that things don't get mixed up.

Saturday was such a fantastic day. We got to the station with enough time to get parked and get everything onto the platform without having to rush. Beth was excited, and loved seeing the other trains coming and going, and there was a little dog on the platform that kept yapping at anything that moved and she thought it was hilarious. Jamie said she'd woken up once during the night, but she'd been awake for quite a while and he was surprised that she wasn't a bit grumpy that morning.

We talked the whole way there, mostly about Beth and work, and a bit about music and films. He loves music, and Helen did too, and they used to go to a lot of the big festivals every summer, with Beth - he said that this year will be the first time he won't be going to Glastonbury. I commiserated, because I've seen the line-up and would love to go, and he said I could have their tickets because it would be a shame to waste them. He looked a bit sad then, and said he couldn't imagine going without Helen, so I changed the subject and got him onto film scores and then films, and it turns out we have similar tastes in those too.

We got to Blackpool with no hitches, and took a taxi to the hotel, right on the promenade. The landlady met us at the door and gave Beth and Jamie a huge hug, with tears in her eyes. She's ever so nice, really mumsy. Our room was on the first floor at the front, and the hotel is so big that it has a lift, which was handy. The landlady said she'd changed the bed set-up after Jamie's calls, and had put in three singles, and she looked at me and Jamie and said she hoped that would be okay and we both went as red as each other and said, "Yes of course it's all right." so she knew straight away that we're not together in that way.

We dropped our bags off and went out for lunch. Jamie said he knew a few places to eat, but if I didn't mind he'd like to try some new ones. I didn't mind - I was worried that he'd get memory overload while we were there, and I didn't want him to be unhappy. We found a nice cafe near the pier and had cheese toasties, which they served with salad. The coffee wasn't up to much - too milky, and a bit own-brandish - but the food was nice. We went down to the beach afterwards - I sat with the buggy while Jamie took Beth down to the water's edge, and then for a ride on the donkeys. He had that awful tortured look on his face when they came back, and I could tell he was having a hard time keeping it together. I half expected him to suggest we went home, but he didn't, he just kept being cheerful for Beth and pointing things out to her and making sure she was okay.

We walked down the prom a bit, towards the fair, and Beth loved looking at everything – there's so much noise and colour and movement – then we turned back towards town and she saw a poster for the Tower Aquarium and got excited about it, so we ended up going there. She loved it, and the atmosphere of the place seemed to have a calming effect on her because she was excited but quiet about it, and I realised they must have been there before because Jamie had tears in his eyes at one point.

I was aching a lot by the time we came out of there, and I could tell that Jamie was finding it really difficult just being there, so I asked if we could go somewhere to sit down for a bit and we went into a cafe that had only opened that day. They had 'proper' coffee so we both had one, and Beth had a milkshake, and I took a couple of painkillers. We had a look at the menu while we were talking, and it was pretty good so we decided to have our tea there. Jamie said we could eat at the hotel - we'd booked in for dinner, bed and breakfast - but I could tell he needed to break from tradition so I said I'd rather try this new place and he nodded.

We took our time eating, and then strolled slowly back to the hotel so that we got back there about 6.30. I went into the TV lounge and left Jamie to take Beth up for her bath. I got chatting with the landlady - she has a Polish name, which I've no idea how to spell, and Jamie calls her Mrs P - and she's so nice, and obviously thinks the world of Jamie and Beth, and Helen. I thought Jamie would have come down after Beth had gone to sleep but there was still no sign of him by 8 o'clock so I went up to the room, and he was in the shower so I just changed my shoes and got a cardigan and went back downstairs. I watched telly until 10 but he still didn't come downstairs and by then I needed another painkiller so I went up. He was sitting in one of the chairs by the window, reading, wearing pyjama pants and a t-shirt. He only had the bedside lamp on and he asked me if I wanted the big light on, but I didn't want to wake Beth so I said no and took my stuff into the bathroom to have a shower and get ready for bed.

I can't remember the last time I felt so nervous. I can't remember the last time I wore thick cotton pyjamas, either, but that was the least of my worries. I didn't know whether to get straight into bed or to sit and talk with him for a bit, so when I came out of the bathroom I asked him what time he was thinking of going down to breakfast and he said 9-ish and he was still reading so I sat opposite him with my book and read for a while. I'd only read a couple of pages when he closed his book and said, "This is a bit awkward" and, "I'm sorry" and when I asked why, he said to just say when I wanted to go to sleep and he'd put the light out. So I said I can sleep with the light on, it doesn't bother me, and I was ready for bed then but I said to not put the light out because of that, and I got into bed with my back to the room and left him reading. He went to bed soon after me, though, because I was still awake, and I heard him crying even though he was very quiet.

Beth didn't wake at all during Saturday night, and we all slept through until just after 8 on Sunday morning. I nipped into the bathroom to get dressed while Jamie dressed Beth, then I sat and played with her while he did the same. Thinking about it now, I'm surprised at how easy it was - not half as awkward as I thought it would be. Beth was a bit quiet at breakfast and didn't eat much, but she'd eaten so well on Saturday that neither of us thought anything of it.

We left the hotel around 10.30 and took a tram ride as far as the Norbreck Hotel, which is north of the town by Bispham and is supposed to look like a castle. Mrs P said they had a child-friendly restaurant there with a playroom so we thought we'd go up that way, look around, and stop for lunch. There's not much to see for an eight-year-old kid, but the sea view was gorgeous and she really loved being on the tram. We had lunch - nothing to write home about, and Beth wasn't impressed - then we took her in the playroom for a bit, but there were three very boisterous boys in there so we didn't stay long. We got the next tram back into town and got off at the fair.

Beth fell asleep in her buggy so we ended up wandering around and looking at the rides, and we went for a coffee to kill some time. When she woke up Jamie took her on a couple of the slow rides which she loved. I took some photos but I was using his camera and I'm not sure if they'll turn out okay. We walked back along the prom - slowly because I was aching even more by then - and stopped near the pier for another ride on the donkeys (got some more photos, and I really hope they come out okay), then we went back to that new cafe for our tea. Beth didn't eat much, but Jamie and I coaxed her with some of our quiche and chips, and she ate most of her apple crumble and some of my cheesecake. Jamie said that last year Beth had wanted to ride on a lot more things but this year she didn't seem so bothered, and I said she's getting to the age where she probably thinks she's too big for all that. I think we both thought she was missing her mum, but neither of us was going to say it.

We walked back along the prom and past the hotel, then circled round to the play park for half an hour. Beth seemed tired, though - she wasn't laughing and squealing like she usually does - so we headed back to the hotel. I left Jamie to bath and bedtime again, and said I'd stay downstairs until bedtime but Jamie said to come up to the room any time since I was staying there too, so I waited until 9 and then went up. He was sitting on the floor next to Beth's bed, talking quietly to her and stroking her hair, so I just sat by the window and watched the people and traffic outside. He came and sat with me when she'd fallen asleep and told me she'd had another of her 'wee fits' as he calls them, but it wasn't as bad as they've been up to now so he said he hoped they were easing off.

We sat there talking for an hour or so, mostly about different seaside towns and childhood holidays, then we went to bed at the same time. I had to get up to go to the loo in the night, and he was on the floor next to Beth's bed again, holding her hand. I hadn't heard anything, but he's her Dad with super-sensitive radar so she must have woken up at some point. I went over to check on them and they were both asleep, so I woke him up and told him to get back into bed, which he did.

Yesterday (Monday) we were up at 8ish and down for breakfast by 9ish again. Beth was a bit grumpy, and Jamie said she probably didn't want to go home. She wasn't saying much, though, just sort of grumbling and whining. She didn't touch her breakfast, so Mrs P made her a little packed lunch to take on the train. The same taxi driver came to pick us up and take us to the station, and he was very helpful too, carrying our bags to the platform for us. It was hot on the train, and Beth dozed off again almost before we'd left the station. She didn't wake up until we got off, and then she started crying and clinging to Jamie so he had to carry her out to the car rather than put her in the buggy, so I put our bags in the buggy and tried to wheel it out to the car park - not easy when you're on crutches! Someone in the ticket office took pity, and came out and took over, thank god. Beth had fallen asleep again by the time we got the luggage and buggy in the car, so I stayed with her while Jamie nipped into the Spar on the way home to get bread and milk and something for lunch. She was making a funny gurgling noise in her sleep, so I straightened her head a little bit in case she was blocking an airway, and she let out a sweet little sigh. I didn't realise at the time, but now I know what that was.

When we got to their house, Jamie and I took the buggy and luggage in first and I went to put the kettle on while he went to fetch Beth from the car. He came running into the house, carrying her and shouting for me to ring an ambulance. He said she wasn't breathing and did I know first aid? I had to tell him he knows CPR - he's been on all the courses - so he put Beth on the sofa and started that while shouting at me to phone for an ambulance, which I did.

They were asking all sorts of questions about her and I had to keep asking Jamie and it felt like hours before the ambulance got here, but it couldn't have been more than a few minutes, really. They came straight in - the door was still open, and some of Jamie's neighbours were outside so they must have told them it was the right house because no doubt they heard all the screaming and yelling - and they took over from Jamie, and then I realised that there were two police officers with them. One of them went to Jamie, and the other one took me into the kitchen and started asking me questions about who I was and who Jamie and Beth were and what had happened, and I started telling her but then Jamie was shouting and crying and it sounded like there was a scuffle, so I went to see what was happening and the police officer and one of the paramedics were holding him down on one of the chairs, and the other paramedic was talking into a radio, and Beth's lips were blue.

I was going to ask why they'd stopped the CPR when it dawned on me: Beth was dead. The gurgling, and the little sigh - just like Mum. She'd died in the car, and I hadn't realised. I thought I was going to be sick, and an officer put her arm around me and took me back into the kitchen and started making tea and I thought how weird that was, that she was making tea in a stranger's house, but I suppose they recognise shock and think that a cuppa helps. Sometimes it does, but not when you feel like that. I wanted to go to Jamie but she said I should stay where I was, because we both had to answer some questions while the authorities were informed. I suppose at that stage we were both suspects since it's not normal for an eight-year-old little girl to die in her daddy's car. So I told her about Dr Burgess and everything I could remember, and we drank tea and she made notes and I tried to listen to what was happening in the lounge.

When she'd finished questioning me, the police officer went off into the hall to talk into her radio and I went into the lounge to check on Jamie. He was still answering questions with the other police officer but when he saw me he stopped and looked so devastated and horror-stricken and shocked, I went and sat next to him and just put my arm round his shoulder and he grabbed onto me and cried. The officer waited a bit, then said he was nearly done and asked Jamie some more questions, and asked me some too - some of them I'd already been asked - and then he asked if there was anyone we'd like to phone, to tell them what had happened, and I said I'd ring Elspeth and Ben because Jamie was in no fit state to ring anyone.

I phoned from my mobile in the kitchen, because I didn't want Jamie to hear what I was telling them. Stupid, I know – as if he didn't know already. Ben was so upset, and asked if they should come home, and I had to talk to Adam in the end because Ben just couldn't handle it and he was making me cry and I was trying not to cry so that I could keep an eye on Jamie. I told Adam there's no point in them coming home early - they couldn't do anything - but he said he'd talk with Ben about it and they'd let me know.

Then I had to ring Elspeth and that's the hardest thing I've ever had to do, even harder than telling Uncle Phil about Mum because at least he was expecting it. So I rang Elspeth and I think she could tell straight away that something was wrong because when I said it was me she just said, "What's happened?" and she must have thought that I was ringing about Jamie because she asked me if he was okay and I said, "No, not really." but then I had to tell her that I wasn't ringing about him because she was going, "Oh god, oh god, oh god." and then I just had to tell her, "It's Beth." She went all quiet, and I had to tell her what had happened. She took it quite well - she was crying, but not hysterical - and she said she'd ring later and talk to Jamie.

By the time I got off the phone, the paramedics and the doctor had gone, and so had Beth, and the police officers were sitting with Jamie and he looked like a white statue. I thought the police would stay, or take us to the station or something, but they didn't - they just asked if we'd be okay and I said yes, and they left. I found out afterwards that the GP had spoken with Dr Burgess, and then he told the police that it was most likely a natural death, so we weren't really under suspicion. I saw them to the door, but I couldn't go straight back into Jamie because I was shaking and felt sick again, so I just stood there with my head against the door for a bit.

Then I heard him throwing up and I ran in there and he was on his knees, hurling into the fireplace and crying. I made him sit back in the chair and went to get him some water, and he kept saying, "Can't breathe, can't breathe!" and I was beginning to panic a bit because I've seen him lose it before but this was going to be so much worse. He drank a bit of the water but then threw it right back up again, and I was just going to get some tissues when the doorbell rang and it was the GP again. He said he just wanted to check on Jamie and I said I was so glad he'd come back and told him about the sick and everything, so he went into the lounge and crouched down in front of Jamie and talked to him for a bit.

I went to get cleaning stuff from the kitchen and when I went back into the lounge the doctor had Jamie leaning over with his head almost between his knees, taking deep breaths. He stayed for a while, talking to Jamie and getting him to drink some water (which he kept down) and then when Jamie thanked him, the doctor turned to me and said he'd call back in the morning (today) and he gave me a little bottle of tablets and said they'd help Jamie sleep if he needed them, and he pressed it into my hand like he was saying 'Keep hold of them' or something and I just filled up. He took me into the hall and said to ring him if I had any concerns at all, and he wrote his number on a piece of paper, and then he said it would be best if Jamie wasn't left on his own for a bit, so I nodded and said I'd stay with him.

When I went back into the lounge, Jamie was still sitting in the chair, his shirt all wet from sick and water, and he was just staring towards the window. The room stank of vomit and it made me gag a bit, but I knelt down in front of him and put my hand on his hand and he looked at me slowly, and he was frowning like he didn't really know where he was or who I was. I asked him if he wanted to get changed and he looked at me like I was speaking a foreign language, so I touched his shirt and he looked at it and nodded but he didn't move, so I pulled him to his feet and took him up to the bathroom. He was shaking and I thought he might be sick again, but we managed to get his shirt off and I filled the sink for him to have a wash while I went to get him a clean top from his bedroom. He was really shivering hard by the time we were done, so I suggested he get into bed, and he did but I had to go in and take his shoes off him.

I told him to shout if he wanted anything, then I took his shirt downstairs and started cleaning up the mess in the lounge and it was only when I went to get fresh water that I realised I was crying, so I sat down and had a good sob to get it out of my system. I went back upstairs after half an hour to check that Jamie was okay and he was still shivering under the duvet but he didn't say anything, so I nipped back down and made him a cup of tea and made him sit up and drink some of it. I didn't think he'd noticed that I'd put sugar in it, but after a few sips he legged it to the bathroom and was sick again, so I said sorry and told him that Mum always said to have a sweet cup of tea when you've had a shock. I think it's an old wives' tale but I didn't know what else to do to stop him from shivering.

He climbed back into bed without saying anything, but when I picked up his mug to go back downstairs he asked me to stay with him so I sat on the bed, and he told me then that the doctor had said that Beth's scan results had shown up some problems and that there was no way Jamie could have known this would happen and there was nothing we could have done. He said the doctor was Dr Burgess's brother-in-law and both their wives were friends of Helen's, and it sounded like he was just talking for the sake of talking, and I didn't know what to say. I just wanted to cry but I didn't want to set him off again, and I was having a hard time keeping the tears back, so I said I needed the loo and went into the bathroom to wash my face and blow my nose and calm down, and when I went back into his room he was on his side and crying again, so I got on the bed behind him and put my arm over him on top of the duvet and we had a good long cry together.

I don't know how long we were there but the phone started ringing, so I went down to answer it and it was Elspeth. She asked me some more questions and I was able to tell her a bit more this time, and I said I'd ask Jamie to ring her later when he came downstairs. She said she'd arranged time off work and was coming down for a bit, and I was so relieved that I'd have kissed her if she'd been there. I'd just put the phone down when my mobile went off and it was Lisa - she'd overheard some women talking in Asda, and she was ringing to find out what was going on because the women sounded convinced that Jamie had been arrested for smothering Beth in her sleep, and one of them had been ringing someone else to pass on the gossip. So I told her what had happened and ten minutes later she was on the doorstep. We had a hug and a cry and I made us some tea and we talked, not about anything in particular but just passing time. She only stayed an hour or so, but I was so glad of her company.

By the time Lisa left it was gone 5 o'clock and I was starting to feel hungry - we'd only shared a sandwich between us on the train, and that was before noon - so I went upstairs to ask Jamie if he wanted anything but he didn't. I told him that Elspeth had phoned but he didn't say anything. I went back down and made a sandwich, and then for an hour or so I was non-stop on the phone - first Lucy rang, because I'd forgotten to ring her like I said I would when I got home, then Darren, because I'd said I'd ring him too, then Ben. It was really hard, going over it all for Lucy and Darren, and then with Ben again because he was still upset from earlier. He and Adam were still in Brighton, because they didn't think there was much they could do by coming home early and I agreed, but he felt a bit bad about it and he said they'd come round as soon as they got home.

I sat and watched the telly for a bit then - no idea what was on, and I dozed off at some point. The news was on when I woke up, and I was stiff and needed the loo so I went upstairs but the bathroom was locked. I waited a few minutes, then started to worry - I couldn't hear any noise in there and I didn't know how long Jamie had been in there - so I knocked on the door and asked if he was okay. I waited a bit and was just going to knock again when he opened the door.

Now the sight of him in grey Calvin Klein's and a Fratellis t-shirt would normally have melted me on the spot, especially since he had seriously sexy bed-head hair going on, but he managed to look like a lost 12-year-old and I just wanted to hug him. I said sorry for disturbing him and told him I'd just put the kettle on if he wanted a drink, and he just nodded and went into his bedroom, but he was in the kitchen when I got back down there, making us both a cup of tea. He was white, but the 12-

year-old look had gone and I sat there wishing to god he'd put his jeans back on because I was having very, very inappropriate thoughts. He must have stripped off in bed, cos I know I left his jeans and socks on. Thankfully he sat down, so I was spared the sight of his long (hairy!) legs and cute little bum, but not before I caught a glimpse of his package. I came over all hot and had to stare at my tea for a bit because I was so scared he'd see how turned on I was, and I felt sick with myself for even feeling that way. Then I noticed he wasn't drinking his tea so I told him to drink up and that took my mind off it.

I told him I'd spoken again with Elspeth and Ben, and that Lisa had called round, but he just nodded. He drank his tea for a bit, and then he said he keeps getting déjà vu back to when Helen died, and it all feels a bit surreal. I said it's understandable, because it is, really, isn't it? It's not even three months since Helen died and he's nowhere near getting over that, and now this has happened so it must feel really weird. Sickening, horrible, and weird.

I told him Elspeth was hoping to talk to him, and I said I'd call her back if he didn't feel up to it, but he said he'd call her and then I think he realised what time it was - nearly 10 o'clock - so he went into the lounge and rang her. I gave him ten minutes then took him a fresh cup of tea, and he was talking quietly and he'd obviously been crying but he looked okay. He came back in the kitchen after another ten minutes or so and said thanks for the tea, and then he sat down and said, "I realise it's a bit late to be asking, but would you stay here tonight?" and I told him I'd already made my mind up that I was staying, whether he wanted me to or not, and he almost smiled at that.

Then he looked at me for what felt like a long time and I said, "What?" and he got up really quickly and said he'll make up the spare bed and off he went upstairs, which made me wonder what he'd been thinking, but I followed him and gave him a hand with the bedding. When we were done I took my bag up to the room, then had a shower and got ready for bed, but he was still downstairs so I went down to say goodnight and he was sitting in the lounge in the dark. I asked him if he wanted something to help him sleep, but he didn't so I just said goodnight and went to bed.

I got up to go to the loo in the middle of the night - too much tea! - and his door was still open so I could see that he wasn't in bed, so I went down and he was still there, sitting in the dark. I told him he needed to sleep and when he didn't answer I went over to him, and then I could see that he was asleep so I nipped back upstairs and got his duvet and put it over him, but that woke him up. I thought he'd have snapped at me - Gavin was a right git if he got woken up in the night - but he didn't, he just said thank you and said he'd been trying to get used to the idea of being on his own, because he's never lived alone before. I said he doesn't have to be alone, and he was going to say something else but I said, "It's nearly 3 o'clock - go to bed" so he picked up his duvet and went. I think he'd have sat there talking all night otherwise, and he looked knackered, so I'm glad he didn't argue.

I slept through until just after 9 this morning. Jamie was already up when I went downstairs - he was on the phone. I made us some toast and coffee, thinking he'd come through to the kitchen when he was done, but he didn't so I went through and he was just standing at the window looking out at the garden. I asked him if he was okay and he said that it was Dr Burgess on the phone - he and Beth had had an appointment with him this morning to discuss the test results, and Dr B had phoned to go over what the GP had told him yesterday. He said that there was a growth in Beth's brain, possibly caused or made worse by the accident in February, and it would have required surgery. Dr B didn't actually say that it had killed her, but Jamie said he thinks that's what Dr B is getting at. I patted his shoulder and next thing I knew he was hugging me really hard, and shaking, so I hugged him back and tried not to think about how lovely he smells up close. He wasn't crying, but it took him a while to stop shaking and then he stepped away from me, and I suggested we have some toast so he followed me into the kitchen and he actually ate a round of toast with his coffee, which surprised me.

The rest of the day turned out to be hectic and kind of weird. A police officer came round not long after we'd finished our toast and was talking to Jamie for about ten minutes - he said it was about the coroner's procedures - and then not long after he'd gone, Jamie's GP came round to see if he was alright and he stayed about twenty minutes. I stayed out of the way in the kitchen. Then just before lunch time, Ben and Adam arrived. The three of us had a little hug and a cry in the hall, then they went into the lounge to see Jamie and I made us all some tea. The lads were really upset, bless them, and when they left Jamie went upstairs for half an hour or so - I think he just needed some quiet time on his own, so I left him to it.

When he came down, he said he needed some air and he grabbed his jacket and went out. I was on the phone with Lisa so I didn't get chance to say anything to him, and I had no idea where he was going. Lisa had asked me if the school knew about Beth, so when I finished talking with her, I rang the school and told the Head Teacher and she said she'd heard a rumour but didn't believe it. She was so upset and asked me to let her know when the funeral will be. Then Elspeth rang to say she was on her way and her train would get in at around 5 and could Jamie pick her up from the station, so I wrote that on a post-it and stuck it on the fridge, then went up to change the bedding on the spare bed. I chucked them and some towels in the washing machine, then collected all my stuff and packed my bag again. I didn't think Jamie would want me sleeping in Beth's room - and I didn't want to, anyway - so I was all set to go home, since I assumed that Elspeth would be having the spare room.

I'd just done that when the AD rang, and I had to tell him that Jamie was out but then he wanted to know what had happened so I had to go over it all again and it made me cry a bit, which was embarrassing. The AD said he didn't expect Jamie to go in to work tomorrow but it was up to him (J) to do what he felt was best for him. I didn't say anything, just said I'd pass on the message, but then he asked me if I was okay to go back to work tomorrow and I said I'm still limping a bit but otherwise fine, so he took that as a 'Yes' and I could have kicked myself. Then Ben rang and asked if Jamie and I wanted to go for tea at their house, but I said Elspeth was on her way so he'd probably want some time with her, but Ben said she could go too so I wrote that on a post-it and said I'd get Jamie to ring him back. I added notes about the school and the AD, just to be sure I didn't forget anything.

Jamie came back around 3 o'clock and the first thing he said was sorry for leaving me on my own, but he just needed to get out for a bit. I said I don't ever want to hear him say sorry again. We went over the notes I'd written, then he saw the washing machine and my packed bag, and twigged that I was going home and he said, "Will you not stay?" in that leg-melting Scottish way of his and I said Elspeth would be having the spare bed, and then he blushed (bless him) and said he'd sleep on the sofa. I wasn't having that, though, and I managed to get him to agree to drop me off at home when he went to pick up Elspeth.

Jamie went to make some calls then, and I made us a sandwich while he was talking because we'd somehow forgotten to have lunch. He came and sat in the kitchen and started eating, and then he put his sandwich down and sat back in his chair and I thought he was going to cry again but he didn't. He said it all feels too normal, like nothing's happened, and he feels weird and numb. My first thought was that he's contradicting himself (normal isn't weird and numb) but I knew what he meant, and I was going to say something about emotions being all over the place but he said it was different when Helen died, he said he felt raw and it was like physical pain, but now it's more like an ache in his chest but the rest of him feels nothing. And I knew I was out of my depth, and I was scared of saying the wrong thing, so I just reached over and patted his hand and he grabbed my hand and leaned over and put his forehead on our hands. It wasn't very comfortable but I just sat there, wondering what to do.

I tried stroking his hair a bit but he didn't move, then he started talking but I couldn't hear him because his face was nearly on the table, so I told him I couldn't hear and he looked up, and he said he's tired of feeling nothing but the pain in his chest. I still wasn't sure what to say, so I just said it won't be there forever, and he looked kind of deflated and said, "Maybe it should be" like he deserved it or something, and I couldn't stand it.

I got up and pulled him into a hug (he stayed sitting down) and I told him it will get better, it's just that it's all happened so close together and it's all such a horrible shock, and he was hugging me back and shaking and it really crossed my mind that he might be heading for a breakdown and I thought about calling his GP, and without thinking I kissed the top of his head, and he said, "I miss that" and he told me how he and Helen had been very tactile, always hugging, and the same with Beth (and I'd seen that for myself), and he missed it. And oh how I wanted to do more than just hug him, but I just said, "Me and Ben are always good for a hug" and he nodded, but then he moved back and pushed me, not hard, so I was at arm's length away from him, and he was holding me by the arms and just looking at me, and then he went really red and let me go and picked up his tea, so I was standing there wondering what that was all about, so I said, "What?" and he said, "Take no notice - my head's up my arse just now" and he wouldn't look at me so I took a chance.

I mean, going on what he'd been saying, and the way he looked at me, and then blushing like a schoolboy, what else would he have been thinking about? So I put my hand on his shoulder and kissed the top of his head again, and I was going to say that he might feel better if he talked about stuff, and the next thing I know he's on his feet and we're snogging, which blew what I was going to say out of the water. It was lovely, of course, but I remembered last time and I didn't want that again, so I pulled away from him and told him to think about what he's doing, and it all got a bit confusing for a bit because he thought I was rejecting him but I wasn't and I had to make him shut up and listen, and I had to tell him I'd like nothing more than to take it further but I didn't want him doing something he'd regret.

He said he just wants to feel something that's not pain and part of me felt it was totally wrong but the other part of me wanted him so badly, so I pulled him back for a kiss and then hands started moving and we were stripping each other off in the bloody kitchen! And oh my god he may be thin but he's in great shape and what a shape he is. I couldn't take my eyes off him. And then he's helping me to sit on the table and the minute he was inside me I started coming - straight away! Never done that before - and he froze. He had his eyes closed and I asked him if he was okay and he said "Yes." and then "No." and he looked at me and said "It feels like adultery." and he started to move away but I held him there and said "Just enjoy how it feels for a moment." and he shifted his feet a bit and I came again, and he groaned and started moving properly, and I have never come so much or so quickly in my life.

I had to grip onto him and the table and it was horrendously uncomfortable, but my god it was amazing. And then he stopped again and he looked really worried and said he's not using anything so I told him I'm on the pill, but that seemed to kill the moment and he pulled away from me, taking my hand so I could stand up, and I could see he was having serious second thoughts even though he was still huge and hard, so I asked him if he wanted to finish and he didn't say no so I took him into the lounge and we finished it on the sofa. It was very quick but fantastic, and after he'd come I just held him there on top of me for ages, stroking his back and shoulders.

Now he may be thin, but he's very long so he weighs more than you'd think, and eventually I got uncomfortable and wriggled a bit, and he moved to the side of me with his hand on my hip and I smiled at him but he just looked at me with that sad, lost look and it broke my heart and he must have seen the change on my face because he rolled off the sofa and started going on about what kind of sick bastard he was, taking advantage of me, and what was he doing even thinking about sex when his daughter had just died, and only bits of it were making sense but he was obviously having a massive guilt attack.

I got up and grabbed his hands (he does that hand waving thing a lot when he's agitated) and I told him he didn't take advantage of me, and if it gave him a little break from the pain then I'm glad that I was there to help with that, and I thought he was going to cry but the phone started to ring and we both looked up and realised it was 5 o'clock, so he answered the phone and I grabbed some kitchen towel and cleaned the mess off the sofa. It was Elspeth, and she was at the station, so we both got dressed and I grabbed my bag and we went to meet her.

We didn't say anything to each other until he parked at the station, and then he said he'd ring me later which I took to mean when Elspeth was in bed, so I just nodded. I waited in the car while he went to find Elspeth, and he'd obviously told her I was there because she wasn't surprised to see me and gave me a hug when I got out to say hello. I got in the back so she could sit next to her brother, and then I saw Beth's car seat and that made me want to cry so I kept my eyes on the window. They dropped me off at home, and when I got in I went straight in the bath and had a bloody good cry because I finally got to shag him and it was amazing but so very wrong, and I could tell he was regretting it and probably wouldn't want to see me again. And he hasn't rung, and I need to get to bed because I've got to be in work for 9 tomorrow.

1.30 am

I've just got off the phone with Jamie. He texted me to ask if I was still awake, and I wasn't but it woke me up and I texted him back and said yes so he rang me. He said sorry for not ringing earlier but Elspeth didn't go to bed until after 12 and he needed a bit of time on his own to think, and that made my heart sink. He said he felt bad about taking advantage of me, and he was so mixed up emotionally he couldn't think straight, and he promised it won't happen again, and he'd understand if I didn't want anything more to do with him.

I asked him if it was wrong to have enjoyed it, and he got a bit tongue-tied at that, so I said I'd enjoyed it and I don't feel used but I'm worried about how he feels about it. And he said, "It doesn't matter, I can't do that - I still feel married" so I said okay, that's fine, but I need him to know that he's not to feel bad about taking advantage of me and all that crap because if I hadn't wanted to do it then I'd have told him no and he went quiet for a bit then, like he hadn't considered that, and then he said, "Shit" and "I'm so sorry" and he put the phone down.

I was going to ring him back but he obviously didn't want Elspeth to know he was on the phone, so I texted him and said, 'It really is okay, please don't feel bad' and it took him ten minutes but he rang me back, and before I'd even said hello he said, "You're a wonderful friend and I don't want to lose that, but I can't handle anything other than friendship, okay?" and I said, "Okay" and then he said thank you and said he needed to get to bed, so we said bye and he went. I'm glad we've got it sorted, and I'm glad he's okay with it all, even if he isn't really - he probably still feels guilty as hell, but because of Helen not me (I hope) - and I just hope there's no awkwardness between us next time I see him.

Wednesday 7 May

Got to work for 9 this morning (took a taxi). Ben was cross with me for not ringing him for a lift, but I didn't know what shift he was on and hadn't wanted to disturb him if he was on a late one. Vinnie has put me on desk duty until my limp improves, which basically means I'm doing all the paperwork that he hates - no trips with the kids, no kitchen duties, hardly anything interesting - until he thinks I'm okay. At lunchtime we all had a chat about Jamie and Beth, and it was very subdued. I finished early to go to physio and Gemma dropped me off there on her way home. I've got new exercises to try, and I have to increase my walking. The physio (I think she's French?) said I can stop using the crutches from tomorrow. Didn't tell her I haven't used them since Monday. Got a taxi home because the stuff she had me doing made my foot ache like mad. Darren came round on his way home from work, but he didn't stay long. He asked a bit more about the weekend, and said he's got the hospital job and starts at the beginning of June. I opened a bottle of wine to celebrate, but we only had one glass as he was driving and I really wasn't in the mood for celebrating anything. Hayley came round at 7 and we finished it off while I got some more crying out of my system, then we caught up on the soaps I'd recorded. No word from Jamie.

Thursday 8 May

Woke up to find a text from Jamie on my phone - he'd sent it after I'd gone to bed but I didn't hear it - inviting me round for tea, saying he'd pick me up from work. I couldn't make my mind up what to do at first. The thought of there being awkwardness between us made me want to stay away, but then it hit me that he was offering to pick me up from work, so he obviously wasn't feeling awkward, so I texted back and said yes. Work was tedious (I hate paperwork) but Lisa went out for bacon and egg baps for lunch, so that made a nice change.

Jamie was waiting for me in the car outside when I finished. He said he'd spent the last hour in the park, because Elspeth had had him clearing out Helen's clothes and he'd felt a row brewing so he'd come out of the house and left her to it. Elspeth was putting scones in the oven when we got there. She gave me a hug, and biffed him lightly on the arm, and made us some tea. When Jamie went upstairs, she told me she'd got him sorting things out, because (she said) he hadn't even changed the sheets on his bed since Helen had died. I'd no idea - not as if I've been in there much - but I could understand it because I went through a little phase like that after Gavin, not wanting to lose the smell of him off the sheets. Didn't say that to Elspeth, though. She said she was worried that Jamie wouldn't be able to move on if he kept Helen's clothes and things around him - not that she wanted him to get rid of everything, but there's no point in clothes being kept, is there? I just nodded - I actually think that's Jamie's decision - and I said I'm sure he's glad of her help. I'm not sure about her timing though, but maybe she just wants him to not think about Beth?

When Jamie came back down, he had three binbags with him and put them outside the back door. We had tea after that, a yummy chicken/pasta/pesto thing with mushrooms and peas in it, followed by some of Elspeth's scones. We talked quite a bit and they told me that the funeral is booked for Monday morning. Elspeth's going home tomorrow but coming back Sunday evening for the funeral, then going back again after it, and Jamie's going back to work next Tuesday. Elspeth asked me about my foot and I told them about physio, and about work. And then, when Jamie was on the phone, she took me to one side in the kitchen and asked me quietly how I thought he was coping. I said I think he's still in quite deep shock - I told her what he'd said about feeling weird and numb but like nothing's happened, and how his emotions are all over the place and sometimes he doesn't make much sense but on the other hand he's over the anxiety and panic attacks like they never happened at all - and she nodded and agreed with me.

For a moment, when she asked, I thought she might know about or suspect what had happened on Tuesday, but I don't think she does. She said she's made him make an appointment with his counsellor tomorrow and asked me to make sure he goes! I'll have to get Ben on to that as I'll be in work, but I told her okay. Then she said something really sweet - she said she was so glad that Jamie had friends like Ben and me, because if we weren't around she'd be so much more worried about him and would probably make him go home with her, but she felt she could trust us to look after him. Of course that then made me wonder if Jamie will now move up to Scotland, but I'm not going to mention that. I ended up staying till 9ish - we spent the evening watching the telly and talking, although Jamie didn't have a lot to say, then he drove me home.

Lucy had phoned while I was out so I rang her back. She was just checking up on me, making sure I was okay, and I said I was fine. I can't tell her about Tuesday. I want to, but not yet.

Friday 9 May 10.30 p.m.

Ben gave me a lift into work this morning. He said he didn't want to say anything in front of the others at work yesterday, but he'd called round to see Jamie after work on Wednesday and he could tell that there was something not quite right with Jamie and did I know what was going on? I swear that man can read my bloody mind, or maybe Jamie's. I wasn't going to talk about it in the car, though, not on the way to work, so I just said what I'd said to Elspeth - I think he's in shock, he's been acting a bit weird, etc. - but I really do want to talk to him about it at some point. He gave me that look, like he knows there's more to it, but we were pulling into the car park then so he let it drop.

Vinnie had me writing out a load of reports all morning. It was boring but it'll look good in my NVQ portfolio. At lunchtime, Gemma made a huge salad bowl with that yummy homemade dressing of hers, and a couple of trays full of mini pizzas. We're going to miss her when she goes off to have that baby! Ben phoned Jamie while we were eating, and suggested he pop in this afternoon while it's quiet (Vinnie was off to the AD's office for a meeting) which surprised me a bit. Ben said afterwards that J had been in town when he rang and had said he was just kicking around the shops after taking Elspeth to the station because he didn't want to go back to the empty house. He'd invited him and Adam round for tea, but they're going to the theatre with friends so Ben had to say no.

Jamie arrived about half an hour later, and he sat in the lounge talking with Ben and the rest of us (not all together, as we still had stuff to do) and he seemed quite relaxed to be there. Gemma got a bit tearful, and he was so sweet with her, like it was her who needed to be comforted more than him. I had to crack on with Vinnie's paperwork so I couldn't stay with him for long, but he came through to the office after a while and I brought him up to date on most things so he's not completely in the dark next week. He asked me what time I finish and then asked me if I'd go for tea, so I said yes and he said he'd hang around till I finished. The kids were chuffed to bits to see him when they got in from school, and he spent the last half hour talking with them and Ben and Gemma in the games room. I went through when I was finished and when he got up to go, Carly gave him a huge hug and he looked a bit embarrassed, bless him, and said he'll be back in a few days.

On the way to his house he said today was the first time he was faced with being there completely on his own, and he couldn't do it. I asked him if he wanted to come to mine, but he said he's got to get used to it and it'd be better to do that sooner rather than later but he'd really appreciate some company for a bit. But then when we pulled up outside the house he said, "Hang on" and kept the engine running. He just sat there with his hands on the wheel but he didn't say anything so I said, "What?" and he looked at me like he had something really dreadful to tell me and I started to get worried. Then he said he didn't know if he could trust himself, because he keeps thinking about Tuesday and he said he's finding it hard to not want to do it again and he's finding it all very conflicting and confusing, so maybe he should take me home.

I waited until he looked at me (he hadn't since he started talking) and I told him that I find him attractive but I'm very worried about me taking advantage of him because of that, and he gawped a bit but didn't say anything. I said if I was a true friend I'd stay well out of this until he knows where his head's at, but I'm finding it hard to not think about it too. So there we were, in the car, with our cards on the table and my heart was pounding because I was so scared he'd be disgusted with me. Then he said, "I'm still in love with my wife" and I thought that was it - it was over, whatever 'it' was. But then he said he's very mixed up, and desperate to stop feeling the pain, and doesn't want to end up hurting me, and he was just babbling on about what he shouldn't be doing or thinking and how difficult it is to make sense of his feelings, and he wasn't making a lot of sense, really, so I suggested we either go in and have a cup of tea and talk about it, or he takes me home, and he switched off the engine and we went in.

We went through to the kitchen and I sat down, leaving him to make the tea because I wanted him to keep busy while we talked, because he looked tense and a bit embarrassed. I said we need to have a really honest talk about this, or it could end up being a horrible painful mess, and he nodded, so I asked him if it was simply a case of missing the sex and he looked at me briefly and shook his head. He said it's not just about the sex, it's about affection and feeling something other than pain and sadness, and he tried to say sorry but I brushed that aside and said it's natural to feel that, and to miss the affection - why should he be sorry for missing it? I said I don't know what the rules are on this but he's got to go with how he feels, and I'm not prepared to do anything that will make him feel worse.

He passed me my tea but stayed standing by the kettle, like he was afraid to come any closer, and I felt awful because I thought I was coming across as clinical and I didn't want to do that but I didn't want to let my feelings for him get in the way of being sensible. And then he started telling me about their sex life, how it was good but limited because Helen had been abused by her stepfather and it had taken Jamie a long time to encourage her to open up to him. I was wondering why on earth he was telling me that, because it's really none of my business, but then he said that what we did the other day - sex in the kitchen and the lounge - was totally new for him and that's probably why he can't get it out of his head. So I'm sitting there, thinking (not unkindly) that he's probably only ever done it missionary style in bed with the lights off, and my head went to some dirty places and I didn't dare say anything for fear of letting on that I was getting incredibly turned on.

Then he said he loves her, and doesn't ever want to stop loving her, but he needs to feel something other than the pain of missing her and Beth. So what he's saying is he doesn't fancy me but he needs a shag (and I'm thinking, if he shags like that I don't need him to fancy me… I will surely go to hell). So I just asked him if he'd really be okay with it that way, and he shook his head and said he's not okay with anything, that's what makes it all so confusing. And then the phone rang and he went to answer it (it was Elspeth, ringing to say she'd got home safely) so I made us some fresh tea and tried to think of what to say to him to let him know that I'll do anything he needs, without me coming across as desperate.

He didn't come back into the kitchen so I took our mugs in the lounge, and he was sitting on the sofa with his head in his hands. I sat on the armchair and asked him if he was okay and he looked at me with absolute anguish and said, "No I'm really not" and then he asked me if I'd please go home, so I got my jacket and went. I wanted to stay but it felt like we were heading into dangerous ground and I didn't want to put temptation in his way, so to speak, because I was feeling really horny and really wanted to comfort him physically, and I don't think he wanted that. I asked him to phone or text me if he wanted company, and I'd go back. So I came home - walked all the way, slowly, and it wasn't too bad - and made myself a sandwich, and rang Lucy, and Darren, and Hayley, watched the telly, had a bath, and mooched about for a bit. I thought he might have phoned but he hasn't, and I'm getting really worried.

11.45 p.m.

Just got a text off Ben - Jamie is staying with them tonight. He said he can't talk but will fill me in tomorrow.

Sunday 11 May

Jamie rang me yesterday morning, apologising for 'being a bastard' on Friday. I told him he wasn't, and that I understand why he's all over the place, and he's really got to stop saying sorry. I said I hope I didn't upset him with any of the stuff we talked about and he said it's helped him get some clarity, which made me think, 'Oh here we go - bye bye, Natasha' but then he asked if I'd mind (!) a little walk in the park later, so we arranged to meet there.

Ben phoned me just as I was going out and I was mortified when he told me that he and Jamie had had a very long and thorough talk and he now knows everything. He was a bit miffed that I hadn't said anything, but I told him I'd been waiting for the right moment. He said not to put too much into it, though, because he and Jamie often talked about sex and relationships - they're good friends after all, even if they are of a different persuasion, and this is no big shock to him.

BUT he said that Jamie now knows I've had a crush on him for months, because Ben let it slip, thinking I must have told him. So I asked Ben what I should do and he said to just remember that Jamie is grieving and he's still very much in love with Helen, so if anything happens it's never going to lead anywhere, and I said, "I know all that but what should I DO?" The bugger laughed at me and said he's not even going there, but then he said he's really worried that Jamie and I will end up hurting each other so it's down to me to be the mature and sensible one because J just isn't thinking straight. Wonderful.

So anyway, I met Jamie in the cafe at the park yesterday afternoon, and we had a cappuccino and I had some of their homemade carrot cake. He said he feels an idiot, for messing me about and for needing to stay out of the house rather than be there alone, and I said he's too hard on himself and perhaps thinks about things a bit more than necessary. I was going for diplomatic, not sure if it worked, but he changed the subject and said he was going to eat out later and asked if I'd go with him, his treat. He said he didn't want to eat alone, and he wanted to pay me back a bit for all I've done these last three months, but I said I'd go with him if we went halves and he eventually agreed. We had a wander around the park but I had to sit down quite often cos my foot was hurting, and after the fourth time he said he'd go and get the car and run me home and I was too achy to argue.

I asked him in because I knew he didn't want to go home. He hesitated a bit but then came in with me, and then I realised it was a mistake because it just felt awkward because we suddenly didn't know what to talk about, so I put the telly on and asked him to channel surf till he found something interesting because I needed to tidy the kitchen, and he got up straight away and said he'd go and I really did think he should go because it was getting unbearable, knowing that we were both thinking about the same thing. And I said to him that I'm supposed to be the sensible one but he makes it very difficult, and he looked kind of apologetic and hopeful, if that's even possible, and I just said, "Oh fuck it!" and started kissing him.

He kissed me back for a bit, and I could tell he was as ready for it as I was, but then he started having second thoughts again and he said, "I can't" so I said, "Let me." and I backed him against the wall and undid his pants and went down on him. He was trying to talk – "I've never ..." and "We didn't ..." and "She ..." - and I had to tell him to shut up, he could tell me later. I just wanted him to have some release, so we could get past it and just spend time together without wondering if we were going to end up shagging. It didn't take long, and I've never enjoyed that particular activity so much in my life (thought I was going to come too, at one point, because he was so very turned on by it) and when he'd come he sagged against the wall like he was going to pass out. And then he slid down and put his head in his hands and started to cry, which is totally NOT what I wanted to happen.

I put my hand on his head and kept saying sorry, and I felt awful and so guilty. After a minute or so he wiped his face and looked at me, and then he said that was the first time anyone had ever done that for him: Helen hadn't been able to and he hadn't really had any decent relationships before her. So I smiled, and he smiled a bit and squeezed my hand and said he couldn't work out what he'd done to deserve someone like me and it was on the tip of my tongue to tell him he could pay me back later, but I thought it'd be best to say nothing.

I left him to sort himself out and went to brush my teeth, then I made that coffee I'd planned on making when we got in, and we sat in the lounge and he said I'm not making it any easier for him to work out what he should be feeling. I said I'm sorry for that but wouldn't it be simpler if he just let himself feel, instead of trying to analyse it and work out if it was right or wrong? And anyway who's to say what's right and what's wrong? And he said that's part of the problem - it feels right and wrong at the same time, and I had to agree with that. But then I had to ask, "Does it feel good, though?" and he said it really does, which made my heart skip a bit, because I thought if we're both getting our rocks off it can't be all bad, can it?

Then I noticed his hands were shaking and when I looked at him he didn't look happy at all, and it must be horrible for him going from feeling okay to feeling shit in a split second like that, because I just knew that reality had kicked in and he was having the guilts again (I can just tell from his face). And I don't know whether it's best to leave him to it or hug him, because either way it could be not what he needs, so I just nudged him and said, "Think about something else" and he nodded and drank his coffee.

And we were fine for half an hour or so, just drinking coffee and commenting on the telly, but then he said, "I need to know what we're doing, what you expect from me." I knew what he meant, and I said, "We're enjoying each other's company and I don't expect any more from you than that." and then I told him that Mum always used to say, "Take comfort where you find it" and I don't see anything wrong with that. He said, "You're a very extraordinary woman" and I said he'd have liked my mum. And just to make sure he understands where I'm coming from, and doesn't think I'm offering him pity-sex, I told him I don't have a boyfriend but I occasionally see Darren, and I don't have a possessive outlook on life or on relationships and I'm very definitely not the clingy type but I'll be a friend to Jamie in any way that he needs me to be, and if that includes sex then I'm not complaining. And he said my openness and honesty stuns him sometimes but he likes it, which I suppose is a compliment.

He said he honestly believes that his current obsession with sex is some kind of defence mechanism (he'd discussed it with his counsellor on Friday - there's me mortified again), a way of not facing the reality of what's happened, and of course missing what he used to have. I said he's hardly obsessed if he's constantly trying to avoid it, and he smiled a bit at that. But I suppose what he's saying is that once he gets to grips with what's happened and starts to grieve properly, he'll go back to being the old Jamie and he won't want to shag me, which will be a shame for me but healthier for him. Why is life always so complicated??

So I think I must have had in mind that this wasn't going to last forever, because I leaned over and said, "I think it's me who's a bit obsessed" and I kissed him and next thing I know we're going at it on the sofa, half-dressed, but it wasn't very comfortable so I took him through to my bedroom and it was amazing. He's obviously desperately trying to just lose himself in it but he's tender with it, not just banging away for the sake of it, and even though he doesn't kiss me while we're shagging he's very attentive and doesn't mind me telling him what to try (in fact I think it turns him on, so yay for that!) and can he makes me come like crazy.

We stayed there for a while afterwards, just lying there and not talking, but then his phone started to ring and he got up to answer it and I realised it was nearly 4 o'clock and I hadn't done a thing all day, so I got up too. He was still talking when I came out of the bathroom, and when he went in there, and when he came out, and then when he'd got dressed and joined me in the kitchen he said Elspeth would be coming down with their Mum, and Dougal was travelling up from London, so he'll have a house-full for Sunday night. I took that as his subtle way of telling me he'd be okay because he wouldn't be alone.

We went out for dinner around 7. I expected Jamie to want to go home first and get showered and changed, but he stayed with me all day, which was lovely. Jamie parked in the car park and we were on our way to the restaurant when two women passed us and threw him a dirty look. I heard one of them saying he'd murdered his daughter, and I know Jamie heard them too because he stopped and looked back at them with absolute horror on his face. He turned to me and asked me if that's what everyone thought. I said, "No of course not" and tried to get him to take no notice, but he wouldn't have it. I tried pulling him along but he said he couldn't do it and he headed back to the car, so I went with him but I was trying to get him to see that they're just two stupid gossips who know nothing of the truth, but he was sickened by the thought that anyone would think such a thing. We sat in the car and I watched him thinking, and I could tell he was going from sickened to annoyed to angry but he didn't say anything, and he wasn't listening to me when I told him to ignore them, and after about ten minutes he started up the car and drove to his house.

I followed him in – he wouldn't have taken me home if he didn't want me there, right? - and he'd gone straight to the kitchen and was leaning against the sink, shaking and staring out of the window, and then he just shouted something and swept his arm out and knocked everything flying off the draining board, sending cups and plates crashing all over the floor. I jumped back and it hurt my foot but I didn't say anything because I just wanted him to get it out of his system, but then he picked a cup up and hurled it at the wall, and he was going for another one so I stepped in then and took it off him and he just crumpled into me and started crying and swearing and going on about something or other (he's hard to follow when he's upset like that) and I just held him until he stopped. And then he sighed, and wiped his face, and hugged me with his chin on top of my head and said sorry. I kneed him in the leg for saying it.

I told him to go and sit down while I made some tea, but he wanted to clear up first so I let him do that and then I took our mugs through to the lounge. He said he's never had a temper and it bothers him when he loses it like that, and I said not to worry about it because all this will pass and he'll be back to his usual self and he sighed again like he didn't really believe it. And then he was gearing up to apologise for ruining our dinner out, so I cut him off and asked him if he fancied a takeaway, because I know a really good Chinese restaurant that delivers and he said okay and it turns out that he and Helen used the same Chinese quite a lot, so he knew the number and rang in our order. And yes I ended up staying the night and yes we ended up shagging for half of it and it was bloody amazing.

Jamie was a bit antsy when we got up this morning. As soon as I was up (we'd spent the night together in the spare room - there was no way I was going to share his/Helen's bed) he stripped the bed, and said he needed to get the place straight before everyone arrived. I asked him if he wanted me to change Beth's bed and he went white, but then he nodded, so I did that. It took me a while because it made me cry and I didn't want him to know. I took all the bedding down to the washing machine so he wouldn't have to see her sheets and things, and then while he was still cleaning the bathroom I made us some toast and coffee.

He came down and started on the lounge and it was like he was trying to avoid me so I asked him to come and eat, and when he came through to the kitchen I asked him what was wrong and he said he felt bad because I'd stayed there when he needed my company but now he feels like he's fobbing me off back to my own place because his family are coming, and I thought that was so sweet of him, and I told him I'm fine with it - it was what I expected - so he should stop worrying. He said it didn't feel right, but he appreciates my understanding. God he's so polite and formal sometimes! It's very sweet but it takes some getting used to, especially after a yob like Gavin. It makes me wonder whatever the hell I saw in him. Anyway, Jamie brought me home after we'd finished tidying up, and he said he'll ring later but I'm honestly not expecting him to, with a houseful of family there. I'd said earlier that I'll see him at the church in the morning and he nodded, like he was trying not to think about it, and I can't blame him - I'm dreading tomorrow.

Hayley offered to take me to Asda this afternoon, so we went there and she stayed for tea. Darren rang while we were eating and I think he was hoping I'd invite him round, but I didn't. He's asked me out for dinner or drinks this week and I said I'd let him know. I don't want to go out with him anymore, but I'm not going to tell him that over the phone. When Hayley had gone, I rang Ben to find out what time he and Adam are going to the church tomorrow and bless him he offered to pick me up. I was going to walk since it's not that far, but it will be nicer to get there with someone with me rather than on my own.

It's nearly midnight and Jamie hasn't phoned, so I'm going to bed. I didn't really think he would, but I've stayed up anyway just in case. Me = stupid.

Tuesday 13 May

There were a few people at the church when we arrived yesterday morning - I recognised the Head Teacher, and Dr Burgess, and a couple of parents from Beth's school. More arrived while we were standing outside (Adam wanted a smoke before we went in), but in the end there weren't half as many people there as had attended for Helen's funeral. Jamie and his family were nearly ten minutes late and we were all getting a bit worried by that time. Dougal and the limo driver had to help Jamie out of the car and he looked awful. He was white, and could barely stand up, and he hadn't even shaved. Elspeth was struggling to help her Mum get out of the car, so I went over to help her while Ben took over from the limo driver, and Elspeth told me that they'd had to call the family GP out because Jamie had had some kind of breakdown. He was sedated, which was why Ben and Dougal had to walk him into the church.

I started to cry, and Elspeth squeezed my hand and kept me with her as we helped her mum inside. So that's how we ended up on the front row with Jamie and his family - Ben and Adam on either side of Jamie, me between Adam and Elspeth, Jamie's mum next to Elspeth on one end of the pew and Dougal on the other end next to Ben. I don't remember much about the service. It was quite short, and Dougal got up to read a lovely little tribute that Jamie had written (I think he'd planned to read it himself, but he was in no fit state) and the songs were all kids' ones that I knew from Sunday school. I think I cried through all of it.

The actual burial was awful because I was standing sideways on to Jamie and could see him clearly for the first time since he got there. He was still being practically held up by Dougal and Ben, and he was crying so much that I'm sure he never heard a word the vicar said. They struggled to get him back to the car - I think he was so far gone by that point that he could hardly stand up, let alone walk - and it was then that I noticed the GP was there too, and he helped get Jamie into the limo and stood talking with Dougal for a bit, and when they left he followed them in his car.

There was no reception afterwards; Elspeth told me in the church that they would be going back to Jamie's house if anyone wanted to join them there, but Ben and Adam and I weren't really sure what to do. I ended up going with B & A to their house for a cup of tea, and I had another bloody good cry while I was there. I think because I've been trying to keep it together all week it just backed up on me and I needed to get it out. The boys were lovely, bless them, holding me and telling me it was okay. They both had to go to work at lunchtime, but I'd booked the whole day off so they dropped me off at home on their way in.

I rang Jamie's house but no-one answered. Elspeth rang me back about half an hour later and told me that they were having a 'time of it' with Jamie, and the GP was making arrangements for him to go into hospital. I asked her to keep me posted, but she said that she and her mother were booked on a train home at 2 o'clock so Dougal would be taking over. She said her mother had a hospital appointment at home on Tuesday (today) so they couldn't stay any longer, but Dougal had arranged another day off work and would stay at Jamie's house until they knew for sure what was happening. Dougal was going up to the hospital with Jamie, so I said I'd go round there and go in the taxi to the station with Elspeth since she'd probably need a hand with their Mum getting on the train. I got there as quickly as I could, but Jamie and Dougal had already gone by the time I arrived.

Elspeth and her mum were really upset but we didn't have much time as the taxi was on its way, so I did what I could to calm them down and said I'd help Dougal if he needed it. I went to the station with them and helped them on the train, then took the same taxi to the hospital. Elspeth had told me which ward Jamie was being admitted to, so I went up there and sat in the waiting room until Dougal came out. He looked shocked to see me, and a bit wary. I said I hoped he didn't mind me just turning up but I was worried and wanted to know if he (Dougal) needed a hand with anything, or if there was anything I could fetch for Jamie. He said he'd packed an overnight bag for Jamie and didn't think he'd need anything else. He said Jamie was sedated and would probably be out of it for the rest of the day.

I could feel myself starting to cry again, so I asked him what had happened, and he did that thing with his hair that Jamie does - running his fingers through it so it stands up, all ruffled - and he looked so like his brother for that moment that it hurt. He said that Jamie had just started to freak out when he was getting dressed for the funeral and he reckons that it was just a massive reality check - it must have just kicked in that Beth was dead and he was going to be burying her and it utterly overwhelmed him. He and Elspeth tried to calm him down but they couldn't get through to him, so Elspeth called the GP out. The GP wanted to have Jamie admitted straight away but they didn't want him to miss the funeral, and that's why he'd been sedated, just enough to calm him down for the service, but it had practically worn off by the time they got back to the house and Dougal said it was a good thing that the GP went with them because he was able to see first-hand how Jamie was acting, and he arranged straight away for the hospital admission.

Dougal didn't have to tell me what he was admitted

for - I knew as soon as Elspeth told me the name of the ward, because it's in the new psychiatric wing with everything named after counties. Anyway the GP came into the waiting room then and told us that Jamie would be assessed in the morning and then a decision would be made as to what happens next. I wanted to stay, but it's a secure unit with strict visiting rules so I didn't even ask. Dougal offered me a lift home, and I asked him to let me know if there's any news - told him my number's on Jamie's notice board in the kitchen. I rang Ben at work when I got in and had another cry while I was telling him about it. He came round after work, and after a lovely long chat with him I felt a bit better.

Elspeth rang me just after 9 last night - she said that she'd rung the hospital, and Jamie was comfortable (they always say that, it doesn't mean anything), and she said she'd asked Dougal to let me know when there's any news. She said Dougal's only looking to stay another day as he's hardly got any time off due to him, and I said straight away that Ben and I are here for Jamie, and she said she knows that and is very glad of it because the trip down and back from Glasgow is not an easy one, and she's got parents and kids and a job to see to as well. She asked me if I thought Jamie was serious about moving back up there, because it would be much easier for her if he did, but I said I wasn't sure. I don't want to hurt her feelings, but I'm pretty sure that he wouldn't want to go back there now - he was only thinking of it because of Beth. I felt exhausted after talking with Elspeth, so I had a bath and went to bed, and cried myself to sleep.

I was woken up by the phone ringing this morning - it was Lisa, because I'd forgotten to set my alarm and I was late for work. I managed to get in by 10 o'clock, but Vinnie wasn't very happy with me and said something about getting my priorities right, and I told him to piss off and was on the verge of turning round and coming home but Lisa stepped in and sorted it out. I don't remember what she said because I was crying by then, but he left me alone and after a hug and a little chat with Lisa I got on with the bloody paperwork.

I felt sick all morning because I was waiting for my phone to ring, and when Ben arrived at 12 with no news either I really thought I was going to be ill. Then Elspeth rang me just after 2 and she was a bit cross that Dougal hadn't been in touch with me, but she said he probably couldn't find my number. Anyway she said that Jamie was still in hospital and would be there for a few days. She said he's having intensive counselling and something else (couldn't hear her properly because Gemma was on the other phone, and she never talks quietly) and she said he could have visitors but only in the evening, and she said Dougal was going back to London but would come back at the weekend. So I asked if me and Ben could visit Jamie and she said she thought it would be okay, and to let her or Dougal know if there were any problems. I closed my phone and burst into tears and Ben, bless him, took me through to the kitchen and made me a cup of tea, and while I was drinking it he went and told Vinnie that I should go home, and then he brought me home and said he'd pick me up later for visiting hour at the hospital. I swear if he wasn't gay, I'd marry that man tomorrow (assuming Jamie wouldn't have me).

Ben picked me up at 7 and we went up to the ward together. Ben reckons that Elspeth must have phoned them because when we gave our names the nurse looked like she'd been expecting us and we were let in straight away. Ben went through first - patients are only allowed one visitor at a time - because I suddenly got worried that Jamie might not want to see anyone. He was only in there a few minutes, and when he came back he said Jamie was not very talkative so maybe we shouldn't stay long.

When I got to his room, Jamie was sitting in one of those big fake leather armchairs next to the bed. I don't know why, but I expected him to be lying in bed and wearing striped pyjamas, but he had jeans and a t-shirt on. Daft, the things you think of, isn't it? He looked up when I went in but he didn't say anything and I'm pretty sure he was sedated, because he was blinking slowly like they do in films. I asked him if he needed anything fetching and he shook his head, so I said what about some music, I could bring him his iPod, and he looked at me then as if to say 'how did you know I'd want that?' but he just shrugged and shook his head again.

There was so much I wanted to say but I was too scared, not knowing what exactly was going on with him or how lucid he was, so I just said I'd come again tomorrow and I came away. Ben said he was drugged up to his eyeballs, and neither of us were happy about that, but we've no way of knowing if that's true. Ben brought me home, and I gave Elspeth a quick ring cos she'd asked me to let her know how he is, and I think we spent ten minutes trying to reassure each other that he'll be okay. I've spent the evening online, trying to get information on psychiatric treatment but I haven't really found anything to put my mind at rest.

Wednesday 14 May

I've just got back from visiting Jamie. Ben and I called at his house to pick up some clean clothes and stuff for him, and we also took his Walkman and some CDs and a couple of new-looking books off the shelf in the lounge. He's got mail piling up, but Ben said we should leave that for Dougal to sort out with him at the weekend. I took his phone, too, which he'd left here on Saturday. Elspeth asked me last night if I'd seen it anywhere, cos Jamie had mentioned on Monday that he couldn't find it, and I found it under a cushion on the sofa. I've still got the charger for my old Samsung and it fits his phone, so I charged it up last night and took it to him this evening.

Ben went in first again and he was in there about 10-15 minutes. He took the clothes and things (shaving kit, I think, and some toiletries), and when I went in afterwards I gave Jamie the other stuff. He was wearing the same clothes, and sitting in the chair, and he didn't take them from me so I put them on the cabinet next to his bed. He did take his phone though and said thank you. I was shocked at how shaky his voice sounded. No wonder he's not saying much.

I didn't know what to talk about, so I sat on the bed and just rambled for a bit - told him about work, and things on the news, and the charts, and the rumour about an old vintage record store opening up on the High Street - and he was listening, I think, but he didn't say anything and I found it quite hard to keep going so I just said I'll see him tomorrow and got up to go and he said goodbye and I didn't dare look back at him because I just wanted to cry.

Ben asked me why I was upset and I said, "He's just sitting there" and he told me they'd talked about work (the AD asked Ben to get a sick note, so Ben talked about that with Jamie) and how Jamie spent his day. I was surprised that Ben had asked him about that but Ben said he thought it would be a good idea to keep Jamie focused on why he's there, so I'll have to try that tomorrow instead of rabbiting on about unimportant stuff.

Saturday 17 May

It's been a mad few days. Mad week, really. Mad month. I'll be glad when it's over. I don't like May anymore.

Darren and I had a massive row on Thursday. He waited for me to finish my shift and took me home, and he was going on about going out for dinner or something and I just wasn't in the mood. Vinnie had been moody all day and I hadn't been able to do anything right as far as he was concerned, and I was fretting about going to see Jamie and wondering how he'd be with me, and it was time of the month too - not a good combination.

I told Darren I wasn't really up for going out and he said I'd been putting him off all week (which I suppose I had, since he'd asked me every day since Sunday) so I said I was sorry but I can't help it if I don't feel like going out, and he said, "What do you want from me? Just be bloody honest with me." I said he knows how I feel because we've had this conversation before, and he said he feels like I'm just tagging him along, which I'm not and I said so, and it all just went from there. He said he's been patient and tried to understand (I assume he meant about Jamie) and I lost my rag then because he sounded so bloody pompous like he was my bloody husband or something, and I can't even remember what I said but he just said "Fine" and "See you" and I got out of the car and slammed the door and came in.

Ben couldn't go with me to see Jamie on Thursday night because he and Adam were going somewhere (I forget where) so I got the bus to the hospital. I'd bought Jamie the NME and a couple of albums and he didn't smile but he sounded really chuffed when he said thank you so I took that as a good sign and asked him what he'd been up to. He shrugged and said, "An awful lot of talking" and I was glad his voice sounded more like normal. I was dying to ask him what he talked about but it wouldn't have been fair, or right, really, so I asked him about the food (he pulled a face) and about the book he's reading (he said he keeps reading the same bits, forgetting what he's read) and then we got on to music and he picked up a bit, but I could tell he was tired. He didn't seem as dozy as he had on Tuesday and Wednesday, but I think they're still sedating him or something, because he seemed slow and lethargic even when he was trying to show interest in what we were talking about. The buzzer went at 8 so I had to go, but he said, "Thanks for coming" which made me smile because he seemed so much more aware than he had been on my other visits.

I rang Darren when I got in. I'd had time to cool down and think about things after he'd gone, and on the bus to the hospital and then back home, and I felt like I owed him an apology, and that's what I said. He said he still thinks I'm wasting my time on Jamie, and he thinks it's a shame because I'm a lovely girl and he doesn't want to see me getting hurt. I said I'm not talking about Jamie but I'm sorry it didn't work out between us, and he said, "No you're not, Tasha - you never even gave us a chance" and he hung up on me. I still feel bad but I don't think I'm going to be able to put it right between us, at least not yet.

I rang Elspeth then, and told her how Jamie had been and she was relieved. She said she'd spoken to him a couple of times during the afternoon (she'd rung him on his mobile) and she said he sounded ... well, not okay, but a bit better than he was earlier in the week, and I said he seemed much better that night, so we were both a bit happier about that. I was just getting ready to go in the bath when Lucy rang, just checking in. She said she'd come up for the weekend if I wanted the company but I said I'm okay, got lots to do. I just know if she came here I'd end up telling her about me and Jamie, and I'm really not ready to do that yet.

Did the 8 - 4 shift at work on Friday and it was busy all day. Mikey wouldn't get up and he missed the school bus so I had to ring school, and the uppity secretary there was going on about telling his social worker and I ended up having a row with her, and then because Lisa had gone to the doctor with Erin I had to keep Mikey in the office to stop him from going out (he thought he'd got away with the day off) until she came back and could run him to school. He wasn't a happy bunny.

Erin's got a stomach bug - not food poisoning, like she kept insisting all day on Thursday - and she spent the day either in bed or in the bathroom, and me and Lisa had a few clean-up sessions after her which was just lovely. Vinnie then had me working on the Quarterly Report which is due next month - he said he wants to make sure we get started early on it rather than leave it till the last minute - and he did my head in, so I was glad when the AD turned up at lunchtime and I was left to get on with it on my own. Then the NVQ assessor turned up - I'd forgotten she was coming, but luckily my folder was still in the office - and she was very encouraging, so that wasn't too bad. It had been lovely and sunny all day so I walked home through the park and bought some blueberry muffins and some flapjacks from the bakery on the way home - one each for me and Jamie.

Jamie was on his phone when I got to the hospital, so I nipped out to the loo. When I got back to his room he'd finished, and he said it was Dougal on the phone asking if he should come up for the weekend. Jamie had told him not to bother, and I frowned at that but didn't say anything. I gave him his cakes and he nearly smiled but didn't open them, he just put them in the drawer and said he'd have them later.

He said he wants to get out, but he doesn't want to go home, and he's no idea how long he's going to be in hospital because no-one will say when he can go home - they keep saying "We'll see how things go" and "See how you feel tomorrow" and things like that - and I said then that maybe he could go home for a while if Dougal came to stay, but he shook his head and said Dougal doesn't really want to come, he's only offering because he feels he should, and that made me so angry.

I was going to tell Jamie he could stay with me, but I don't think that would help, so I said he needs to listen to what the professionals are saying because they know what's best, and he just nodded but it was half-heartedly. He said he'd listened to the new albums and we talked about the tracks on them, and I said I'd bring some of my music in if he fancied a change - you can only listen to an album so many times, after all, and he's got all day. He said he'd be glad of that because there wouldn't be much happening over the weekend, as the counsellors only work Monday to Friday. I said that visiting hours are different over the weekend, too - there's an afternoon session as well as the evening one - so would it be okay if me or Ben came to see him, and he said, "Yes that would be nice."

He said Ben had phoned him earlier because he couldn't visit (he didn't say why) and then he said we really don't have to come every day, but I said I want to and he looked at me with that lovely intense look he has that makes me shiver, and I thought he's really getting better because that's the Jamie I know, but then he shook his head and looked away and he looked really sad, so I wonder what he was thinking. The hour flew by and I couldn't hang around, much as I wanted to, or I'd have missed the bus home - I only just made it to the stop as it was.

I rang Elspeth when I got in - she wants me to ring her after every time I see him - and she's chuffed that he seems to be doing so well. She talks to him a couple of times a day, but she's always glad to get my perspective on it since she can only go by his voice and what he says to her. She said she knew that Dougal would have backed out of coming back for the weekend if Jamie was still in hospital, but she's sure he'll come up when Jamie's discharged. She said the two of them had had a long talk on Sunday night and had more or less made it up with each other, but Dougal's a bit selfish and would see a trip here as a waste of time if Jamie's still in hospital. I suppose it's a long way to come for two hour-long visits, but it wouldn't have bothered me. I had to go then because someone was at the door, and then things got a bit crazy.

It was Mrs Lewis from upstairs and she was hysterical. I couldn't get her to calm down so I had to go up to her flat with her and she took me in the bathroom, where Mr Lewis had fallen between the bath and the loo and he was stuck. I asked if she'd phoned for an ambulance but she hadn't and she wanted me to help her get him up. He was out cold, and he's a big man - I don't know how the hell she thought we'd be able to move him - so I sat her down in the lounge and called for an ambulance, but I had to make her take the call because it would have taken too long for me to get the answers to their questions. I ended up going to the hospital with her because she was hysterical and they wouldn't take her in the ambulance - I phoned for a taxi - and when we got there a lovely male nurse took charge of her and got her calmed down, and I ended up sitting there with her in A&E for nearly three hours (it had to happen on a Friday night, didn't it?) until Mr Lewis was properly admitted, and then we came home together in a taxi. She was still a bit weepy but she thanked me, and said she'd be okay so I left her at her door. It was gone 12 by then and I was knackered so I went straight to bed.

My phone rang at 2 a.m. and it was Ben asking me if I'd had a text or call from Jamie. I checked, and I hadn't. He said he'd just had a text from him, asking him to come and get him from hospital because he couldn't sleep and he was sick of being there. I was a bit gutted that Jamie hadn't texted me, but that's not important. I asked Ben what he was going to do, and he said he can't do anything - it's a secure unit, and he's not family. He rang me back half an hour later and said he'd spoken to Jamie and he was okay, but he didn't say what they'd talked about. I told him I'd be going to see him in the afternoon, and Ben said he'd go in the evening so I asked him to pick me up then. Finally got back to sleep around 3 I think.

I'd forgotten to switch off my alarm and it went off at 7 this morning, but I went back to sleep and slept in until 10. I got to the hospital just after 12.30 and stopped at the little shop to buy some sweets and magazines. Jamie wasn't in his room when I got up to the ward and I had a little flash of panic, but one of the nurses came past and told me he'd just gone to the bathroom, so I waited by his door until he came back. When the nurse came back from wherever she'd been going I asked her if it would be okay to go down to the gardens with Jamie for a bit, and she said yes.

Jamie wasn't long, but he looked like he'd just got up - he was wearing just a t-shirt and boxers, with nothing on his feet, and his hair was all over the place - and he looked at me and asked me what the time was so I told him and he looked sort of confused. He said he thinks being in hospital is making him lose his mind and I couldn't help smiling at that, but he didn't think it was funny.

I said it's a lovely day and asked him if he fancied going down to the garden for a bit and he nodded and pulled on his jeans, but I had to remind him to put his trainers on or he'd have gone down there barefoot. He was shaking a bit as we left the ward - I suppose it's the furthest he's walked since Monday, although he probably wouldn't remember much of that - and when we got down to the garden he stopped at the door, holding on to the frame, and I remembered then that the last time he'd been there it had been with Beth, after her scan, and I could have kicked myself. So I said we could go to the other one - the little square one without a roof, in between the cafe and the A&E - but he said o and went in.

It was too hot, though - the glass roof makes it feel like a greenhouse even with some of the windows open, which is lovely in the winter but stifling in the middle of May - so we ended up going to the outside one, which is a suntrap but at least there was a breeze. He said it was nice to breathe fresh air, and he really wanted to get out even if just for a couple of hours, but I said he'd have to check with the nursing staff about that and he looked at me as if to say he knew that wasn't going to work.

I said he looked rough today and he nodded and said he's having trouble sleeping because although he's in a room on his own, the place is noisy all the time, and he said he'd been up half the night and eventually one of the nurses had given him something that knocked him out. I told him about my little 'adventure' with Mr & Mrs Lewis, and he smiled then - first one this week! - and he said, "You're everyone's guardian angel." I said, "Oh I'm no angel" and I think he blushed!

He became quiet again and asked me if I'd been at the funeral on Monday, because he can't remember seeing me, so I told him where I was sitting, and he said he remembers very little about it. In fact, he said, his last clear memory is of our day at the fair in Blackpool (the day before Beth died) and everything else after that is fuzzy and jumbled, with a lot of blanks. I said it'll come back to him but he's probably best not to try and force it, and he said he feels like he wasn't even there on Monday and that's not right. I just squeezed his hand because what is there to say? I'm sure he'll remember soon enough and I didn't want to push him into doing it now, and anyway that's hopefully what the counsellors are working on, amongst other things. He said he's no idea what happened on Monday, and he has no recollection of how he came to be in hospital, so I said he should maybe ask Elspeth but he said she's being evasive about it, so I said I'll find out what I can.

We chatted about other stuff, nothing much really, and we were just talking about going to get a cup of tea when the nurse from his ward came in and said visiting time was over. That hour goes so fast! She looked a bit miffed about having to come all the way down to find us, so I said sorry. I went to kiss Jamie's cheek as we were saying goodbye and he pulled me into a hug instead, quite a nice one until I realised the nurse was standing there and getting impatient, so I pulled back and let him go. Cow.

I rang Elspeth from the bus, on my way into town, and told her that Jamie is desperate to know what happened on Monday. She said she'd ring him later. I was rather hoping she'd tell me because I'm nosey like that, but I don't suppose it's any of my business and it'll probably be better for Jamie to hear it from her, as she can answer any questions he might have. I had to get the bus home from town because my foot was killing me by the time I'd been to a few shops. Must remember to mention that to the physio next week. I had a couple of hours to kill before Ben would pick me up so I went back to bed for a nap and slept until 6! I just about had enough time to get changed and have a quick butty and a cup of tea before he arrived.

The Cow Nurse was still on duty when we got there but, credit where it's due, she let us both go in together. Ben had brought some cake that Adam had made (coffee and walnut - yummy) so I nipped out to the corridor and got us some tea and we had that while we were talking. Jamie and Ben talked a bit about cricket and sporty stuff on the telly, but mostly Jamie was telling us about the troublemaker in the room next door who's been spoiling for a fight all week and finally got Jamie cornered this afternoon by the bathroom! Nothing happened because a couple of nurses heard them arguing and pulled the other guy away, no questions asked - he's known for it, apparently - but Jamie said it made for an interesting five minutes. He must be bored out of his skull :(He said the man goads everyone and causes chaos at the group therapy sessions, but the staff don't seem to be doing anything about it, and he said that's one of many reasons why he wants to get out of there. We both just nodded because neither of us are sure about whose decision it is, but Ben suggested to Jamie that he have a chat with his GP about it, since it was him who arranged the admission. Ben and I don't think he should be on a secure unit, but we didn't see what happened on Monday so there may have been good reasons for it (I doubt it, though).

We had to go then, and Jamie looked really relieved when I said I'd see him tomorrow, so it must really break the day up for him. On the way out, Ben asked one of the nurses if we could take Jamie out tomorrow - maybe just for a ride in the car, or to the park or something, just for a change of scenery - but she said that would need the okay from his consultant who wouldn't be in until Monday. We were gutted but at least we can try again after the weekend. In the car on the way back to mine, Ben said he won't come tomorrow afternoon. He said he'd have done so if we could have taken Jamie out, but since we'd be stuck in his room he said he'll leave that to me and will come with me in the evening. He's so sweet, and so thoughtful. Why aren't all men like him?

I rang Elspeth when I got in. She said she'd had a long talk with Jamie this afternoon, going over what happened on Monday, and she'd been shocked at how little he could remember about it. He was upset when she told him the details - apparently he'd hit Dougal, and sworn at all of them, and at one point he'd been so totally out of control that it had terrified their mother - but she thinks he still doesn't really remember anything. It's as if he's wiped the whole day from his memory. We talked about shock and grief and all that and what it can do to your mind, and we're neither of us sure if we want him to remember, at least not until he can handle it properly. I told her he was itching to get out, and that we'd asked about taking him out for a little while, and she said she'll talk to Dougal and find out what they can do in terms of swaying the consultant's decision about that. She doesn't think he should be on a secure unit, either and she really wants him moved from there as soon as possible.

2.15 a.m.

Just got off the phone with Jamie. He sent me a text message and we texted back and to for a bit at first, and then he rang me. He said it's noisier than ever tonight, with people shouting and running around. He'd looked out on the corridor a few times but hadn't seen anything, so he's no idea what's going on but he's awake and bored and was really apologetic for texting/ringing me but he feels really isolated there and he doesn't think that's helping.

I asked him if he could get some sleeping tablets or something, but he said the stuff they've been giving him - a liquid - knocks him out cold for ten hours and somehow that's worse. I said there's not much I can do, really, but he said it helps just to talk because it relaxes him. I could have just sat there and listened to his voice for hours but I started yawning and he said sorry again. He said he'd have another go at getting to sleep since things seemed to have quietened down. I told him to ring me back if things kick off again, but I'm going back to bed.

Sunday 18 May

Today was quite a nice day, all things considered. I had a lovely long lie in until 11ish for starters, which was a really nice treat, and I had breakfast in the garden because it was so warm. Then I got a taxi to the hospital and had a lovely hour with Jamie in the garden there, sitting in the sun and talking about gigs and the summer festivals and no-one came to rush us back upstairs at the end of visiting so I actually got an extra 20 minutes with him by the time we realised what time it was. I got the bus home and sat next to Mrs Lewis who'd been to visit Mr L (he's cracked his hip) and when we got home she came downstairs and gave me a fruit loaf that she'd made, as a thank you for the other night, bless her.

I spent most of this afternoon in the garden, reading and sunbathing, then after tea I had a shower and got changed in time for Ben picking me up. He said he and Adam are going away again next weekend (Bank Holiday weekend), to visit Adam's parents in Oxford, and he asked me if I'll be okay getting around and stuff by then. He's such a darling. When we got there, Jamie had his earphones in and was doing a crossword and they're such simple things but it was so good to see him doing something. I know he's been reading and listening to music, but it's nice to actually see it.

I took the fruit loaf with me and we had some of that with some tea. It's not as nice as the one Adam makes, but it was okay. Jamie said he'd had visitors after I'd left earlier - Dr Burgess's wife and the GP's wife, both of whom had been friends of Helen's. They'd been to visit their aunt and called in to see him afterwards, bringing him a bottle of squash and some grapes. He said they didn't stay long, only a few minutes, and he said it was probably because he got a bit emotional because Helen used to talk about them a lot and they'd been good friends to her. Ben and I reckon they were spying on him for the GP, but what do we know?

Now I'm back home and I'm going to have an early night. I said I'll do Gemma's 8-4 shift tomorrow because she's got a doctor's appointment at 9, and after this weekend I feel like I still need to catch up on some sleep.

Monday 19 May

Jamie might be going home this week! :)

He phoned his GP this morning and, fair do's to the man, he (Dr Mallory) called at the hospital to see Jamie this afternoon and they had a long talk. Mallory is going to liaise with the hospital counsellors and the one that Jamie was seeing before and see if they can agree a programme for Jamie that will mean he can be discharged. The doctor said that Jamie could actually leave at any time, but he'd advise against it until everything's set up, so Jamie's agreed to that. He had a good session this morning but he knows he's got to convince them that he'll be okay at home, and he told Ben (I was fetching tea) that he's a bit worried about that, so now Ben's thinking about postponing their trip to Adam's parents.

Elspeth already knew, when I rang her - she's spoken to Jamie a couple of times today. She said she's worried that he'll not cope on his own, but I think he's stronger than she thinks he is, and maybe she's basing her feelings on what happened last week. I didn't say that, though - I just said we'll all be as supportive as we can and see what happens. I can tell from the things that she says that she's really thinking about getting him to move back up there.

I hope that's just her being a bit over-protective and that it'll wear off when things settle down.

Tuesday 20 May

Physio today was horrible. I mentioned the pain I had on Saturday and she had me doing all sorts of different movements so that she could try and work out what was going on, which meant that it was hurting in exactly the same way by the time I'd finished the session. Thank you, Helene, I'll remember to keep my mouth shut next time. She's given me some new exercises and told me to look out for a particular kind of trainer that will support the arch of my foot (she wrote it down for me).

I got a taxi to work because I couldn't be bothered standing around and waiting for a bus. I toyed with the idea of going to see if they'd let me in for a quick visit with Jamie after my physio appointment, but it was around the time of his counselling session so I didn't bother. If I'd thought about it in advance, though, I could maybe have arranged to have lunch with him or something - wish I'd thought of that last week, really. Anyway I got to work just after 11 and, because I was limping, Vinnie set me to sorting out the admin filing cabinet and updating all the referral files, and other paperwork stuff, and then after the team meeting he had me working out next month's rota too. Git. Ben's on late shift today and tomorrow, so Lisa dropped me off at home after work and I got the bus up to the hospital after tea.

Jamie was a bit quiet when I got there, and it took a

couple of goes for me to get him to open up. In the end I just asked him what was wrong and he tried to get out of it but I just looked at him like he was wasting his time and he told me. He said he'd been to his house today, with his counsellor - the one he's been seeing for a while - as part of his staged discharge. That's all he said so I had to ask him how it had been and he shrugged and said, "Emotional." He said everything was okay, though - he'd had positive feedback from the counsellor and then went over a few things this afternoon with the hospital team, and they seem encouraged. It's just that he was a bit surprised at how upset he'd got, going into the house and especially into Beth's room (which he said was a mess, thanks to Dougal not tidying up after himself). I said it's to be expected, isn't it? I still well up a bit when I go past Mum's house, not that it's very often, but it still has an effect on me. He agreed, but he's obviously not too pleased with himself. I said I think he's expecting a bit too much of himself if he thinks he's not going to get upset - it's only been a couple of weeks after all. I didn't want him dwelling on it, so I gave him the Smiths album we were talking about the other night and that changed the subject, and after that he was okay but I hope this doesn't mean his discharge will be delayed.

Elspeth rang me when I was on the bus on the way home, asking me how I thought Jamie was doing. I told her what he'd said and she said he'd been really upset this afternoon. I can't understand why they're so thrown by this - he's lost his wife and his daughter within three months, how else is he supposed to be?

Wednesday 21 May

My phone started ringing when the alarm went off this morning, which was confusing. It was Elspeth on the phone, asking me to call in on Jamie because he'd been assaulted and she needed to know that he was okay. The hospital had phoned her after it had happened, in the middle of the night - policy, apparently, similar to ours - and they'd said he was not seriously hurt and was actually asleep by then, but Elspeth wanted me to go and check on him because she didn't want to ring him that early (7 a.m.). She'd rung Ben but his phone was off (he switches it off when he's on the late shift) and she'd told the hospital she would be sending one of us round there.

I ordered a taxi and flew round to the hospital. The nurse on desk duty said Jamie was still asleep but I could pop in for a minute or two. He was sleeping with his back to the door, his legs all tangled up in the sheet, and I had to go round the bed to get a look at him. I don't know what I expected, but he looked fine - a little cut on his lip, some blood on his t-shirt, and a graze on his arm, but otherwise fine. Elspeth had said that Jamie had woken up around 2 a.m. to find the nutter from the next room going through his things, and when he tried to ask him what he was doing, the guy had attacked him. Jamie didn't stir at all while I was there, so I left him a note asking him to ring me when he woke up, and I rang Elspeth on the way out.

I got to work about 20 minutes late but Vinnie didn't get in until 11, so he's none the wiser. I told Lisa where

I'd been and she was worried, but fine about me being late. I rang Ben at lunchtime and told him what had happened, just to keep him in the loop - he said he'd call Jamie before coming into work. Jamie rang me just before 1, wondering why I'd been there, so I had to tell him and I think he was a bit embarrassed that his sister got me involved but I said it's no trouble. He said he's fine, and the other guy has been moved to another hospital so hopefully the place will be a bit calmer now.

I'd built up some overtime so I finished at 3.30 and went home via Asda - bus there, taxi home. Ben rang me from work. He said he'd spoken to Jamie and everything seems okay, and that was after another counselling session so that stopped me from worrying for a bit. I had a lovely long chat with Lucy after tea. She and Will are going to Devon for the bank holiday weekend, lucky things. She said she'll find out on Friday whether or not she's got the promotion, so the weekend will be to either celebrate or drown her sorrows.

I got to the hospital a bit early tonight but went straight up anyway. Jamie looked like he'd just had a shower, and the cut on his lip looked really red and sore. He still hasn't shaved, and I'm starting to like the beard on him. I got a tiny smile off him when I arrived, and he said he'd told Elspeth off for having me fly round there so early this morning. I said I was up anyway, and on my way to work, and besides I'd wanted to know for myself that he was okay, and he told me then what had happened - pretty much what Elspeth had told me, but I didn't interrupt. The guy had done this before, apparently, in the week before Jamie was admitted. Jamie was advised that he could make a formal complaint, but he said the guy clearly has enough problems so he's not going to bother. It crossed my mind that Jamie should complain about the hospital not keeping him safe from harm, but that's up to him.

He said he hopes to be out by the weekend, mostly because it's a bank holiday and the weekends are long enough without an extra day tagged on. I think mentioning the bank holiday made him think of Blackpool, though, because he suddenly went all quiet and got that awful, sad look on his face, so I just squeezed his hand because I couldn't think of anything to say. He's got to get used to having reminders like that, and pretending he's not thinking and feeling that way isn't going to help. After a minute or so he bumped my shoulder and told me he likes the Smiths' album and can't believe he missed that one, which got us talking about safer things and he was okay after that. The cute little male nurse - the one who looks about fifteen - came and told us it was 8.30, so I was there much longer than I should have been but he wasn't cross, bless him.

I rang Elspeth when I got in and asked her if she thinks Jamie could get out tomorrow or Friday, but she said she doesn't want him rushing it and would go with what the doctors advise. When she said that, I realised that that's the sensible way to be, and it made me realise that I want him home for selfish reasons: I miss him. I miss pre-hospital Jamie.

Thursday 22 May

Elspeth rang me at work this morning. She said she'd had Jamie and Dr Mallory on the phone, both talking about Jamie going home. The doctor is fine with it in principal, but the team as a whole would be happier if there's some support in place and Elspeth as next-of-kin was asked about that. I love that they're so concerned about making sure he'll be all right, even though they'd have no power to keep him in if he were to decide to just leave. I wonder if Helen's friends have anything to do with it?

Elspeth rang me because she can't come down this weekend - her youngest has chicken pox - and Dougal has already gone away on a pre-planned trip to Paris, and she wanted me to try and persuade Jamie to stay where he is until one of them can spend some time with him, as he won't listen to her, and she knows that Ben's going away too. I said I'll try but I know he's keen to leave, and she knows he has friends here who won't let him down, and I said if push comes to shove he can stay with me for the weekend if it gives him a break away from the hospital. She seemed a bit thrown by that, as if I'd offered the moon or something, and I had to remind myself that she doesn't know I've stayed with him at his house.

She rang me back half an hour later and said she'd told Dr Mallory that she'd feel happier if Jamie stayed in hospital until the professionals are 100% sure he's okay, but he'd said that in their opinion he was no danger to himself and they couldn't really insist on keeping him in, they could only advise him to stay for further therapy. So she told me the upshot is that if Jamie wants to go home there isn't anything anyone can do about it. I knew that already and I can't understand why she didn't, because I'm sure the doctor would have made it plain to her and Dougal, if he'd said as much to Jamie. Anyway she was ringing me to ask me to try and keep him company as much as I can over the weekend, because she's really very worried about him being alone. I asked her if she'd talked with Jamie about that - if he knew she was calling me - and she said "No" which is unusual because they don't keep much from each other (although obviously he hasn't told her everything, thank god). So I said I'll be close, and she seemed happy enough with that.

So when Ben and I got there tonight we half expected him to be packed and ready to go home, but he wasn't. He said he'll have another counselling session in the morning and see how he feels. I think he might be having second thoughts, maybe thinking about being on his own in the house. He's got to do it sooner or later, but maybe he's just not ready yet. I wanted to tell him that I'll stay with him, or he can stay with me, but I don't want to sway his decision - I want him to be ready on his own. Ben asked him if he thinks he's ready, and what he'll do if he gets home and finds that he isn't, and Jamie said he doesn't really know what 'ready' means but he wants to go home.

He said the sweetest thing, then, and probably the most meaningful/sensible thing he's said since he's been there. He said, "If being ready means I won't get upset and I won't miss my girls, then I don't want to be ready." Ben gave him a hug and looked like he was going to cry. Ben said that he and Adam will be around and Jamie was appalled that they might have cancelled their trip, and said he'd rather wait until next week than have them not go away. In the end he was very persuasive and talked Ben round.

So the arrangement is that Jamie will have his counselling session tomorrow morning and then he'll ring Ben to tell him what he's doing - staying in or going home - and they'll take it from there. Ben's on the 9 - 3 shift tomorrow and I'm on 10 - 6, but Ben said he'll nip out from work to run Jamie home if he wants to go before 3, so that's not a problem. I said I'll go to Jamie's from work if he wants some company, and Jamie nodded. Ben and Adam are planning on leaving for Oxford after Adam finishes work, so B will be able to stay with Jamie for an hour or so after he finishes at 3, and then Jamie will have about an hour on his own before I get there. That's just me thinking of it now - we didn't discuss it.

On the way home, I told Ben that I'll do some shopping in the morning and make sure Jamie's got bread and milk, etc. He said he's really not sure about going away, and I had to have a talk to him about trusting Jamie to know what he's doing. Yes, I'm just as worried as he and Elspeth are, but at the end of the day we've got to just be there and let him do what he needs to do. He's not a kid, and he's not going to do anything stupid, and he's said himself that if he feels he can't cope he'll just take himself back to the hospital. I'm not sure how that works, exactly, but at least he's being realistic about it.

Got home to a message from Darren - he's having a leaving do at the Washington next Friday and hopes I'll be there. I didn't ring him back - I'm going to see how things go for Jamie before I commit myself to a night out. Dancing will be out of the question, anyway, so I'm not too sure about being in a club all night without being able to boogie. We shall see.

Friday 23 May

I've just nipped home to get some things. Jamie's asked me to stay with him, so I'm going back there as soon as I've picked up my overnight stuff and a change of clothes for tomorrow. He's okay, he even seems quite cheerful, but he said he doesn't want to be alone tonight and asked if I'd mind staying - as if I'd mind!

Monday 26 May 5.45 p.m.

Lucy got the promotion on Friday! I'm so happy for her, and I've sent her a 'Congratulations' card - hopefully it will be there when she and Will get back from Devon.

When I got to Jamie's house after work on Friday, he was listening to Radio One, and he told me he'd been reading. He'd have been on his own for just under two hours, and I got the impression he'd stayed in the lounge all that time, which had me very worried. He said Elspeth had phoned twice since Ben had brought him home, and he said she was making him nervous with her concern so he'd told her not to ring again until Saturday! I asked him if he'd eaten, and he hadn't, so we ordered a pizza and I suggested a trip to Asda on Saturday because I'd only got him the basics that morning and he hadn't shopped for food for a couple of weeks.

He said it's ironic that home was always his haven and when he was in hospital he was desperate to get away from the noise and the lack of privacy there, but now he was home he found the silence unnerving. That puzzled me a bit because he's always got music on so it's never silent, and Beth was never a loud child, but I suppose he's just missing the fact that there used to be three of them and now he's on his own.

When we got back to his house, I took my bag upstairs and changed the bedding on the spare bed - Elspeth and her mum had slept there and much as I like them, I just didn't want to sleep with the same duvet and pillowcases. I took a peek in Beth's room and saw that Dougal had left the bed unmade, and he'd left a few mugs and a plate on the chest of drawers, so I took them downstairs to wash them. It must have been a horrible reminder for Jamie the other day when he saw it like that.

We spent most of the evening watching telly, and then around 11 we both started yawning and yawning, setting each other off, so I said I was going to bed and he said he would too. He told me to use the bathroom first and when I'd finished I called, "Goodnight" down the stairs but he came out of his room, so I said it again and went to bed. I lay there listening, though, and didn't settle until I heard him switch his light off.

On Saturday Jamie slept in till after 11! I was sitting in the garden reading when he came down. I wish he'd wear boring, ugly pyjamas because the boxers and t-shirt ensemble just makes me want to jump on him, and the fact that he's completely oblivious to how sexy he is makes him all the more attractive, which doesn't help. I love that he's comfortable enough around me to not even think about it, but still.

I made him some toast and coffee and we sat outside for a while, then he went off to get showered and dressed. He was a bit quiet, but I didn't think anything of it. When he came down he asked me if I wanted dropping off at home and I thought he just wanted to be on his own, which puzzled me, so I said okay but asked if he wanted to do the food shop first, and he said yes so we went there, and while we were going round I asked him what he was planning to do for the rest of the day and he said nothing, I suggested a walk and he agreed, and after we'd unloaded the shopping we walked down to the park.

He was chatty enough but it was only when we sat down on Mum's bench that he let slip what was bothering him, because he asked me if I was nervous about staying with him! I asked him where that had come from, and he said he'd seen that I'd stripped the bed and assumed I didn't want to stay again, so I had to explain why I'd done that and, bless him, he was more embarrassed than I was! So I asked him if he wanted me to stay again, and I think he didn't want to say because he was probably thinking it was a huge inconvenience, so I just said I'm happy to stay if he doesn't want to be on his own, and we left it at that.

My foot was killing me by the time we got back to his house, so he made me sit on the sofa with my feet up while he made us a cup of tea. I took some painkillers, and then he came and sat with me at the other end of the sofa and massaged my foot which was lovely and relaxing. We spent the rest of the afternoon just lounging around, listening to music and reading and drinking tea - it was heaven. Elspeth rang, and I heard him telling her he was fine and he actually laughed at something she said, which is the first time I've heard him laugh since Blackpool. The counsellor rang, too, and he's made arrangements to see him on Tuesday. Ben rang me while Jamie was on the phone, just checking that all was okay, and I told him not to ring but to enjoy his weekend away, and I said I'd ring him if there were any problems.

Sunday didn't start off so great. I got up just after 9 and Jamie wasn't in the house. I rang him, but he'd left his phone in the lounge, so I had no idea where he'd gone, or when. There was no point in me going out to look for him because I had no clue where to start, and anyway his keys were on the table so if I went out he wouldn't be able to get back in. I felt sick, I was so worried, but I didn't want to raise the alarm in case he'd just nipped to the shop or something, and I was overreacting.

I waited until 10, then texted Ben and he rang me straight back and we talked about where Jamie might have gone. I could only think of the park or the shops.

Ben suggested I leave Jamie's keys with his neighbours and pin a note to the door telling him where they were, then go to the park and see if he was there. So I did that, but I couldn't see him anywhere in the park and I soon realised that I could walk around there all day but still miss him, so I headed back to his house and as I turned the corner I saw him further up the road in front of me, so I called him but he didn't hear me. He was reading the note when I got to the gate, and he looked at me with total confusion, like he couldn't understand what was going on. I didn't know whether to laugh or cry or hit him or kiss him, so I just said I'd been worried when I got up and he wasn't there, and we went inside.

He went through to the kitchen, put the coffee on and apologised for worrying me. He said he'd been to the church to see if he could remember anything about Beth's funeral, but he couldn't get inside because services don't start till 10 and it was locked. He'd wanted to go to Helen's grave (Beth is buried with her mum), but he didn't have any flowers with him, and the grounds men had been cutting the grass in that area, so he'd ended up sitting in the remembrance garden. He didn't say that he'd cried, but I could tell that he had.

I think it was a combination of the built-up two hours of worry and overwhelming relief that he was back (and hormones), but I just burst into tears, and he pulled me into a hug and kept saying sorry.

I pulled myself together and I asked him to please not do that again, and he said he just wasn't thinking straight.

He'd been awake in the night a lot, trying to remember things, and he'd got up with that in mind and had just taken off. He'd forgotten I was there, which in a way is a good thing because it means he's getting used to it being just him in the house. He apologised for that and said if he'd been thinking straight he'd have left me a note or at least taken his phone and keys. I'd figured that much for myself. We had coffee and toast, and I asked him if he wanted to go back there, and that I'd go with him if he did. He said yes.

So we drove down to the church and got there just as the mid-day service was finishing. We waited outside until no-one else came out, then we went in and we sat down at the front, where we'd sat on the day of the funeral - I told him who was sitting where - but he obviously couldn't remember any of it. The vicar came over and shook his hand and asked how he was, and Jamie told him that he was trying to remember the funeral and, bless him, the vicar stayed with us and went through the order of service. How does he remember everyone? Or is it because it was a child's funeral, and they stick in the mind more? Anyway, he was very sweet and kept checking that Jamie wanted him to continue, and he went through the whole thing, then he took us outside to the grave. Next to the headstone there's a little wooden cross with a number on it for Beth, and loads of flowers that are mostly dead now, and Jamie broke down when he saw it (which I'd been expecting since we got there) and the vicar just held him and let him cry, while I held Jamie's hand and cried quietly myself. The vicar said to call back any time and offered to call round and visit

Jamie at home, but Jamie just thanked him and we went back to his house.

I just let Jamie drive without saying anything but when we got back inside I asked him if it had helped and he said, "No, not really," but he was glad he'd been. He went upstairs then, and I think he went back to bed. I kept myself busy, bringing the washing in and ironing pillowcases and tidying up a bit, and I phoned Ben to tell him everything was okay. Jamie came down after an hour or so, a bit rumpled but I don't think he'd been sleeping. I made a pot of tea and we sat at the table for a while, but he didn't say anything. He looked like he wanted to, so I just waited - I didn't want to put him off or distract his train of thought by babbling about nothing important - then the phone rang and it was Elspeth and it all came pouring out to her.

He said it bothers him that he still can't remember anything about the funeral, and he's worried that he's having a mental breakdown and wonders what else he's forgotten or will forget, and he's not sure he wants to carry on living in the house without Helen and Beth, and he's not sure of what he's thinking and feeling. Of course he had to then explain to Elspeth about the trips to the church, and she was obviously asking him questions that I couldn't hear, and some of what he was saying made no sense to me because I was just hearing one side of the conversation, but he was so upset that I couldn't stand it and I had to go out in the garden to keep myself from crying. He came out after a while and said Elspeth wanted to talk with me, and while I was on the phone he went upstairs to wash his face I think. Elspeth asked me straight if I thought Jamie should be back in the hospital and I said I didn't think so, because he's no danger to himself or anyone else, and wouldn't they just drug him to calm him down? She said that might bring him some peace, but I know how Jamie feels about that sort of thing and I said I didn't think he'd want that, and she admitted that he'd already said as much to her. She asked me to ring the GP if he got any worse, because he'd advise what's best for Jamie, and I agreed.

I went up to the loo after that and had a peek into Jamie's room but he wasn't there - he was in Beth's room, sitting on her bed and just looking at the shelf unit that holds all her toys. I was standing in the doorway and he looked at me and scratched his head, like he didn't know what the hell was going on. He grabbed the pillow and put it to his face, but then put it down again and said it doesn't smell of Beth anymore, and he lay down on the bed and said he can't smell Helen in their room anymore either.

I went over and knelt down so he could see me, and I said they'll always be in his head and his heart, and there will be other smells that will remind him of them, like roses and ginger and wool remind me of Mum. He just nodded and closed his eyes, and he looked so white and so tired that it really worried me, so I asked him if I should phone Dr Mallory. He said, "No thanks," then, "Just give me a minute or so." I started to get up to go downstairs but he asked me to stay, so I sat with him and held his hand, and we stayed there for what felt like ages.

I have no idea how long, really, but it must have been at least half an hour because I heard the town hall clock strike 4 and it had struck 3 o'clock when I'd been in the garden.

I thought he'd gone to sleep, but when I pulled my hand away to get up, he opened his eyes. He said I'm an oasis of calm and he was so glad of it because I help him switch his head off. I just smiled - I didn't want to say anything in case it sounded flippant or jokey. He squeezed my hand then and got up, saying he'd make us some tea, so I followed him downstairs and put some teacakes in the toaster while he put the kettle on. It was such a lovely day that I took our plates outside and he brought the tea out, and we sat out in the garden for about an hour just soaking up the rays and watching the birds and not really talking about anything in particular.

And then, just like that, he went all quiet and sad again and he said he doesn't know how people get through this sort of thing and he doesn't know what he's supposed to do. I said there's no 'supposed' about it, he'll just get through it in his own way like everyone else does. He said he's tired of feeling 'like this' and then he said part of him doesn't want to stop feeling that way, because he can't imagine not missing them. He's said this a few times before and I don't know what else to say except to tell him that he won't stop missing them, but it will get easier. It's like he forgets he's had these conversations and he needs reminding on a regular basis that things will change. I just hope he mentions it to his counsellor. I wanted to try and keep his spirits up so I suggested we go for a drive somewhere and find somewhere to eat - somewhere out of town, somewhere completely new - and he didn't look at all enthusiastic but he agreed.

We ended up about ten miles away, in a pub called The Crow & Herald which seemed to be in the middle of nowhere. We had to wait forty minutes before they started serving meals, so we sat outside with half a Stella each and looked at the menu and had a wander around the garden. Jamie said he was sorely tempted to get blind drunk, and I offered to drive him home but he knew my foot isn't healed enough for that so he said no, but maybe he'd pick up some bottles on the way home. I can totally understand why he feels that way, and I felt the same way - getting completely off my face was a very attractive idea - but I felt I had to stay sensible, because he'd been so erratic in his moods that I couldn't be sure he wouldn't go off on one. Then he came back from the bar with our second drinks; he had a pint and a large glass of wine for me. I asked him what he was doing and he said we could get a taxi home, and I jokingly said it would be cheaper to stay the night and he took me seriously and even though I said I was joking he went to find out how much they charge for B&B. It actually was cheaper than a taxi back would have been so he said, "Shall we stay?" and I can't refuse him anything, can I? So we ended up having a lovely meal - lasagne, chips and side salad for me and salmon salad for him - and we got completely rat-arsed and stayed the night.

We didn't have anything with us for an overnight stay, so we ended up sleeping in our underwear and yes it was a double bed. I don't even remember going up to the room, but I woke in the night needing the toilet and I was snuggled into his back with my arm around him, and his hand was on my hand on his chest. Pissed as I was, it still made me smile.

6.15 p.m.

Just got off the phone with Lucy. She and Will have had a great weekend in Devon and she was asking what I'd been doing and I was really close to telling her everything about what's been going on with Jamie, but I didn't. I don't want to do that on the phone, I want to talk to her face to face when that all comes out.

Jamie and I were both so ill this morning that we missed breakfast. There's no room service so we had to make do with drinking loads of water and tea in the room, and thankfully we didn't have to check out until 12. We had phone calls from Ben and Elspeth, and both of us managed to sound fairly normal so no-one's any the wiser about what we did last night. Not that getting pissed and staying in a B&B is anything to hide, but as Jamie hadn't told Elspeth, I wasn't about to tell Ben.

Neither of us were hungry, but I said we should at least have a sandwich and a coffee or something before even thinking about driving back, and in fairness the sandwiches were really nice and the coffee was good and strong so it turned out to be a good idea because we both felt better afterwards. I'm still not sure that Jamie should have driven, but we weren't stopped and we made it back without any problems.

I asked him to drop me here so I could have a shower and get changed, and I said I'll walk round later if he still wants company, but he's been so quiet today that I'm not sure if he's had Natasha overload or something. Or maybe it's just how he is when he's hungover. He said he was going to go back to bed for a few hours, so I asked him to ring me when he gets up. That was about three hours ago, and he still hasn't rung. Do I ring him or text him, or leave him be?

Tuesday 27 May

Jamie turned up on my doorstep just before 7 last night. He'd been to sleep for a couple of hours, and when he woke up he'd felt anxious and wanted to get out of the house so he'd come to my flat. I said it's probably the hangover wearing off that had made him feel a bit weird, and I thought he'd just stay for a cup of tea and he or we would go back to his house, but when he came in he asked me straight away if he could stay over, and when I said okay he went back out and got a bag from the car.

Neither of us had eaten since lunch time, so I made us some cheese toasties and we spent the evening watching telly and he was very quiet. When it got to 11 o'clock, I said I had to go to bed because of work in the morning, so I told him to help himself to whatever he wanted and I went to bed, but he was still up when I went to the loo at 1.30 so I went through to the lounge and asked him what was wrong. He couldn't tell me - he was so emotional, trying so hard not to lose it, that he couldn't say what was wrong - so I just asked him if it was the idea of sleeping alone that was bothering him (since he hadn't gone into the spare room) and he nodded, looking really sheepish but still miserable, so I made him come with me to my room and we slept together again like we did in the pub, with me snuggled into his back. I lay awake for ages, though, because I was - and still am - really worried.

This morning, Jamie was already up and dressed before my alarm went off. When I went through, he was sitting in the lounge with my headphones on, listening to something on the stereo. He switched it off and said sorry for last night but I told him not to be daft. We had toast and coffee and then he took me to work. He had an appointment with Dr Mallory at 9.30 (arranged on Friday as part of the discharge process) and one with his counsellor at 11, then he was going home to cook as he'd invited me, Ben and Adam for tea/dinner as a 'thank you' for all our support and help.

Ben was already in work when I arrived, and we managed to have a bit of a chat. They've had a great weekend, and he said he'd been a bit worried about going away but he was really glad he'd gone in the end because he'd realised that he and Adam really needed a break. I didn't tell him about Sunday night, or about last night because I thought it would feel a bit like betraying Jamie's trust, even though Ben's probably his best friend.

Work went quickly and it was a fun day, something

that's been missing for a while. Nobody said it but I'm pretty sure we were all thinking it: is it just coincidence that Vinnie's on holiday this week? I don't think so. Even the AD commented on how light the atmosphere seemed today, although he assumed it was due to the extended weekend off that some of us had had. He asked me and Ben about Jamie, how he's doing and if we thought he's any nearer to coming back to work. We both said the same thing - he's up and down, but mostly okay - and we avoided answering the return to work part.

Ben and I got to Jamie's just after 5, and Adam was about 20 minutes behind us. My biggest surprise was that Jamie had had a shave – that lovely beard has gone! I like him clean-shaven (he looks a lot younger) but I'd started to really like that beard.

Adam brought four bottles of wine, and Jamie thanked him but said he's sworn off alcohol after the weekend, so that cat was out of the bag ... Ben was initially a bit miffed/surprised (he's the only person I know who can do that) but he and Adam thought it was hilarious when we told them how ill we'd been in the morning.

Dinner was bloody lovely - it was like a big Chinese buffet - crispy chicken, three different types of rice and some noodles, some prawn things and a red noodle salad, and lots of veggie dishes, and loads of other things that tasted yummy but I have no idea what was in them. Ben and Adam were all over him for recipes! It's nearly indecent how perfect this man is - good looking, sexy, polite, thoughtful, intelligent, bloody amazing shag, and he can cook like a dream too! I keep wondering when we'll find out he's an axe murderer or something. God I shouldn't say that, but sometimes it's like he's too good to be true. Okay, he belongs to someone else (still) and probably will never think of me as anything but a friend, and he clearly has a needy/negative/erratic side to him when he's down, but apart from all that he's perfect boyfriend/husband material. If only he were in the market ...

Anyway, we had a lovely evening and Jamie seemed much more relaxed and less edgy than he had this morning. While the boys were doing the washing up - they insisted - I commented on his lighter mood, and Jamie told me he'd had a good session with the counsellor and he'd gone over a lot of things with him, and he felt a bit better about some things (he didn't say what). I'd love to know what they talk about, but I'm not going to ask. He also said he'd had a long talk with Elspeth this afternoon, and that had put some things into perspective. I was very tempted to ask him what he meant, but it wouldn't be fair to put him on the spot like that and anyway it's none of my business. I just said I'm really glad that he's finding some clarity, and he said that I do that for him because I'm so 'together' and 'wise' whenever he feels himself unravelling, which made me blush.

Ben and Adam went home just after 9. They offered me a lift but Jamie said he'd run me home later - and that got me a 'oh yeah?' look off Ben when J wasn't looking. When we'd waved them off, he said he hoped I didn't mind him saying that and I said no, as I'm not due in work till 12 tomorrow, and he said, "Let's have a cup of tea" and I kind of got the feeling he was up to something, which was really weird and a bit unnerving.

We went down to the kitchen and he made the tea, and I should have known what was going on but I didn't see it coming - I was so glad to see him all relaxed and cheerful that I kept ignoring the nagging thoughts that it was just a front. Then when he handed me my tea I noticed that his hands were shaking, and he could see that I'd noticed and he dropped the facade. He said he'd made up his mind this morning that he was going to stay home alone tonight and he'd been fine with the idea all day, but now he was getting nervous about it and he had no idea why he should feel that way about his own home, and he hated it.

I pointed out that he's never spent the night alone in the house (to my knowledge - certainly not since Helen died) so it's understandable, and I asked what his counsellor's thoughts are about it. I know it doesn't work that way - the counsellor is there to prompt him to think for himself, not to tell him what to do - but I wondered what direction their discussion had taken. Jamie said they'd talked about what he's feeling and explored reasons for it, and it all makes sense and it's not that he doesn't understand it, it's just that he finds it hard to get past the feeling of not wanting to be alone and he doesn't like feeling uncomfortable in his own home.

So I asked him if it's one of those 'now or never' things

and he said he didn't think so, but he really doesn't want to keep putting it off. I asked him if he'd talked with Ben about this and he has, and Ben thinks he shouldn't push himself but should wait until he feels okay about it, but Jamie's worried he'll become dependent on having people around (which is what's happening). I'm just worried that he's getting all worked up over this when it's really not that important, in the grand scheme of things, but I didn't say that to him.

We talked about it a bit more and in the end I phoned for a taxi, because we thought it would be easier for him if he didn't have to go out to take me home and then come back on his own. So I've been home for about an hour and I just can't help sitting here and wondering what he's doing. The urge to phone him is driving me mad, but that's not going to help, is it? I told him to ring or come round if he gets to the point where he really can't stand it, but I hope he doesn't because I know that it's really upsetting for him.

Wednesday 28 May

I've no idea what time I eventually got to sleep last night/this morning. I know I didn't go to bed til nearly 1 o'clock, and I lay awake for ages wondering if J would ring or turn up. Anyway, my alarm went off at 10 and it felt like I'd had about 5 minutes' sleep, so I've felt rough all day. I got the bus to work because I'm supposed to be walking a bit further each day and I wanted it fresh in my head for this afternoon's physio appointment. It wasn't too bad, actually – my foot was aching a bit by the time I got there, but not half as bad as it has been. It was a nice short day at work - in at 12, off to physio for 2 o'clock and back for 3.30, then finished at 5 - which is just as well because I've been yawning all day, and I'm looking forward to a long hot soak in the bath. Physio was okay too, and she said I'm doing really well and should be able to drive again in a week or so - hurray!

I texted Jamie when I was on the way to physio, just to ask him if he was ok, and he texted back 'Yes thanks' and I sent him a smiley in reply and that was it. Ben said he'd phoned Jamie at lunchtime to ask if he wanted anything picking up from the shops, and J had said no, so we were both chuffed that he was getting on with things on his own. Then Elspeth rang me when I was on the way into town after work, asking if everything was okay because Jamie had been 'tetchy' with her when she'd phoned him earlier and she thinks he sounded depressed. I honestly don't know what she expects of him, but I said he's been okay but I'd check in with him on my way home and would ring her if there's any problem.

I called round there after I'd been to the shops, and I could hear music from the gate so I knew he wouldn't hear me ringing the doorbell, so I used my key and let myself in. He had The Scissor Sisters blaring out full blast from the stereo - I just hope his neighbours were out - and he was standing at the back window of the lounge, singing along at the top of his voice to *Comfortably Numb* and moving a bit (not quite dancing) to the music.

I went down the hall and through the kitchen,

thinking he'd see me coming from there but he didn't so I think he might have had his eyes closed. I said hello and he swore and jumped back - it was quite funny, really. He turned the sound down and said, "Hi," and looked really embarrassed. He knows they're one of my favourites though, so I just said, "Love that track" and smiled, and he nodded. I told him I was on my way home and just thought I'd pop in and see how he's doing, and he asked if I had time for a cuppa and I said, "Always" so he went and put the kettle on. I followed him and sat down at the table and he asked if I was all right, so I just said I was tired (didn't tell him why!) and I told him about physio and he was really pleased about me being able to drive again soon.

I was dying to ask him about last night but I couldn't think how to ask without it sounding like I was checking up on him. Then after a bit - I can't remember what we were talking about (nothing important) - he asked me what was wrong. He said I looked like something was bothering me so I just came out with it and said I was wondering how he'd been overnight, and he smiled a bit and said I'd be a hopeless gambler because I can't hide anything (oh God I hope that's not true!). I had to prompt him to tell me, though, and then he said he'd been okay - better than he'd expected - but it had taken him a long time to get to sleep. He said the house is too quiet and I said it just takes a bit of getting used to, and he nodded.

Then he said the AD had phoned this afternoon and asked him about returning to work, and he said it had been a difficult conversation because although he's got nothing to do he doesn't feel ready to go back and he doesn't know why, so he finds it difficult to explain to the AD, and it's all been left up in the air but the AD clearly wants an answer by the end of the month (which is Saturday). I asked him if that's something he could explore with his counsellor and he agreed, but he's not seeing him till next Tuesday, so I suggested meeting the AD half-way - go back on a part-time basis for now and see how it goes - and J said he'll think about it.

Then he asked me if I was in a rush and would I like something to eat, and I wasn't hungry but I said I'd have another cuppa if he was making one, so I stayed until 7ish and then said I'd better get going and, bless him, he looked so disappointed so I kind of back-tracked and said I had nothing planned and was he up for some company, and I could tell he was kicking himself for being so needy so I said why don't we go out for a drink or something and he said yeah, so we did. I thought we'd walk round to the Pig and Whistle, but he went straight out to the car, and when he saw me looking surprised he said he thought I meant The Crow & Herald, and there was a bit of to-and-fro between us over where to go, but we ended up going there.

He talked a lot while we were there. He said he doesn't much like his own company and doesn't know what to do with himself when he's on his own, and he said he thinks that's because he's never lived alone: he shared digs in Uni, met and married Helen when he was 21, and when Helen had Beth he was allowed to stay with her overnight each time, so they'd never been apart.

He's never mentioned it before, but he told me that they'd have had three children, but the first two miscarried quite late in pregnancy, before Beth was born. He said they never knew what caused the miscarriages but they'd both blamed themselves: he'd thought it was his fault, and he knew Helen thought it was something to do with the abuse she'd suffered from her stepfather, but they never talked about it. He said he'd never met the bastard but he'd haunted their entire relationship. I said it didn't look that way from an outsider's point of view. To me, their relationship sounds strong and loving and very special. Stupid thing to say, really, because then he was struggling to not cry. I asked if it helps to talk about them or would he rather change the subject, and he said, "It helps, but it hurts." I said, "I know what you mean." I meant that I felt that way - and still do, sometimes - about Mum. Then he said I never mention my dad and I just told him he died when I was 12 and he let it drop.

I went to the loo then, and when I got back to the table he'd bought more drinks (coke for me, soda water for him) and he said he wonders how different Helen might have been if her Mum had been a bit more like mine, and we got talking about how Muriel wasn't supportive when Helen told her what Bill (the step-dad) was doing, whereas Mum would have cut his bits off. He didn't go into detail but I think Bill was interfering with Helen from an early age and having full sex with her by the time she was in her teens. J said Helen left Australia as soon as she was old enough to have her own passport, and to this day Muriel insists it was only to get a British education. I said it's amazing to me that Helen trusted blokes enough to even want to go out with one, let alone get married so young, and he shrugged and got all modest and shy. Then he jokingly said he wore her down with his persistence, but I can't imagine him being anything but gentle and understanding, and that's almost certainly what won her over.

He said he'd had no idea that sex would be such a big issue and it took a long time for them to get to that stage of their relationship. I started getting a bit embarrassed because on the one hand he clearly wanted to talk about her but on the other hand I really didn't want to hear just exactly what he was missing. I mean, I know he's kind of hinted before that they weren't experimental - I don't think they ever shagged anywhere but in bed, and he'd never had anyone go down on him before me - but he'd said it was good, and he'd loved her so much that it was probably as lovely and loving as he wanted it to be, because it was her. So I'm sitting there going 'Lalalala' in my head in case he started saying how great it was and all that, but then he took a sip of his drink and didn't say anything more and I wondered if I'd missed something and he was expecting an answer.

He wasn't. He just said, "You're far too easy to talk to." I said, "Is that good or bad?" and he smiled and said, "I'm not sure just now." He told me that Ben was the only other person he'd really talked to outside his family, and it made me realise how isolated they - him and Helen - must have been, because they only had two or three friends and those were people they knew from work, so I said, "You don't get out much then?" and he said that he and Helen used to love going to the cinema or out clubbing, but that all stopped when Beth was born, and they'd go cycling at the weekends with Beth on the back and they'd go to some of the big festivals every summer, but they mostly stayed in. I said if he ever fancied a night out he only had to say, because me and Ben - and most of the guys at work - are always up for that. He nodded but he looked a bit sad, so I don't suppose he's ready to go out on his own yet.

I was yawning like mad by that point, so he suggested we get going. He was a bit quieter in the car, which I assume was because he was thinking about going back to the empty house. I was gagging to ask him to come in with me and stay the night, but I'm resolved that that's got to come from him, because my making it easy for him really won't help him get to grips with the situation, will it? He brought me straight home, and I gave him a quick peck on the cheek and got out of the car before I changed my mind.

I got in to find a snotty message on the phone from Darren, saying he assumes I won't be there on Friday since I haven't got back to him, so I rang him and apologised and said of course I'll be there, but he was so off with me that I might not bother. Moody git. Had enough of that with Gavin.

Friday 30 May

Well, so much for my resolve. Actually my resolve was fine, but he had different ideas, and now I'm not sure what to think.

Jamie rang me when he got home on Wednesday night, because I'd left my shopping there, and he offered to bring it round. I said no at first but then I remembered the milk was in there and he insisted, and he was here in less than ten minutes, bless him. I'd not long finished updating this thing when he rang, and I was in the middle of getting undressed because the bath was running, so I pulled my tracksuit on to answer the door and he thought I was going out for a run. We got that cleared up and without thinking I asked him in and put the kettle on while I was putting the shopping away, then he reminded me that the bath was still running so I asked him to go and turn it off. He started to leave then, but I'd made us a cuppa and persuaded him to stay for that, but he drank it quite quickly and then he went.

I thought it was a bit odd because usually he's not keen to go back to being alone, but I just thought maybe he really was getting used to it, or maybe there was footy on the telly or something. Anyway I had my bath and went to bed, and I was just dozing off when he texted me: 'Please can we talk?' I rang him. I think he was surprised that I rang him straight away, like maybe he half-thought I'd be asleep and wouldn't get the text until the morning. Anyway I asked him what was wrong and I think that threw him too - I think I need to try and stop being so direct with him - because he stammered for a bit, saying nothing was wrong and he was sorry for bothering me so late (it was nearly 12), and then he said he felt really selfish for disturbing me and said it didn't matter and he was saying goodbye but I stopped him and asked him what he wanted to talk about, and he said "Anything." and he said talking to me calms him down.

He said he was sorry for blabbing on about Helen earlier and he hoped he didn't make me feel uncomfortable, so I put him at ease on that one and said I'm glad he feels comfortable enough with me to talk about whatever he wants. So he talked about the job situation and said he'd decided to ring the AD and talk about a part-time return for now, and he said something about another of Elspeth's kids having chicken pox, and something about his niece's exam results, and I was listening and talking back to him, but I was tired and yawning, and after a few minutes of this I just said, "You can't get to sleep, can you?" and he said no. I said he could come round and stay here if it would help (and I honestly was thinking of the spare room) and there was no answer and I thought he'd put the phone down so I said "Hello?" a couple of times and then he said thank you, but then he said "I can't do that, but thank you for saying it." I was a bit disappointed so I asked him why not, and there was that silence again, so I said, "Jamie? Are you okay?" and then it all came out.

He said the week between us getting back from Blackpool and Beth's funeral is still a big blur, but in the pub he'd kind of got some memories back about him and me, and that shut me up then because I hadn't realised he'd blanked all of that out as well, and I realised that this was what he wanted to talk about when he'd texted, and why he hadn't wanted to stay earlier. Talk about embarrassed - I didn't know what the heck to say. He said then that perhaps we should leave it for now, seeing as it was late, and he said he really shouldn't have brought it up and he was sorry that he didn't wait until morning, but I said that that didn't matter because if he wanted to talk about it then so did I, and I said if he wanted to come round rather than talk on the phone then I'd be fine with that, but he wouldn't.

He said he just needed to know what had happened - not so much that he wanted details, but he was worried that he'd forced me into it and had taken advantage of me - so I said we'd both been very emotional and needy, and it had just happened, he certainly had nothing to worry about and if anything I should have been the one to stop it because I wasn't the one who was crazed with grief. I told him what we'd talked about at the time - how it felt right but wrong, and how he'd said it made him feel unfaithful but he really just wanted an escape from the pain, and what Mum said about comfort where you find it, and what I'd said about being here for him in whatever way he needs, and all that stuff.

He'd gone quiet again so I asked him if he remembered anything now, and he said he did, and then he said, "Give me a few minutes - I'll ring you back" and put the phone down. So I'm lying there in bed, wondering what on earth he was thinking, and worrying about him being all upset or even freaking out, and I wanted to call him back but at the same time I didn't, because it's important for him to be in control rather than getting prompted all the time. Of course I was wide awake by then, and my heart was pounding, so I got up and put my pyjamas on, and went to make some hot chocolate. I was just heating the milk when he rang back. He just said "Tasha ..." and I said, "Come round." Twenty minutes later he was here.

I opened the door and he just stood there looking really nervous, so I handed him a mug of hot chocolate and let him shut the door and follow me through to the lounge. I sat on the sofa, but he just stood at the other end looking like he wasn't sure what he was doing. I asked him if he was okay, hoping that would get him talking, but he shook his head and turned round, heading for the front door. I hurried after him, but he hadn't opened it, he was just leaning his head against it with his hand on the handle, so I went up to him and asked him if he wanted to stay and he said yes so I took him back through the lounge and said he could sleep in the spare room or with me, but either way I was going back to bed unless he wanted to talk.

He said it would be best if we left the talking for another time because it was getting on for 1 o'clock by then, so I went to clean my teeth and while he was in the bathroom after me, I switched everything off and went to bed, and after a while he came into my room. I was really shocked. I fully expected him to take the spare room, but I pushed the duvet back for him and he got in.

He was just lying there on his back and I could feel the tension coming off him, so I turned over to face him and said perhaps we should talk, but he said he was too tired and mixed up to make any sense, so I just put my arm over his chest and went to sleep. I woke in the night and he'd turned over, and I was snuggled into his back with my arm still round him (I think he likes that). I woke again around six to go to the loo, and I felt awful - really tired, and a bit headachy, and I knew I'd never get up with my alarm at 7 so I turned it off, and texted Ben to say I felt unwell and would ring later. When I got back in bed, Jamie turned and snuggled into my back, with his arm round me - the first time he's done that - and I fell back to sleep like that.

My phone woke us up just after 9. I leaned over to grab it from the bedside table, and I think that woke Jamie more than the phone had. He rolled onto his back when I answered the phone, then he went to the bathroom while I talked to Ben. I told Ben that I'd had a couple of bad nights and I felt tired and headachy, and he knew I'd felt rough on Wednesday so he was sympathetic and said he'd spin it out a bit to the AD. Jamie heard the tail end of my conversation and asked me if I was okay, and I said I was but I could do with some more sleep, and I thought he'd have taken that as an excuse to leave but he didn't - he got back in bed and went back to sleep with me!

When I woke up later, I felt really horny and I realised that Jamie's hand was just under my breast, not quite touching it. He was snuggled into my back again, and when I stretched my legs a bit I could feel his erection against my bum - that's probably what had got me feeling horny, even though it could have meant he was having a great dream about Helen, or he needed the loo. He was still asleep, though, and much as I wanted to, I wasn't going to wake him up because I still wasn't sure how he felt about the fact that we'd had sex. So I just lay there, trying to get back to sleep, and I think I dozed for a little while but I woke up feeling really hot and thirsty.

Jamie hadn't moved, and he still felt quite hard, which made me feel more horny and I got to the point where I couldn't stand it and I went to get out of bed, but he pulled me back and asked me if I was feeling any better. I said yes, and he pulled me closer to him and said, "Can we ...?" and I swear, I nearly came there and then. I moved his hand down inside my pyjama pants and he got the message. While he was doing that, I shoved my pants down and reached behind me to pull his boxers down and pushed myself against him, and I'm not sure he even knew what I was suggesting because I ended up guiding him inside me from behind and he swore when he got there. I was already coming like no tomorrow by then, and that spurred him on but he was slow and gentle like he thought it might hurt me, and it was sooooooo good, but we were both getting really hot so I pulled away from him and stripped off, and he did the same, and then he was on me and in me and dear god he's so sexy he's only got to touch me and my insides are exploding all around him.

We talked for quite a while afterwards. He said sex

with me is amazing and we've done things he's not tried before, but it all feels a bit surreal. He said he feels horribly guilty, because he loves Helen and still feels married, so he tries to kid himself that she would want him to not be lonely. It struck me that he didn't say she'd want him to be happy. He also said he feels guilty because he feels he's using me - our friendship - and I told him that he can pack that in because I enjoy it, and I paid him a few compliments that made him blush in the most adorable way that made me want to snog him senseless.

It hurts him that Helen never really enjoyed sex the way I do, though - I can see it in his face when we talk about it. We talked about him feeling guilty and I tried to get him to see that we can't hurt Helen, we can only hurt ourselves or each other (and I said I'm willing to risk getting hurt because he's worth it). We talked about how he can still love Helen and probably always will, even though he's technically no longer married to her (that was him saying that, not me), but I said that that needn't stop him from enjoying himself and finding friendship and more with other people. I think he gets that, he's just having a hard time letting himself actually do it guilt-free.

We talked for ages, and he seemed really relaxed and as if things were starting to make sense so I asked him if he's okay with all this now, if he can live with this as it is without feeling bad about it, and he said he doesn't know, he needs to play it by ear if it's okay with me. I laughed and told him I'm getting mind-blowing sex into the bargain so why wouldn't it be okay, and he blushed again.

He got serious and said he really doesn't think he knows what he's doing or feeling half the time, so I said he needs to save the self-analysis for his counselling sessions and the rest of the time just go with the flow. And then he said, "Like this?" and he was on me again, which took me by surprise but in a good way. Dear god he's an amazing shag. I've never known anyone with such quick recovery! I feel sorry for Helen because she missed out on so much with him, poor woman.

We finally got up around 1, I think. We took turns in the shower and while he was in there I made us toast and tea for breakfast/lunch (is that what 'brunch' is?). He came out of the bathroom, towelling his hair dry, and his trousers were so low on his hips I could tell he was going commando and it took every ounce of resolve I had left to not jump his bones then and there.

I rang work after we'd eaten, just to let Ben and the others know that I was okay and that I'd be there today. Jamie asked me to find out where the AD was, and then he phoned head office and spoke to him about returning to work. I was really surprised by that. I know he'd talked about it, but I didn't think he was ready to even start thinking about it yet. Anyway he got it sorted out, and he'll be going back next week for a few hours a day and then they'll review it each week. He said he's not sure if he's doing the right thing, but the AD has been really supportive and patient (not the words I'd use) and Jamie feels he owes it to everyone to at least give it a try. I said hopefully going back to work will keep him from kicking his heels at home all day, and he said that's mostly the point - he needs to stop wallowing at home and get back into a routine.

He nipped home after that, but he came back for tea (I had a go at making lasagne with Quorn, and it wasn't too bad) and he stayed the night. He's now been introduced to a new position – me on top - and something tells me he likes it. He had a bit of a cry afterwards, though, and when I got him talking he told me he doesn't think Helen ever had an orgasm - it certainly wasn't obvious, if she did - and seeing me coming so forcefully and so often has made him realise how little she must have enjoyed it. I said I obviously don't know, but I can't see how she wouldn't have enjoyed making love with him because (1) she loved him, and (2) he's very good in bed, and he hugged me tight for that. Is it weird that we discuss his dead wife's feelings about sex, after we've shagged? I think it probably is, but I don't much care - I just love the fact that he's relaxed enough with me to talk about whatever pops into his head.

Jamie dropped me off at work this morning, and he took me right to the door, which surprised me - I didn't think he'd want anyone to know we were 'together' at that time of the day. No-one saw him, though, or at least if they did, no-one said anything. Lisa and Gemma asked if I was okay, and for a second I almost dropped myself in it because I'd forgotten about phoning in sick yesterday. Ben came in at 10 and we had a good day until Darren came in this afternoon, to bring in his name badge and to return some files, and to make sure all the paperwork is done for him leaving. Today's his last official day but he's been using up the last of his holidays this week.

There was talk about tonight and who's going and how they're getting there, etc, and I'd completely forgotten all about it but didn't let on. Ben offered to pick me up and because I didn't answer straight away, Darren jumped right in and said, "D'you have to check with Jamie first?" and I could have died. Ben was horrified that he'd drop me in it like that, and Lisa looked like she knew anyway, but Gemma was all "What? Huh?" and I didn't know where to look. I just said, "What's he got to do with it?" and before Darren could answer, Ben said he thought my physio had already told me no dancing and I could have kissed him. I said to Darren that I'll be there if I feel up to it, and he just said, "Yeah, whatever," and changed the subject.

As he was leaving I went up to him and wished him good luck and he apologised. I called him an idiot and he smiled, so I think we're okay. I really don't care anymore what he thinks, but I need to find out how Jamie would feel about this coming out at work. Maybe I can get Ben to sound him out about it.

Anyway, Lisa brought me home after work, and I've phoned Lucy (she and Will were thinking of coming down tomorrow but I've put her off, saying me and Hayley are going out for the day), and I've told Ben that I don't need a lift (he laughed at that, because he'd already figured out that I wasn't going), and I've had a bath and tidied up and now I'm waiting for Jamie to come round.

We're going to do nothing more exciting than order a pizza and watch telly, but I've got butterflies because it's him. I know he doesn't love me and I know he never will, but I'm fairly sure that I love him, and if this is all I can have with him then I'm happy with that.

Wednesday 4 June

Jamie's back at work and it's been a bit weird, but it's okay. Lisa definitely knows what's going on, but Gemma and Vinnie don't, and I've asked Ben to have a little word with Jamie and find out how he feels about 'going public' because I'm on pins about it all blowing up - I don't want him to be embarrassed about it. He's doing mornings, and he seems fine about it but Vinnie is still running the show. I'm not sure if that's because Jamie wants him to, or if Vinnie doesn't want to hand over.

I'm going over to Jamie's house in a bit - it'll be my first time driving on my own since I broke my foot. I drove last night, just to try it, but Jamie was with me in case I couldn't manage it. He's cooking for me and Ben and Adam tonight, and I'll probably stay over. He's stayed at mine nearly every night except Saturday, when I stayed at his house after we'd been to the pub (Crow & Herald), and Monday, when he was upset after going to the stone mason to get Beth's details put on the headstone, and I stayed with him again. He keeps saying he really wants to try living on his own, but every time he's there alone he says he can't stand the thought of the emptiness. I know that Elspeth has suggested that he sells the house but he doesn't even want to think about it yet. I sometimes think

Elspeth is expecting him to move on a bit too quickly, but I know it's only because she worries about him.

Lucy and Will are coming up at the weekend. If Jamie's okay with it, I'm going to tell Lu what's going on.

Friday 6 June

Jamie and I had a long talk about the situation last night. We'd had a bit of a chat about it on Wednesday night, and Jamie was really struggling with the idea that we actually have a situation - I think he just didn't want to admit to himself that he's doing stuff he'd never have dreamed of doing if Helen was still alive. He was very sweet about it later, though - he said he's certain he'd have cracked up or something worse if it hadn't been for me (and Ben, but mostly me), but he's not comfortable with the idea of him and me being in an official relationship, and it took me a while to convince him that that's fine with me and I'm not hurt by it.

And I'm really not - I'm quite content to just do what we're doing without labelling it 'a relationship' - but he needs to understand that others might see it differently. So now, after last night's talk, he's a bit concerned in case there are repercussions at work - he's not sure where the AD stands on managers 'dating' the employees, not that that's what's happening exactly, but it's as much as the AD would need to know. Jamie says he's fine with me talking to Lucy - although he's not sure about meeting her and Will, at least not yet - but he's not ready to say anything to Elspeth.

I love that we can talk about stuff like this - really uncomfortable and difficult stuff - with absolute honesty, without either of us getting wound up. Okay he sometimes gets upset, and that's understandable, but we talk it through and work it out, and I can't even imagine getting into a slanging match with him - it's so different from how things were with Gavin, he'd blow up at the drop of a hat. Jamie's so calm and sensible and mature, and keen for everything to be talked through and sorted out and resolved - I love that about him.

Anyway, we also talked about him staying with me while Lucy and Will are here, but he doesn't want to do that, not with them not knowing what's been going on, which is why he's fine with me talking to Lucy about it. It means he'll be staying at his house on his own tomorrow night, but I've made it clear that he can come round here at any time if he finds he just can't stand it. I've given him a key - seems only fair, since I've had a key to his place for nearly 3 months - so he can let himself in if it's really late.

I'm going round there now. I may or may not stay over - we're going to see how it goes.

Sunday 8 June

I ended up staying at Jamie's on Friday night. We had another really long talk and it all got a bit emotional, and we ended up in bed - his bed this time, not the spare room like we usually do - and I've no idea what time we got to sleep.

I can't remember now what started us talking about it, but we got onto the subject of relationships and sort of picked up from Thursday's talk, and he said he felt he was being unrealistic about it all - about our 'relationship' for want of a better word - because we're clearly more than just friends and yet he can't get himself to think beyond that. I tried to get to the bottom of why it's so important for him to label what we have, and he said he just needs to know what we're getting into, and I said we've been over this before and surely it's more important to just appreciate what we have than to try and define it.

He said I have a very unique and unusual way of looking at things, and he can't get his head around it, so I asked him straight out what he thinks of me and he was going, "You're very attractive and honest and sexy..." and being very complimentary, but totally missing the point. So I said, "You think of me as a friend, don't you? But not a girlfriend" and he went pale, so I had to quickly tell him it's all right, I understand. I know he still loves Helen, but I'm just trying to get him to see that he doesn't need to think of me as anything but 'Natasha' and there's no need to try and categorise what's going on between us.

It just messed his head up even more though because he can't get past the idea that he's still married and in love with his wife, but he really enjoys what we've got going between us, and the conflict is eating at him. So I made him think about what Helen would really want for him - would she want him to be lonely, unhappy, isolated, ill

- all the things he's been through since she died - would she want him to be like that for the rest of his life? And he couldn't say, "Yes she would" because he knows that Helen loved him. We were both knackered by that point, and he was upset and it was upsetting me, so I said we should leave it for now and go to bed (to sleep) but when I came out of the bathroom he took my hand and pulled me into his room.

We've laid on the bed before, and slept there, but we've never shagged in there so I just thought we were going to sleep together, but he started kissing me and rummaging under my pyjamas and then we were shagging in his bed. And I actually got him to kiss me while we were doing it, and he got so turned on by it that he came very quickly, and there is something incredibly sexy about the way he says "F- fuck!" when he's coming. And bless him he apologised for being so quick, and he told me that it was because he'd never done that before because Helen couldn't handle being kissed during sex. God I feel more sorry for that woman the more I hear about her - that bastard of a stepfather ruined what should have been a beautiful thing for her.

So, since we were talking (again) about his previous sex life, I asked him what they used to do and I was right - just ordinary face-to-face lovemaking with no kissing and, from the sound of it, very little foreplay or after-snuggling. He doesn't mean to disrespect her, far from it, I can tell from the things he says that he never felt he was missing anything, she was everything to him, and if anything he's sad that she missed out. Talking about it turned me on, though, because there's so much that he hasn't tried yet and I really hope I get to show him all that.

I was stroking his chest and his arm while we were talking, and I moved my hand lower down his body and he shivered, and it just popped into my head to try something, so I started kissing down his chest and stomach and then down his leg and back up the other one and he got hard again, so I started kissing there too and then moved back up to his mouth and snogged him while I stroked him and made him come. And the sounds he made while I was doing that made my insides twitch (it's making me horny now, just thinking about it).

I needed to come too, then, so I carried on kissing him but started working on myself and he pulled away and asked if he could watch, so I let him and that is much more erotic than fantasising about him doing things to me. I asked him to fondle my breasts while I was doing it, but when I was close I told him to finger me and he did it at just the right time, and the groan that came out of him was bloody lovely and helped me along very nicely. We took a minute to clean up, then I snuggled into his back and we talked about it for a bit, and eventually we fell asleep. He's not easy to sleep with though – he tosses and turns a lot, and I spent half the night trying to get the duvet back off him.

I stayed with Jamie as long as I could yesterday. I tried to persuade him to come back to mine and meet Lucy but he wants to wait, so I didn't push it. We got up around

11 and he made scrambled eggs with toasted muffins for breakfast, and we just lounged around for a couple of hours until Lucy rang and said she was half an hour away, and that's when I came home. Lucy and Will arrived just after 2, and after they'd unpacked and freshened up and we'd had a little catch up we all went into town for a mooch around the shops. Lucy was looking for work clothes but she didn't find anything. We stopped for a coffee, and while we were there I texted Jamie to ask him if he wanted to join us but he didn't answer and I felt bad for pushing it when I'd said I wouldn't.

We'd decided to go out for dinner and when we got back here, Lucy and I got some girl talk in while Will was in the bathroom. I told her that Jamie and I have started seeing each other, and when she asked, "Since when?" I just said in the last couple of weeks - I couldn't tell her about before. She was surprised, but pleased for me, but also a bit concerned in case Jamie's just on the rebound. I told her that I know it's probably that, and that it most likely will not go anywhere, but she knows that I'd sworn off relationships after Gavin anyway so she knows I'm not looking for commitment, life-long or otherwise. Of course she asked me when I'm going to introduce him, and I had to say maybe next time - I said he was a bit shy, and she thinks that's sweet. I was so relieved to tell her, even if I haven't told her everything.

I got a text from Jamie just as I was going to the bathroom - he said he'd been out earlier and had left his phone at home, and he thanked me for the invite and said, 'See you tomorrow'. Lucy, Will and I had a lovely evening - we went to the Queens Hotel and had their 3-course Saturday special, which was really nice - and they made their announcement over dessert: they've set a date, July 18th next year, and Lucy wants me to be her bridesmaid. She'd have been in big trouble if she hadn't at least asked. I bought them a bottle of champagne to celebrate, and we all got a bit giggly, and it was lovely. I texted J when we got home, just to check he was okay, but he didn't answer so I assumed he'd gone to bed. Lucy, Will and I sat up talking for hours, and only went to bed when Will started to doze off which I think was around 2.

This morning I made us all a big fry-up and we were eating that when Ben rang to ask if me and Jamie fancied a country-pub lunch with him and Adam. It nearly became awkward, because Ben was all for making it a six-some when I told him that Lucy and Will were here, and I had to go into the bedroom to tell him quietly that Jamie wasn't up for meeting Lucy just yet, but I asked him to ring J and invite him to go with them and he said he would.

Lucy and Will left just after 1 - they wanted to get back early as they had arranged for someone to come and look at the garden, as neither of them have had time to do anything with it and it's getting embarrassing. They want me to go down there for a visit, with or without Jamie, so I need to get that organised. I tidied up and did some washing and had a shower and was just going to ring Jamie when the doorbell rang. It was Ben, Adam and Jamie and two of them were very tipsy and gave me a big hug then staggered into the lounge and almost fell onto the sofa. Adam gave me a kiss and apologised - he'd planned on just dropping Jamie off as he'd asked, but Ben had insisted they all come in and he (A) hadn't been able to do anything about it.

I put the kettle on for coffee and tried to have a conversation with one sober and two very nearly drunk men, which was confusing but funny. They'd had a lovely lunch in the King's Head, which I've never been to but I've heard good things about, and Adam told me quietly that they'd talked a LOT which made me squirm with embarrassment for a moment, wondering what on earth Jamie might have said, especially if he'd had a bit too much to drink, but Adam winked and said, "Nothing juicy" and Ben called over "He won't be pressed," which made him giggle for some reason. Adam waited till Jamie went to the bathroom, then he told me that J had been asking for advice and he hopes that he and Ben have helped set his head straight.

I was about to ask what about when Ben came over and put his arms round me and said, "I love you Tash." and he said he loves Jamie and he's so happy that we're so good for each other, and Adam and I rolled our eyes at each other because he was getting so smooshy, but it's really sweet when he's like that and I hugged him back. Adam led him back to the lounge and I took the coffee through, but Ben wouldn't drink it without milk and sugar so I fetched that too, and some biscuits, and by that time Jamie had come out of the bathroom. He stood in the doorway for a minute, taking deep breaths, and I thought he was going to be sick but he just looked at us and smiled apologetically and sat down. Ben asked after Lucy and I told them about her and Will setting the date, and he and Adam were chuffed, and J said, "Ah that's nice" and he looked genuinely pleased.

While we drank our coffee and they devoured the biscuits, I got them to tell me about the King's Head and the food, mostly because I didn't want Ben blabbing about what they'd talked about in case it embarrassed Jamie. It sounds like a really nice place and they all said we've got to go there sometime soon for lunch or dinner. Once Adam and Ben had finished their coffee, A pulled B to his feet and said they needed to get going. Ben gave Jamie and me a hug, and I helped Adam get him back into the car - I swear the coffee and biscuits made him more tiddly, maybe it was a sugar high - and when I went back inside, Jamie was pouring himself and me another coffee.

He said he hadn't wanted to go with them today because he was still a bit hungover from last night (which explains why he didn't answer my text), but they'd been very persuasive. I said it looked like they all had a good time and he said, "Yeah they're good company.". He said Ben had talked him into coming over to meet Lucy and Will, but he was quite glad they'd gone because he didn't think he'd have made a good first impression. I said, "You don't know my sister." He smiled a bit at that and asked if she's like me, and I said, "A bit" and he nodded. He said he hoped I didn't mind him coming round, like it's a huge inconvenience or something, so I told him I'd been just about to ring him to find out what he's doing later.

Then he asked me if I'd had the talk with Lucy that I'd planned. I told him what I'd told her. He seemed a bit surprised and quite relieved, I think, that I haven't shared every detail. I told him I hadn't planned on telling her every single thing, I just didn't want to hide the fact that I was spending a lot of time with him, and he said, "So you've not told her we're in a relationship, then?" which totally threw me after what we'd talked about the other night. I said, "I thought we weren't?" and he said, "Ben and Adam seem to think we are," and I didn't know what to say. I mean, yeah, if he wants to call it a relationship that's fine with me, but he's the one who's been having trouble even thinking in those terms so it wasn't important to me to label it ... so why was he now saying we're 'in a relationship'? I thought it must have been the booze talking, so I just said okay and he took that as meaning I wasn't happy about it, and then we got into a very odd little conversation.

It was odd because (a) he was a little the worse for wear on red wine and therefore not at his most coherent, and (b) he'd suddenly got it in his head that being in a relationship would be okay (and it's obvious I have Ben and Adam to thank for that), and (c) I was almost completely at a loss for words. He said we're more than friends - much more, he said - and we most certainly are NOT fuck-buddies. He said we enjoy each other's company and spend a lot of time together. Ergo, he said, we are in a relationship. And I'm just sitting there, wondering if he means it or if it's the wine speaking, and not knowing whether to humour him or not, and wondering just exactly what the hell the three of them had said in that bloody pub to get him to this little epiphany.

So I said okay again and then, "That works for me if you're okay with it." For a couple of seconds he looked absolutely clueless as to what we were talking about, then he said, "Um ... yeah." and nodded, scratching at his head like he does when he's trying to think clearly. So I did what any woman would do after such a romantic bombshell - I sent him to the spare room to sleep it off. He went, mostly I think because he was feeling a bit rough by then. I took him a pint of water and put it on the bedside table with a couple of aspirin, and he said something but I couldn't make it out.

He's still in there. I've spent the last hour and a half mulling over what he said and trying to remember what he said the other night, because I'm fairly sure they contradict each other. I really want to talk to Adam and find out what was said in the pub, but I'm not going to do that with Jamie in the next room, even if he does seem to be out for the count. I'll just have to wait and see if he feels the same way when he's sober.

In the meantime I need to try and work out how I feel about it, because if he's offering me a proper relationship then that's pretty much my dream come true - it certainly would have been, six months ago, anyway - but can he do that? Can he move on from Helen so soon?

I don't think he'll ever stop loving her, but will that mean he can't ever love someone else? I know he doesn't love me now, but could he? Does he want to? Or is he not even thinking that way? Do I want him to? I've been happy enough with what we have ... why am I now wondering if I'll get more, just because he's labelled it? God I need a drink.

Monday 9 June

Well it seems I owe Ben and Adam a massive thank you, even if they flatly refuse to tell me exactly what they talked about with Jamie yesterday. It's obvious they discussed 'the situation' but they won't go into details, because apparently Ben had suggested to Jamie that he didn't need to say anything about their talk to me, and Jamie hasn't given much away either. I can forgive them, though, because J is much more relaxed about the whole thing now and that's more important than anything else.

It was nearly 6 when he got up yesterday evening. I was on my second Chardonnay by then (thank you, Lucy) and I'd actually calmed down and was thinking quite sensibly and maturely and objectively, then he goes and appears at the door in his Calvin Klein's and I nearly spilt my wine. He had the decency to pull his shirt on, but the damage was done by then and I'd forgotten most of the sensible and mature things that I was going to say - I had just enough presence of mind left to keep quiet and wait for him to say something. The first thing he said, of course, was sorry - sorry for sleeping so long, sorry for getting drunk - which I brushed off, but we do need to have a serious talk about him saying that so much.

I gulped the last of my wine and asked him if he wanted a drink, and he wanted tea so he put the kettle on. When he'd made it - and one for me - he came and sat down next to me on the sofa and of course he noticed straight away that I was quiet so he asked me if I was okay, and then, before I could answer him, he said, "Have I made a fool of myself?" and that made me smile. I said no, but I told him I was a bit thrown by what he'd said earlier and he admitted, then, that he wasn't supposed to have said anything.

He told me that Adam had asked how he's doing and it had all gone from there, and he'd probably said a bit more than he would have done if he hadn't been hungover (he wouldn't say what, exactly, and I'm not even sure that I want to know) and both Adam and Ben had talked a lot of sense, although from what I can tell it sounds like the red wine had somewhat hindered Ben's delivery and Jamie's understanding of it all - I assume Adam sorted that part out. Anyway the upshot of it is that he's accepted that we are in a relationship of sorts, he still feels guilty as hell about it but he doesn't want to end it, and he's sorry for upsetting me with it all (he was talking about Friday, when we'd both got upset trying to figure out what the hell he was thinking) and then he asked me if he was making any sense.

I'd had two hours or so, and a couple of glasses of wine, to think it over. I think I'd decided that if the wine had got the better of him and he hadn't meant a word of it, I wasn't going to say anything and would just forget what he'd said, but if he said he'd meant it then I was going to say yes to a relationship with him if he felt he could commit to one, but I was going to make it clear that I didn't want to end up being rebound girl in a couple of months, and if there was any chance of that happening then I was not going to commit to the relationship thing. Or something like that. It was very mature and sensible, I'm sure.

But he'd come in all sleep-ruffled and sexy in his boxers, being all earnest and quiet and trying so hard to be sensible about it all, and I knew it was really important to him to get this straight in his head - even if that doesn't last, and he falls apart over it again in a week or a couple of days or a month - so I just said he made perfect sense, and could I have a kiss please? And we ended up making love - slowly and gently with a lot of kissing, not the usual energetic shagging and desperate snogging - on the sofa, and it was absolutely bloody amazing. So amazing, in fact, that I came very close to telling him that I love him. It was on the tip of my tongue, just as I was about to come, but I looked at him and saw the tears in his eyes (he does that sometimes) and I changed my mind. I can't do that to him yet. I'm not sure if he'll ever want to hear it from me, but it's definitely too soon just now. He sobbed when he came, and I know it's the guilt and the regret and the pain, and I know it's a huge emotional release for him as well as a physical one, so I just held him and let him cry. He's done that before, a few times, but it was different this time - it felt like he was letting something go.

He was quiet for the rest of the evening, though, and I really thought he was having second thoughts. There was nothing interesting on telly and I've got the NVQ assessor coming on Thursday, so I worked a bit on my portfolio after we'd eaten, and Jamie had the radio on and was reading. He made us a cuppa around 10 and asked me then if he was okay to stay the night, which really shocked me - why would he feel he had to ask? - so I said he didn't have to ask but he looked really troubled so I asked him what was wrong. He said, "Nothing - just adjusting," and that made me feel so sad for him.

I went to give him a hug but he pulled away and he said, "Just give me some time." I could have cried, but I said, "We don't have to do this," and he said, "I know" and went into the bathroom. I was absolutely convinced that he was going to come out of there and tell me he'd changed his mind, but he didn't. He came out and got dressed, saying he hadn't brought anything with him for staying over and I offered him a clean t-shirt but he said he needed other stuff, and he was gone before I could say anything else.

I thought about going after him but I didn't, because he obviously needed some time alone. I felt nearly sick with anxiety, but there wasn't much I could do, so I had a quick shower and got ready for bed rather than sit here and fret. He came back around 11.30 - he rang the doorbell instead of using his key but I didn't say anything about that, I just opened the door and tried not to look too relieved. He had a sports bag with him and he said he wasn't really sure what to bring, and then he looked really troubled again and it's so obvious that he's having second thoughts but he doesn't want to give in to them.

I left it to him to decide where to put stuff - I said there's space in my wardrobe for clothes, or in the one in the spare room if he'd prefer, and if he's got bathroom stuff he can just shove my stuff over and make space where he needs to - but he just put the bag on the floor in the hall and said he'll do that tomorrow, and would I mind if he just went to bed? I said I'm ready to go anyway, and while I was brushing my teeth he brought some of his toiletries into the bathroom and put them on the shelf over the radiator.

I left him to it and got into bed, and he came through after a few minutes. I was on my side facing him when he got in, but it was like he didn't want to touch me - he lay on his back, right at the edge of the bed, and didn't look at me. I felt really confused and upset, and a bit angry, because he was being so distant and I couldn't get him to open up, which isn't like him at all. I eventually dropped off, but when I woke up in the night - don't know why - we'd turned over and he was snuggled into me with his arm around my waist, so that made me feel a bit better.

This morning, when we got up for work, he was fine. When the alarm went off, he pulled me closer to him - we were still snuggled together - and he said sorry for being so moody last night, he just had a lot of things going through his head and didn't feel able to vocalise any of it. I said next time, he just has to say that that's what's going on, so that I know. I think he could tell that I was a bit hurt, because he kissed my shoulder and said sorry again. He kissed my shoulder! I think that's the first time he's done something like that. We've kissed plenty of times, but I'm pretty sure that's the first time he's kissed me innocently like that, with no sex involved, and it's ridiculous how happy it makes me.

While I was making our coffee and toast, he had a shower and unpacked his stuff, so he's clearly come to a comfortable decision in that head of his, thank god. I don't for a second think that it's going to be easy or stress-free but for now he seems cool about it, and that's all I want.

Had a good day at work - no problems, and even Vinnie was in a good mood, and Gemma made French-bread pizzas and salad for lunch because everyone loves that. Jamie finished at one as part of his part-time arrangement, and it was then that I grabbed Ben and tried to get him to spill the beans on yesterday's pub discussion but he was having none of it. He said it wasn't that important, and they're not sworn to secrecy, but it was up to Jamie to bring me in on it - Ben said he's not in the habit of sharing details of every conversation he has with his friends, even if I am shagging one of them. Cheeky bugger. I knew he was teasing with that, though, and he has a point - I certainly don't tell him about every talk I have with Jamie - so I let it go.

Wednesday 11 June

I've nipped home to grab some clean clothes and sort out the fridge, because I'm staying at Jamie's for the next couple of nights and then on Friday we're going up to Glasgow. It's Father's Day on Sunday and Jamie doesn't want to be here, plus he wants to see his Dad. Elspeth said she thinks their Dad's had a mini-stroke, and they're just waiting for confirmation of that, but otherwise he's settled in at the nursing home and he's fine. I'm chuffed that Jamie has asked me to go with him. I'm not sure what he's told Elspeth, and I've no idea where we're staying, but he's obviously happy for me to go with him.

Monday 16 June 11.50 a.m.

I thought I'd be glad that I booked the day off today. I booked it because I thought I might be a bit tired after the weekend trip, and I was right, but I wish now that I'd gone to work so I could find out what's up with Jamie. We mostly had a nice time in Glasgow, and it was lovely to see Jamie in his home environment, even if it does make his accent more pronounced and hard to understand while he's there, but it wasn't an entirely happy trip for him, and something's upset him badly, and I'm not sure what's going on.

I'd done the early shift on Friday so that I could finish at 2, the same time as Jamie. We'd already packed the car up, so we left straight away. The drive up there is bloody long but it's through gorgeous countryside in places, although J reckons the view from the train is better. We stopped at a services place around 4 and had a cuppa and stretched our legs, and I was glad of that because I'd been driving and my foot was starting to hurt. Jamie drove the second half up to Glasgow and I'm glad of that too because I do not ever want to have to drive into that city, it's mad! He knew where he was going, of course, but even so the whole road system made me nervous.

We were booked into a hotel because Elspeth doesn't have the room and Jamie thought his mum would be flustered if we stayed there - she's crippled with arthritis and very unsteady on her feet but would still have wanted to play 'hostess' and he didn't want her trying to do too much. Also, he wasn't entirely sure how she was going to react to me being there with him, even if we slept in separate rooms. He'd told Elspeth we were coming together, and there had been quite a lengthy talk about that and its implications - she's as supportive as ever, just worried about him - and she wasn't sure how their mum would take it, either. He'd nearly changed his mind while talking to Elspeth, not because of me but because he'll be seeing his nieces and nephews for the first time since Beth died and he wasn't sure if he could handle it, but she talked him round. It turned out to be an emotional trip for him, but I'm fairly sure that he's glad he went.

We went straight to his Mum's house when we reached Glasgow and stayed there for about an hour. Jamie has a key and let us in, but he'd phoned first to give her ten minutes warning that we were nearly there. She'd put the kettle on and was plating up some biscuits, but Jamie took over when we got there. His Mum was very polite with me but didn't make much conversation, she talked mostly with Jamie. I could barely understand a word - I swear his accent becomes unintelligible when he's there. I wasn't involved much but it was lovely to watch them together - he's so sweet with her, and she obviously adores him.

We left there just after 7 and walked round to Elspeth's, which is about five minutes away. She was chuffed to see us and all four of her kids piled on Jamie like they hadn't seen him for years. He gave them all a hug and a kiss, and I could see him and them getting a bit choked, but he pulled them into the lounge and distracted them with little presents he'd bought at one of the motorway services shops. We had another cuppa with Elspeth, and planned the weekend, then after about an hour we went back to the car and went to check in our hotel, back in the city centre.

I don't know what I was expecting, but it was a lot swankier than I'd have thought to book - four stars! - and the room was gorgeous. We unpacked and freshened up, then went downstairs to get something to eat (we both had pasta). As we were finishing our meal Jamie asked me if I wanted to go out for a drink or something, but I was too tired - I'd been up since 6 - and he looked relieved when I said, "No thanks."

We went back upstairs and had a little chat about what we would do over the weekend. Then we got into a 'No, you go first' thing about the bathroom, which he won by running the bath for me and filling it with the complimentary bubble bath (he said he'd have his shower in the morning) but once I'd got in I realised just how big it was and I called him in and persuaded him to get in with me, and that's the first time either of us have shared a bath with anyone other than a sibling, and the first time either of us have shagged in one too. It's a bit slippery but very erotic, something I'd definitely like to try again. We were hot and knackered afterwards, though, and practically fell asleep on top of the bed covers.

On Saturday morning we went into town (the city centre) and wandered around the shops and along the river for a bit. We stopped for coffee, I bought some books, and Jamie bought a card and some fudge-like stuff for his dad – I'm sure he called it 'tablet'… Then we went to pick up Jamie's mum and took her out to lunch at the Argyll Hotel - it's a treat for her that Jamie likes to do when he goes home. She was a bit chattier with me this time, which was nice.

After that, we all went to Elspeth's and spent the rest of the day there, and I got to know her kids a bit more. They're such a sweet bunch, and they all worship their uncle (can't think why) and it was lovely watching him with them. He played football with the boys for a bit, but he also sat and read with Sophie and that must have been heart-breaking for him, with Sophie being only a year older than Beth, but he didn't let it show.

Kelly and I had a little chat, too, and she's a lot more mature than I was at her age. I think she has a niece/uncle crush on Jamie, which is kinda cute, but I didn't say anything. She asked me if I thought he'd still want to go to Glastonbury - he and Helen promised to take her this year, for her 18th birthday - and I said I didn't know but encouraged her to ask him. We had our tea there and stayed until about 9, then took Jamie's mum home, stayed with her for half an hour or so, then went back to the hotel. No bath this time - Jamie had a shower, then I did, and he was asleep by the time I'd finished.

Yesterday was a difficult day for J. We went over to Elspeth's after breakfast, and Kelly, Sophie and I were dropped off in town while Jamie and Elspeth went to visit their Dad. Kelly and Sophie were in full girl-shopping mode and I happily tagged along but wasn't really in the mood for trying things on. I bought another couple of books, though, and some CDs. We only had an hour and a half, then we made our way back to the big square (St George square?) where we'd arranged to be picked up again.

Jamie and Elspeth were a bit late - about ten minutes - and they were both a bit upset. I don't think Sophie noticed, but Kelly and I did. Kelly leaned over and squeezed her Mum's shoulder, and Elspeth patted her hand - I get the impression that visits to the nursing home are unhappy events for her. We went straight to Jamie's Mum's house, and David and Daniel were already there - they'd gone there from their football matches - and we had tea and biscuits with them before we left. Jamie, Elspeth and their Mum had a private little chat in the kitchen for ten minutes or so, and Kelly told me then that her granddad's memory was getting much worse, which is probably what was so upsetting.

Jamie was a bit upset again when we were leaving - he obviously misses them, living so far away, and Sophie's clingy goodbye hug didn't help. He drove us out of the city, and we swapped over at the half-way point again after stopping for tea and a sandwich. He was quiet but not withdrawn, and I didn't push him to tell me what had happened with his Dad - it was private, after all, between him and his family. We got back here just after 7. He'd already asked me if he could stay, and he had his stuff with him so we came straight here.

My foot was hurting again by the time we got here. It's my own fault - he'd tried to insist on driving all the way home but I wouldn't have it, because it's such a long way and he said at the services place that he felt a headache coming on, so I drove the last two hours home. Anyway, when we got there I put the kettle on but he went to run the bath for me and said I should have a soak and rest my foot, bless him, so I did that. I was half hoping he'd come and join me, but he didn't. When I was finished I wondered where he'd gone, then I saw him sitting in the garden and assumed he wanted to be on his own for a bit so I left him out there for 20 minutes or so while I dried my hair and painted my nails, then I made us some tea and took it out there.

There was a friendship bracelet on the table, one of those thin ones made from cotton strands, the type that comes in little hobby kits for kids, and when I put our mugs down he picked it up. He said Sophie had made it for him but she hadn't tied it properly and it had come off, so I took it off him and tied it on his wrist for him, and he looked so sad then. He said that Sophie used to make them for Beth. I didn't say anything, just tried to look sympathetic. Then he told me that his Dad's had a series of small strokes, and it's quite probable that he'll have more, and possibly larger ones. He also said that his Dad had been really pleased to see him, but he'd asked where Helen and Beth were - which is obviously what had upset him the most - and after about half an hour he seemed to forget that he and Elspeth were there and had to be constantly reminded. No wonder they were upset when they came away from there.

Jamie wasn't looking at me while he was telling me all this, and I could tell he was trying very hard to not cry, so I just took his hand in mine and said nothing. We just sat there and drank our tea, but then my stomach started to rumble so I went in to make something to eat and he followed me. He still had a headache, so I suggested an early night and he didn't argue. He woke me up in the night - not intentionally, he was having a bad dream. He was talking in his sleep - that's what woke me up - but I couldn't make out what he was saying, and he was fidgeting a lot and sort of groaning for a while, then he started saying, "No, no, no!" and it sounded like he was getting upset so I pulled him over onto his back and woke him up. He didn't say anything, but got up and went to the bathroom, then I heard him go through to the kitchen. I tried to stay awake, thinking he'd gone for a drink and would only be a minute or so, but I fell asleep.

When I woke up this morning I was on my own - he spent the rest of the night in the spare room, and he's got up and gone to work without me hearing him. I'm really upset about that - I've spent the morning wondering what I've done, or what's bothering him so much that he doesn't want to talk to me. I texted him when I got up, to ask if he's okay but he didn't answer for over an hour, and the answer just said 'Yes' and that's made it worse. He's only in work till 1 today but I've no idea if he's coming here afterwards or if he'll go home, and I don't know what to do.

1.15 p.m.

Clearly I am an idiot. Either that, or I was more tired this morning than I thought I was, to have doubted him that much. Jamie's just phoned me. He couldn't answer properly earlier because he was in with the AD - I'd forgotten he had that meeting scheduled for this morning. I couldn't help telling him that I'd been worried about him, and when I said why, he said he'd come back to bed after the bad dream, but I'd sort of sprawled across his half and rather than disturb me, he'd gone to the spare room. And he said he hadn't been especially quiet this morning, so he's surprised I didn't hear him go. So all that worry was for nothing. Me = idiot. He's still at work but he said he'll pick me up in half an hour :)

6.10 p.m.

Just getting ready to go to the gym. Jamie's had a big row with Dougal over the phone and he's really upset, but he's going to pick me up from the gym and I'm staying with him tonight. No idea what the row was about - haven't really had time to ask because I'm running late.

Tuesday 17 June

Apparently Dougal thinks I'm a gold-digger. He had a go at Jamie yesterday for taking me to Glasgow with him, and 'parading' me as his girlfriend (which he most certainly did not do - we were very, very discreet around his family), and for generally spending time with me. He thinks I'm only hanging around for Jamie's money, and that he (J) is making a huge fool of himself. Jamie wasn't going to tell me any of this, but last night I overheard some of it when he was telling Elspeth what Dougal had said, and he heard me crying in the bathroom afterwards, and I made him tell me all of it.

He said Dougal gets these daft ideas about things, thinking he's being protective, and we should both just ignore him, but I was really hurt and upset for myself and for Jamie. I've half a mind to ring Dougal and give him what for, but I don't want to get embroiled in it. Jamie said Elspeth will probably do that anyway, and J has already told Dougal that he's out of order.

I'm trying to ignore it, but I can't - it just makes me so mad. Dougal knows nothing about me, or about me and Jamie, and he obviously doesn't know Jamie that well either if he thinks he'd let himself fall for that kind of thing. And it just sickens me that Dougal would think I'd want Jamie's money before I'd want him, and it's already making me paranoid about making sure I pay my share of stuff (which I do). Bastard.

I've just come home from work to do some washing, and ring Lucy and Hayley. It's Ben's birthday and we're going out for a meal with him and Adam later, and I'm nervous now about making sure I pay for my food and drinks. We've gone Dutch or treated each other before now and I've never even thought about it, but Dougal's got me worrying about it and I hate it. Plus I'm edgy, and wondering if Jamie's seeing me differently, and it's making me a bit prickly around him. He keeps telling me to forget it but I can't, and the fact that he's barely even held my hand since Sunday isn't helping.

Just opened today's mail. My rent's going up by £50 a month from 1st September. Marvellous. I'm going to have to start dipping into my savings because my pay won't stretch to that.

Wednesday 18 June

I came very close to making a complete idiot of myself last night. We were in Archie's - first time I've been there since the new people took over, and it's fabulous! - and we'd had a lovely meal, but I started getting nervous at the dessert stage in case Jamie tried to pay for me (he'd done it in Glasgow, and had only let me pay for our snacks on the way home). I went to the loo while we were waiting for coffee, and when I got back the waitress was just leaving the table with the bill and cash on a little silver tray, and I got all embarrassed. In my rush to pay him back I dropped a fiver in my coffee, and that made me even more embarrassed and I could feel myself getting upset, and I was talking over Jamie so he wouldn't insist on paying for us both, and then Ben laughed and said, "What's got into you?" and Jamie told me that Adam had paid for all of us as part of his birthday treat for Ben.

I could have died on the spot, and I really just wanted to sit there and cry because I'd got so tense, it was awful. Jamie put his arm around me and pulled me to him, kissing the top of my head, and while I sat there burning with embarrassment he told Ben and Adam about what Dougal had said. They were both horrified, and outraged on my behalf, bless them, but I didn't know where to look. They talked me through it though, and between the three of them they made me feel much better and much less anxious about it all. Jamie brought me home and stayed the night, and he made a very good job of convincing me that he's not remotely interested in what Dougal had to say :)

After work today we went to the cemetery. Jamie had a call this morning to say that the headstone was done and had been returned to the grave, with Beth's details added under Helen's, and he asked me if I'd go with him to have a look. I was dreading it, but I couldn't let him go on his own. They've done a really nice job, matching the lettering and cleaning the whole thing (not that it was dirty, but Helen's lettering would have looked a bit worn next to the new). Jamie squatted down to have a proper look, but we didn't stay long. He'd brought a little bunch of roses, half of them pink and half red, and he put them at the foot of the stone and then he was walking away before I'd realised he was finished. I slipped my hand into his and he squeezed it but he didn't say anything.

When we got back here (he didn't want to go to his house), he pulled me straight into a hug and said, "Can we...?" and we were at it straight away. I worry sometimes that he uses sex to forget, but I suppose it's better than drugs or alcohol. It's not like that every time - the rest of the time it's normal lusty him/me sex - it's just that on days like today I think he just wants to lose himself in the sensation, to get the sadness and pain out of his system.

Sunday 22 June

I've just popped home to pick up clothes for work tomorrow. Jamie said I might as well leave some things at his house since it would save me from having to pop home every couple of days. We seem to both be commuting back and forth between his house and my flat, and it's all very random, but I don't mind.

We've had a nice weekend. We went for a bike ride yesterday, which was a lovely surprise. He hadn't said anything but he's taken Beth's seat off the back of one of the bikes (they're both the same) and he just asked me yesterday morning if I fancied it. I don't know how far we went, but we were out for a couple of hours. My bum's a bit sore today but my legs aren't half as stiff as I thought they'd be, so the gym must be doing me some good.

Today we went for lunch at the Crow & Herald (he

bought dinner and I bought dessert) and while we were there Elspeth phoned, and he's now decided he will go to Glastonbury because he doesn't want to let Kelly down, and he asked me if I'd like the other ticket. So we're going to Glastonbury next weekend!! Hurray! It'll mean sleeping in a tent, which I'm not too fussed about, but OMG Glastonbury!

Wednesday 25 June

Perfect fucking timing - two days before Glastonbury and my period arrives. Hopefully it will be a light one and I'll be clear for Sunday - I've been fantasizing all week about shagging in a tent.

Jamie's been really down this last couple of days. He's anxious about Glastonbury, for a start, because it will be the first time, ever, that he'll be going without Helen, and he's been going for years! Then on Monday night he saw something on TV about Blackpool and he had a bit of a meltdown/flashback episode, which was a bit scary and very upsetting. I'm so glad I was there and he didn't go through that on his own.

He remembered that we'd taken photos, and he got the camera out and looked through them and got terribly upset again. I've offered to get them printed but haven't got round to it yet. He hardly slept that night, tossing and turning and dreaming, so he was tired and grumpy when he got up yesterday, then in the post he got a letter telling him that Beth's inquest will be held on 4th September, which he didn't tell me about until I got him talking last night. I've told him I've had one, too, so at least he won't be there on his own.

He was really tired and sad last night, so we went to bed early and that was when I managed to get him talking and I think that helped get his head straight a bit. He fell asleep eventually and this morning he thanked me for listening. I adore that about him - he doesn't take anything for granted.

He's got a late meeting at the AD's office this afternoon, so I've come home and I'm doing dinner for a change (baked potatoes with cheese and loads of veg) and I've also had a go at the raspberry mousse recipe that Gemma wrote out for us the other day.

Just been on Facebook, and Hayley's posted that she reckons I've finally got a love life. I'm going to have to ring her or arrange a get together. At least she's not mentioned him by name - I'm fairly sure she'll know it's Jamie.

Tuesday 1 July

That was the best weekend ever! First of all, Jamie hired a camper van for the weekend! He said Elspeth had been worried about Kelly being in a tent, so he hired this bloody big mobile home thing with 2 separate bedrooms and a shower - the lot! He didn't say anything, but when I got to his house on Thursday it was parked outside. It was amazing, very modern and very comfortable, and so much better than a tent! Bit of a bugger to drive, but so worth it! Mind you, if I'd known we'd have all that space,

I'd have packed more clothes.

I'm going to try and get this all in order because it's been a fantastic weekend and I want to try and remember everything.

Last Thursday -

I was making sandwiches and getting a flask ready when Jamie got home with Kelly. She knew I would be meeting them there, but I think the fact that I'd let myself in and was doing domestic stuff surprised her a bit. It was a long journey, and we arrived much later than I thought we would. We stopped a couple of times, and Jamie and I took turns in driving, but we were both tired when we got there. Kelly, on the other hand, was practically bouncing she was so excited. It took us a while to find the campsite - there's different ones for camper vans and tents, and Jamie had only been in a tent before - and it was gone midnight by the time we got parked up and settled, so we had a cup of tea, took turns in the tiny bathroom (no bath), and went to bed.

Kelly woke us up early on the Friday morning, squealing and giggling on the phone to her friends. Jamie had had a rough night, so he turned over and pulled the duvet over his head, but I got up and had a shower and got dressed, by which time he'd given up trying to get back to sleep and was making toast and coffee. Kelly was chattering on about who and what she wanted to see and he was patiently trying to tell her that it would be impossible to fit in everything on her list, but I don't think she believed him - either that, or she wasn't really listening.

We were heading down to the main site by 9, and it was horribly muddy but Kelly and I were just so chuffed to be there that even the mud was exciting. Jamie took us to Trash City and the hippy tents and the healing circle - loads of places that I didn't even know were there - and we had the yummiest vegetable curry pastie things for lunch, and Kelly and I bought wacky felt hats and some bracelets and we were having a fantastic time even without the musical side of it. I made a note of all the acts we saw but I can't find it. There were too many highlights to mention!

I noticed a couple of times that Kelly gave Jamie a hug or squeezed his arm, and he'd have that strained look on his face, so I assumed it was something to do with Helen. Apart from that, though, he seemed relaxed and obviously enjoyed being there. He loves to dance, too, which is an incredible turn on. He's not brilliant - Gavin and Ben still reign supreme (and wouldn't Gavin be horrified to know who he shares that crown with! haha) - but he's got some nice moves and clearly isn't shy about dancing in public like a lot of blokes are.

He had another bad night on Friday, though, tossing and turning (more than usual) and mumbling in his sleep. I pulled him into a hug at one point to try and calm him down, and he said sorry and turned over but he was still fidgety right through the night.

Saturday was amazing! We got a bit sunburnt during the day, and Kelly had a bit of tummy trouble (she blamed the curry pastie), and we almost lost her on the way to the John Peel stage because she stopped to talk to some French boys she'd met on Friday, and we made friends with a lovely bunch of people from Wales, and we all got wasted at the cider bus. Fantastic day! The cider knocked Jamie out, too, so we all got a decent night's sleep :)

Poor Kelly was not well on Sunday morning. Jamie and I were a bit delicate but not too bad, but she felt really ill. We pumped her full of water first thing, and made her eat some toast, and by lunch time she began to feel a bit better. We spent most of the day at the Pyramid stage. OMG what an amazing day! For the closing sets Kelly went off with the Welsh contingency, and Jamie drove her mad by constantly texting to check she was okay but in fairness she was well looked after and they even walked her all the way back to the van afterwards. We'd got back before her and I'd rather hoped to have some decent alone time with Jamie but he wanted to wait up for Kelly, which is totally understandable. She was buzzing when she got back, and we invited the others in for drinks as a thank you for looking after her, and I think it was gone 3 by the time they left. Needless to say we were all asleep within minutes.

We slept in till about 10 yesterday morning. I woke up with Jamie's arm around me, which was nice. He'd had a better night, and I think he was glad to be going home. Kelly didn't want to get up at all - I think the whole weekend just caught up with her all at once. It took ages to get off the site - we crawled along in a traffic queue for miles and miles, and Jamie had Kelly ring her mum to warn her that she might not make her train home. She did though. We stopped for lunch at a services place, and stopped to take turns driving again, but we still got back in time for Jamie to drop me off at his house and take Kelly in his car to the station. I had a lovely hug and kiss from Kelly when she was leaving; she's such a sweet kid.

Jamie brought us a pizza back with him from Pizza Hut, but he didn't eat much of his half. He said he was tired, but I knew from the bad dreams and from the snippets that Kelly had told me over the weekend that the festival had been difficult for him, even though he'd enjoyed it. I suggested he have a bath and get an early night, since we both had to be in work for 9 today, and he nodded and went upstairs, although I hadn't actually meant straight away - it wasn't even 7.30 by then.

I tidied up and loaded the washing machine, then realised that he hadn't run the bath or the shower so I called up to ask if he was okay and I just about heard him say "Aye," but there was no sound of movement so after a few minutes I went upstairs and he was sitting on his bed. He didn't look at me, but he looked so sad that I just went in there and stood in front of him and hugged him, not thinking, but he pulled back because the sparkly stud things on my t-shirt must have scratched his face, so I sat next to him and put my arm around him instead.

He said he didn't want to talk, and we just sat there

for a while. After a few minutes he leaned forward, resting his arms on his knees, and it took me a few more minutes to realise that he was crying, he was so quiet about it. I rubbed his back and said, "I'm sorry it's so painful for you." He said he misses them so much. It's fucking heart-breaking to see him like that, knowing there's nothing you can do to make it better. I just rubbed his back and let him cry, and eventually he stopped. Then he said sorry to me! And I'm thinking 'what the hell?' and he said he shouldn't be saying stuff like that to me, which is ridiculous, and I told him so and he shook his head and went into the bathroom, saying something that I couldn't make out. I heard the bath running then, so I left him to it and went back downstairs. I was getting really worried about him, so I put the telly on to give me something to think about while he was in the bath.

He came down about an hour later and made us both a cup of tea and said sorry again. My only defence is that I was tense and worried, because I had a go at him for constantly saying sorry when he has no reason to apologise - it's usually after sharing or showing some emotion, and I can't stand the idea that he thinks that that's not acceptable. I could have been more gracious and less snappy but I wasn't thinking, I just told him to stop saying it. He looked a bit confused, then he said he apologises because he feels that he says and does things that upset me and he doesn't like that, and that confused me because I couldn't think of anything that had upset me, other than him being upset, so I told him that.

He didn't say anything for a while, he just looked at

me and then sat there and drank his tea, then when he'd finished he said he sometimes thinks that I understand him better than Helen did, and he's honestly not sure how he feels about that, but he'd really like to make love to me. Those were pretty much his words and dear god the way he said it would have made me go weak at the knees if I'd been standing up. He called it 'making love' and not 'shagging' or anything else - that alone was enough to turn me on. I managed to say, "I'd like that too." I leaned in to kiss him but he took my hand and led me upstairs, to his bed, and he was so gentle and so loving and it was the best yet. We snuggled afterwards - him behind me - and I know he cried a bit, but he obviously didn't want me to notice so I didn't let on. I just wish that I could do something to get him past the sadness, and the guilt he feels for being with me.

I thought he'd gone to sleep, but when the phone rang a bit later he gave me a little squeeze and went down to answer it, so I followed him and put the kettle on. It was Kelly on the phone, letting him know she'd arrived home safely as he'd asked her to do. She said something that made him laugh and I'd love to ask her what it was because it's so lovely to see/hear him laugh now and then.

Today when we got in to work we found out that the AD had invited himself to our team meeting, to discuss staffing requirements for when Gemma goes on maternity leave. Andy and I said we're interested in extra hours - Andy's saving for Disneyland, and my rent's going up - although neither of us are keen on taking on any more late shifts or overnighters, even though they pay better. The AD didn't commit either way, he just made notes of what everyone was saying.

Afterwards Jamie asked me about my rent and I told him about the letter I got last week. He looked a bit surprised (even hurt, maybe?) that I hadn't mentioned it, but it had arrived in the middle of the Dougal/goldigger episode and I wasn't about to say anything then, and then it was Glastonbury and I forgot about it. At lunchtime everyone was asking us about Glastonbury and Jamie got quite animated and upbeat when we were talking about it, so I'm glad he's got positive memories of it rather than having it all tied up with Helen and Beth not being there. Ben's going to Leeds next month and now he's trying to get Jamie and me to go with him (and Adam)!

I've been to the gym tonight (lost four pounds since last time!) and I've come home to ring Lucy and Hayley and catch up with them. I had a little dig at Hayley over her Facebook comment but we laughed about it, and she's promised not to say anything. She's chuffed for me, but (like Lucy) she says she's worried that he's just using me to move on. They don't know him. He's not capable of thinking like that - he's a bit old-fashioned that way. I didn't say that, though, just promised to be careful and not fall too hard. Didn't tell her I fell way too hard a long time ago.

Friday 4 July 5.50 p.m.

Jamie's on a mood-swing rollercoaster and I'm seriously wondering if he should be back in hospital. It's been a difficult week with one thing and another, but I'd thought he was handling things okay - or at least as well as can be expected - but right now he's got me really worried.

It started on Tuesday. I thought he'd been a bit quiet at work, but I put it down to tiredness etc after the weekend and didn't think anything of it. Then when he didn't turn up after my gym session I rang him and he said he'd forgotten about coming round, and he said he wasn't good company anyway so he wouldn't bother. We'd had such a lovely evening on Monday that I couldn't think why he'd suddenly be so down, unless it was guilt kicking in again, so I asked him what was wrong and eventually he told me that July 1st was the anniversary of their second daughter's death (she was still-born at 35 weeks). God does it ever stop for him?? I told him I was coming round and didn't let him argue. He wasn't in the mood to talk, but when we were going to bed he thanked me for not letting him 'stew' and he fell asleep snuggling into my back. It took me ages to get to sleep, though, because I kept thinking about all the sadness he's carrying around and wondering what I could do or suggest to make it easier.

On Wednesday he was okay, and he was obviously trying to be cheerful, but that all went to hell when we got home after work and I opened my mail. He'd come with me because I'd talked him into coming home with me rather than going to his house - I thought the change of scenery would give his mind a break - and everything was fine until I opened the letter.

This is what it said -

"Don't think you're the only one he's stringing along. Ask him about the girl who works in the bank, and the woman at the leisure centre. You and I are just two on a long list that he's duped over the last few years. I've dumped him. I advise you to do the same."

If I'd been on my own, I'd have had time to think about it and work things out, but he was there and he saw my reaction and asked straight away what was wrong so I showed it to him. He read it and looked at me and asked me what it meant and I said, "You tell me." He just gaped at me and said, "You can't think this is about me?" and I was just so shocked and not thinking straight that I said, "I don't know what to think" and he completely lost his rag.

He said it was bad enough that I thought he was capable of stringing me, or anyone else, along, but I clearly also thought he'd been capable of being unfaithful to his wife, and he was more upset about that, I think. He said the letter wasn't about him, and he was deeply hurt that I would think it was, and before I could say anything else, he left. I went after him but he said, "Just leave me be," and drove off.

I went back in and read the letter a few more times, and checked the envelope, but it didn't give me any clues - the letter's typed, and I don't recognise the writing on the envelope. They didn't put my flat number, though, so whoever it is doesn't know that much about me.

And then it dawned on me - the leisure centre: Darren's favourite place, after the pub. The letter's about Darren, and someone obviously thinks we're still seeing each other. I didn't know whether to laugh or cry, and then I thought of Jamie and went round there straight away. I've got a key but I rang the bell and he was shocked to see me. I said sorry straight away, and told him the letter wasn't about him, and I said I should have known that but it just hadn't occurred to me to think of Darren as we'd never really been in a dumpable relationship (well we hadn't, not really) and I can't remember what else I said but 'sorry' was in there a lot. He didn't say anything but he looked really upset, so I just stood there, not knowing what else to say, and after a bit he let me in.

He closed the door but he just stood there in the hall with his hand in his hair, looking so upset. I stood there too, trying to think what else I could say to him to make it up to him, but he beat me to it and said, "I'm not that kind of man, Tasha." I said, "I know," and I burst into tears. He pulled me into a hug and I said sorry again, but I quickly pulled myself together and then we went down to the kitchen and he made some tea. I couldn't stand that he wasn't saying anything, and that I'd hurt him so much by thinking the letter was about him, so I just talked and talked and said how it was obvious now that it was about Darren but when I first read it my immediate reaction had been that it meant that Jamie didn't have any feelings for me and that's why I'd been so shocked and hadn't thought it through properly.

He put our mugs on the table but didn't sit down, and

my heart was pounding, wondering what he was thinking. Then he said he can't commit to anything other than what we have at the moment and he honestly doesn't know how long that will last or where it will go, but 'two-timing' is something he's never done and never will, and I said that I know that, and I'm sorry I over-reacted and I'm sorry I hurt him, and he looked at me for a bit and then he sat down and said he'd probably over-reacted too. I don't think he did, though: I think he was deeply offended, and he had every right to be. And it just makes me love him even more.

I ended up staying the night there. I wasn't sure where to sleep because he'd been a bit unchatty, but he must have sensed that because when I came out of the bathroom he took my hand and we went into his room. We just snuggled though, and I went to sleep still feeling really bad about hurting him.

Yesterday (Thursday) he seemed fine - he kissed me on the shoulder when we woke up with the alarm, and he was his usual self all day. He finished work early to go to an appointment with his counsellor and he came round to mine after that, and he was fine, even telling me what they'd talked about (Beth, and the other babies, and the grieving process). We went for a bike ride after tea - his suggestion - and when we got back we had a lovely long talk and got the whole letter thing sorted out, and I love the fact that we can talk so honestly and openly about things no matter how awkward it is. We went to bed after that and it was lovely, and we talked a bit afterwards too.

Then today he got up grumpy and said he'd had a bad dream but didn't want to talk about it, and at work he kept himself in the office most of the time - although I know that Ben was in there for about twenty minutes just before lunch, and he said to me afterwards that he (J) had been a bit short with him, and he (B) asked me what was up and I just thought it was the bad dream.

We'd arranged to go to the Crow & Herald tonight with Ben and Adam, but he'd already told Ben he wasn't up for it and when he was leaving work this afternoon he told me too but said I should go anyway. I told Ben I wasn't going, and he's fine - he knows I want to get this sorted out. I went to Jamie's house from work but he wasn't in, so I've come home to catch up on the laundry and tidy up, and I've left him a message on his answering machine, asking him to ring me when he gets in.

I'm worried because he's fine one day and not fine the next day, and this business of not wanting to talk about it isn't really him, it's an avoidance mechanism, and I know I can get him talking if I can just get him started. I know there's been a lot going on this week on top of all the other stuff he's dealing with, but he seems really sensitive and more down than ever and I'm just worried that he's heading for a bad downward spiral. I don't know whether to mention it to Elspeth - she's not picked up on anything, as far as I can tell from my brief chat with her yesterday, and I don't want to worry her unnecessarily.

8.00 p.m.

He hasn't rung, so I'm going round there.

9.15 p.m.

Jamie rang me when I was on the way back from his house. He's in Glasgow. He said he needed to get away, and he wants to talk to Elspeth, and he said sorry for not saying anything (I'd said I'd been worried about him, which after finding his house still empty was a bit of an understatement) but he hadn't really been thinking straight, he'd just got in the car and drove and was halfway there before he realised it.

I was dying to ask him what was wrong and what's so important that he has to drive all the way to Glasgow to talk to his sister, but it's obvious he doesn't want to talk to me, so I just thanked him for ringing and told him to take his time and enjoy the break with his family. He told me not to worry, and I said I can't help it. I was going to say, "Especially when you go running off to Glasgow without a bloody word," but he didn't need that kind of dig, he knows I'm upset. He said he'll be home on Sunday, and he said he'll ring tomorrow.

I think he's going to finish with me. Although why he needs to talk to Elspeth about that, I've no idea. I daresay I'll find out on Sunday. Right now I'm going to demolish another bottle of wine and watch 'Bridget Jones'.

Saturday 5 July 4.20 a.m.

Jamie texted me a couple of hours ago. I didn't hear it - I noticed it when I got up to go to the loo just now. He said: 'I'm an idiot - forgive me?' and I've no idea what he means, unless he's talking about flying off to Glasgow. My head is banging and I'm sitting here at my PC while the kettle boils and I'm trying very hard not to ring him back, mostly because I assume he'll be asleep by now. I hope Elspeth has managed to talk some sense into him, even if it means him going back into hospital until his head's straightened out. I was so worried about him yesterday that I thought I was going to be sick, and I don't know how long I can handle that for. I don't know if I'm doing him any favours by not telling anyone what he's like - maybe his GP or Elspeth would have had him back in hospital long before now if I'd said something. Mind you, I suppose it's out of my hands now, anyway.

10.55 a.m.

Jamie rang me just now, and we were on the phone for about ten minutes, I think. He said he'd phoned earlier, but I hadn't heard it. I've got such a hangover that I'm surprised it didn't sound like Big Ben, but I suppose I must have been unconscious. Anyway he was telling me how he's talked the ears off Elspeth and they're going to visit their Dad and he's going to spend some time with his mum this afternoon and then he's coming home… and honestly he was talking so quickly I wondered if he was on speed or something but now I realise he just sounded relieved and kind of happy. Not 'happy' happy but certainly not depressed, and I really do wonder if Elspeth's got him on some antidepressants or something. And he asked me if I've forgiven him, so I said, "What for?" and he said, "For running away." To be honest, my head's banging and I feel sick and I'm so convinced he's going to finish with me, that I just started crying but I didn't want him to know, so I sucked it up and I said, "I'll forgive you anything," and that made him go quiet.

So I suppose he knows he's not in for a rough ride when he gives me my marching orders. Maybe I should make it hard for him, but I can't. Anyway he asked if he could come round when he gets back later, and I thought about saying I'm going out, but what's the point? Might as well get it over with. So I said yes and now I've got all afternoon to look forward to that. Marvellous.

4.05 p.m.

Elspeth's just phoned me and now I'm really confused. She said Jamie left about an hour ago (so he should be here between 7 and 8, depending on whether or not he stops on the way) and she said she's worried that he's not thinking straight, and she asked me how he's been recently so I told her everything about how he's been this week (except the sex) and she said she knows all that - they talk to each other practically every day - and was there anything else? I couldn't think of anything. Then she said, "You do love him, don't you, Tasha?" and that threw me because I thought if she's been advising him on how to finish with me, why would she be asking me that now? No point in lying, though, so I told the truth (which I'm positive she's known for a while anyway). She said, "I hope that's enough." I asked her what she meant but the kids were shouting in the background and she said she had to go, but she'd ring me back later.

5.25 p.m.

How long is 'later' exactly? Half of me wants to ring her back, and the other half is too scared.

Sunday 6 July

I have massively misjudged that man twice in the space of three days, and he knows it, but he's still here.

This is what happened yesterday -

Elspeth rang me back around 7.30 last night, and we talked for a bit and then I was just going to ask her what she'd meant about 'hoping it's enough' when my doorbell rang, and we both figured that it was Jamie so I said I'd ring her back.

I'd been on pins for most of the evening, dreading Jamie's arrival and trying to rehearse some calm and sensible and mature things to say in reply to his 'It's over' speech, so my hands were shaking when I opened the door but I thought I was keeping it quite together. But he gave me that sweet embarrassed/sheepish smile and said hi, and I burst into tears. He looked so concerned and went to hug me but I got angry with myself for losing control and I pushed him back and said, "Just get it over with," keeping my hand on the door and made him stand in the hall.

He looked really confused, bless him. He said he was sorry for dashing off on Friday, and he doesn't really know what got into him but he's glad he went because it's cleared his head, and then he saw that I was still looking miserable and he apologised for making me worry. Then he twigged that I wasn't going to let him in, and he looked a bit puzzled but he kept talking. He told me his head has been battered this last week or so, and although we've sorted some things out together there were a few things he hadn't mentioned, and they'd been rattling around in his head and eating at him, and he said Elspeth reckons that's where the bad dreams have been coming from. I didn't say anything because I was concentrating on not crying.

He said then that he should have talked to me, because if he had he probably wouldn't have got to such a state on Friday, and he said sorry again and I thought 'Here it comes' and then he looked past me like he was looking for someone and he asked me if he'd come at a bad time, and I just said, "Is there a good time for this?" and then he looked completely perplexed and when I think of it now, it's quite funny, but at the time it just looked arrogant and that got me riled.

So I said, "Just say it, Jamie," whilst trying not to cry, and that's when he realised I was on the wrong page because he said, "What on earth do you think I'm going to say?" and he tried to hold my hand but I pulled away. Mrs Lewis called down just then to ask if everything was all right and I called back to say it was. Jamie looked at me like he had no clue what was going on. He waited until we heard Mrs. L close her door, then he said, "Tasha I promise you, unless I've completely misread everything, I'm not going to say anything bad," and then he asked me if he could come in, because he really needed the loo, so I let him in.

I put the kettle on while he was in the bathroom and I was still shaking, but with him saying he wasn't going to say anything bad I wiped my face and tried to pull myself together - I was really annoyed with myself for crying and for not keeping cool, because I didn't want to come across all desperate and needy. He came out of the bathroom and stood in the kitchen doorway, looking like he wasn't sure what to do.

I gave him his tea and he asked me what was wrong, and I just came right out and said, "Do you want to finish with me?" and he said he couldn't understand why I'd think that, but then he twigged that that was why I was so upset and he pulled me into a hug and said, "No, far from it." I was so relieved that I started crying again. I absolutely hate that I cried over that, but I love that he does that to me. We went through to the lounge and he apologised for stressing me out and for not talking to me about things, and when I'd pulled myself together, he told me the whole lot.

He said he'd realised while we were at Glastonbury that he'd been kidding himself about his relationship with Helen. He said he'd put her on a pedestal (and he mentioned that that was one of the things that he and Dougal had rowed about last year) and even more so after she'd died, like she'd been a perfect saint or something whereas in reality she'd had as many faults as he had. He said he loved her, and he'd been missing her at Glastonbury, but on the Friday he'd remembered that last year they'd had a massive row while they were there, and that reminded him that things hadn't been perfect and the last few years had been quite difficult, but it would never have occurred to either of them to split up. Just before she'd died, they'd discussed ways of making things better and had even talked about having another child. But he said he's come to realise that if they hadn't had children, and especially Beth, they may not have stayed together. He didn't say why, and I didn't ask because I was too stunned to think of it.

Then he said he's spent the week thinking about all this and going over practically his entire history with Helen and feeling torn over his new feelings and the guilt and all that, and he didn't feel he could talk to me about it because he felt too conflicted. Then the letter incident on Wednesday made him start thinking that I didn't trust him, and he felt he needed to make more of an effort with me, and that tied in to the conflicted feelings over Helen, and then he had what amounted to a nightmare on Thursday night that unsettled him so much he couldn't think straight, and that's how he'd ended up on the motorway heading for Glasgow.

By that point my heart was pounding and I just wanted him to get to the point, whatever it was going to be, but he stopped and took a big breath and asked me if he was making a fool of himself. I said no, and told him I wish he'd tried to talk with me about all that. He nodded and said that he should have done. Then he said that when I'd mentioned my rent going up on Tuesday, he'd also started thinking about other stuff, and then he stopped again and he said, "This is where I really hope I'm not misreading things," and he said he's been wondering whether or not it would be sensible for us to move in together.

I must have looked really shocked because he went pale and sort of shifted away from me, and started apologising for not saying anything at the time and for springing it on me out of the blue, and he said it was just a suggestion to save money and it didn't matter and, bless him, he was nearly babbling. I just laughed, because I'd been so convinced that he didn't want to see me anymore and here he was proposing that we live together, but he looked absolutely aghast and obviously thought he'd put his foot in it, so I leaned over and took his hand and smiled at him and he shut up.

I said it was nice of him to offer, but I'm not going to move in with him just to save money, and he got embarrassed and said he'd thought there might be other reasons. So we explored that for a bit and he said again what he'd said on Wednesday, that he can't commit to anything more than what's happening at the moment but he has feelings for me and doesn't want to let go of that. And it's true, we spend half our time at his house and the other half at my flat and it does seem a bit daft to be paying two lots of bills when what we're doing is living together in two places.

I asked him, though, if he was sure about it and if he's ready for it, and he said what he usually says - he's not really sure about anything - but he feels it's something he wants to try and that's good enough for me because at least he didn't say 'it's the right thing to do' or something like that, so I said okay. I reminded him that I'm not skint and said that the rent going up annoyed me in principle more than anything else, but he knows how hard I've been trying this year to keep my bills sensible so that's where he was coming from.

Obviously the choices are either for him to sell his house and move in with me, or for me to give up the flat and move in with him, and I said I don't mind either way but I feel it's more important for him to be happy with the decision because that house holds a lot of memories for him, so we're going to think and talk about it a bit before deciding what to do. I hugged him, then, and he asked me why I'd thought he was going to finish it and I couldn't really say because I'm not sure where it came from, unless the two bottles of wine and him running off to Glasgow had something to do with it. I just called it nervous paranoia and he apologised for putting me through that.

I think he was a bit hurt that I thought he wouldn't be straight with me about something like that, but I didn't know what to think when he said he was on the way to Glasgow, so he understands why I'd started thinking negatively. I told him he's not to run off like that again and bless him he looked so embarrassed. He said he's always been able to talk with Elspeth about pretty much anything, but since Helen died he's come to rely on her for her 'voice of reason' so I asked him what she thought of all this, and he said she's worried that he's rushing into things but she's very supportive. That sort of explains her asking me if I love him, then.

I was going to ask him if he thought he was rushing things - it's not even five months since Helen died - but his stomach growled so loudly that we both just grinned and I suggested we have something to eat. I made scrambled eggs on toast (didn't have much else in) and while I was buttering the toast he came and hugged me from behind and said sorry again, for making me worry so much, and I turned round and kissed him which is how we ended up with cold scrambled eggs, but it wasn't too bad. We talked more while we were eating and he's not bothered about rushing things if I'm not, because there doesn't seem to be a rule on how long you're supposed to wait before it's seen as not rushing things.

Neither of us had had much sleep on Friday night, and we'd talked for more than two hours since he got back from Glasgow, so we were both knackered by 10 o'clock. I said we should go to bed, but he didn't move. He asked me again if I'm okay with everything, so I said yes, and I said it was all a bit unexpected (understatement!) but in a good way, and that seemed to satisfy him. When we got into bed, he didn't say anything but he pulled me close and started kissing me, and we had a lovely slow gentle shag. It was so lovely, and felt so special, that I started to say, "I love you" but he stopped me with a kiss. Then he stopped moving, still inside me, and he leaned his forehead against mine and looked at me and said (whispered, really), "Please don't say it. I can't say it." He kissed me again and started moving again, fucking me and kissing me so tenderly that I was coming in waves, and when he finally came, he said my name, and this time it was me who cried.

We were quite late getting up this morning - sometime after 11, anyway - and Jamie suggested lunch at the Crow & Herald so we went there for 1. He told me some of the things he'd talked about with Elspeth, mostly the stuff about Helen and his idea about moving in together, and he told me a bit more about Elspeth's thoughts on that. She's only worried about him, of course, and she's told him quite bluntly that she thinks he's probably not thinking rationally, but she helped him sort his head out while he was there and she's supportive of whatever he wants to do. He also said he's not mentioned anything to his Mum just yet about the moving in idea, as she'll probably have an old-fashioned view on the prospect of us living together so that's something he'll introduce to her gradually. I asked him if it's something he'd have thought about if I hadn't said anything about my rent, and he didn't answer straight away but then he said he thinks it would happen naturally anyway, eventually, and as far as I'm concerned that tells me he wants to be with me like nothing else does.

Jamie's gone home to pick up some clothes and things,

then he's coming back here. We don't have anything planned, although I really should get over to Asda before it closes - my cupboards are bare! I've just rung Lucy because I haven't spoken to her since Tuesday - she's been out a lot this week - and we've had a good natter but I haven't told her anything. Jamie and I are still just talking about the moving in idea, nothing's been decided, so there's no point in mentioning it to Lucy until (unless?) there's something to tell her.

Thursday 10 July

We've talked about it pretty much every day this week and although we haven't finally decided anything, I think I'm going to give up my flat and move in with Jamie – it seems the most sensible option, and it's the one we talk most about. If we do it that way, I'm going to sell my furniture (except my wardrobes, and the tallboy that was Mum's) and the money I make from that will go into a separate account with the deposit I'll get back when I move out - Jamie suggested that I could do that in case I change my mind, then I'll have money readily available for another flat. I wouldn't have thought of that, but I suppose it makes sense. It might not be me who changes my mind - anything could happen.

I've just told Lucy and she thinks I'm mad and she tried to talk me out of it, but I've said nothing's been decided yet and she finally let it go when I told her about the contingency plan. Of course now she's insisting on meeting Jamie, so I've got to put that to him and sort that out. I'm sure he'll be fine, and I'm sure Lucy's going to love him once she gets to know him.

On Monday, we took the memory card from Jamie's camera into Boots to get them printed. Jamie said that Boots have a service where they print the pictures in a photobook, so we went for that and it'll be ready on Saturday. They're lovely photos, from what I could tell on the camera, but I'm not looking forward to seeing them in that album.

TRSMT festival kicks off tomorrow. Kelly's going with a friend (and the friend's parents) and she rang on Sunday night to ask if Jamie and I would be going, but we're not. Jamie was tempted but he says he's not ready yet - Glastonbury was a start and maybe (if we can still get tickets) he'll be up for Leeds, but right now he doesn't want to go and I'm not going on my own. Glastonbury was fantastic but there's no way I'd want to go to one of those events on my own.

Jamie will be here soon – he's coming here from his counsellor's appointment (Tuesday's got postponed because the counsellor was ill) – and then we're going round to Ben and Adam's for dinner.

Saturday 12 July 1.55 p.m.

I'm home for a bit because Jamie wants some time alone. When we were in town this morning, we went to pick up Beth's photobook, and he didn't even check that it was all okay, he just took the bag and paid for it. Then on the way back to his house, he asked me if I'd mind if he looked at it on his own. He said he knows he's going to get upset and he knows I probably will too, and he was going to say more but I just cut in and told him that I don't mind at all, but he's to ring me if he changes his mind about being alone and I'll go straight there. That was over two hours ago and I haven't heard anything. I'll give him till 2 o'clock and then I'm going to ring him.

What else? Dinner on Thursday was lovely. Adam's a fab cook anyway so the food's always lovely, but it was especially nice because Jamie was really relaxed and in a good mood and there was a lot of joking around and laughter. He's not a miserable person by nature - he was always so much fun at work, before Helen died - but obviously during the last five months he hasn't had much to laugh about, so it was a lovely treat to see him being more himself. He was that way a bit at Glastonbury and more so in Glasgow, and I suppose it will be a gradual thing, it's just that I'm so chuffed to see him that way when it happens because (hopefully) it means he's starting to get back to normal.

Lucy rang yesterday and asked if Jamie and I would like to go down there for the weekend, not this weekend because they've got a dinner party to go to, but some time soonish (which means before we move in together). I didn't think Jamie would want to go, but he's fine with it, so we're going next weekend!

He hasn't phoned, so I'm going to ring him.

Wednesday 16 July

I've got about half an hour to kill until I need to leave

to meet Jamie, so I'm updating while I've got the chance.

I've given my notice to the landlord today, and started sending cancellation notices for the phone, internet, water, etc. There's so much to do! I'm sure I missed half of this stuff when I moved out of Mum's house. I'm tied into the rental agreement until the end of August, and Jamie and I haven't actually set a date for me to move in officially, it'll just be a gradual thing as I move my stuff over there with each visit. The wardrobes will have to go fairly soon, though.

We're okay now, but we didn't have a good weekend. Well, Sunday turned out okay, but Jamie was a mess on Saturday, much worse than I'd expected. He didn't answer the phone when I rang on Saturday afternoon, so I left him a message to say I was coming round and I got there about half two. He was in bed when I got there, sleeping, but I could see he'd been crying. I only went into his room to check that he was there and to make sure he was okay, then I went back downstairs to wait for him to come down.

Beth's photobook was on the sofa so I had a look at it, and the pictures are great (most of them anyway) and the book really sets them off nicely, and of course I had a bloody good cry while I was looking through it. There was an older photo album under Beth's and I had a quick look in there too - it's got family photos in it, mostly of Beth of course, but there's some of her with Jamie and Helen too, and it's the first time I've had a proper look at Helen. There are a couple of framed photos around the house but only one with her in it and it's too small to really see much, so I've never really had a clear idea of what she looked like. I'd built up this image of her of being tall and slinky and glamorous and gorgeous, I suppose because Jamie is gorgeous and Beth's beautiful. Helen wasn't quite the supermodel I'd built her up to be but she was very pretty, and a bit taller than me, with short cropped hair and in all the photos she's wearing trousers and loose tops, although they're quite feminine-looking. Funny how you imagine people to be one way and they usually turn out to be completely different. There weren't many pictures of the three of them together, but the few that were there showed them all laughing or smiling and it must have torn Jamie up going through them, and that made me cry again.

I went out to the garden afterwards and sat out there reading for a while but by 4 o'clock Jamie still hadn't come down so I went up to check on him. He was still asleep and I had a little panic then in case he'd taken some tablets or something, so I woke him up. I was quiet and gentle with him and he woke up slowly, but as soon as he saw me, he started to cry again and that set me off so I sat on the bed and held him in a hug until he calmed down.

We stayed up there and talked for ages, and he was so upset, it was awful. He kept saying that he should have paid to bring Beth's appointment forward and he shouldn't have taken her to Blackpool and he should have noticed more about her agitation and the likes - all things he's said before, to me and to Dr Burgess and to Dr

Mallory, and probably to his counsellor as well - and I had to keep repeating what Dr Burgess had said, about there being no way anyone could have known what would happen, and I tried to reassure him that Beth had had a lovely holiday (which he knows) and what would that weekend have been like if we hadn't gone, and he knows all that but I think he just feels so guilty that he can't let it go. He's her daddy, after all, and he's supposed to keep her safe.

It breaks my heart to see him like that and I was crying as much as he was. I know it's only been two months, but when he gets like this it's as if it's just happened, and he's so distraught, and I'm worried that he seems to forget that he's said all these things before and talked them through and reached some kind of acceptance, if that's the right word. He keeps so much of it inside, and every now and then it will all pour out when something triggers it - like Glastonbury, and like the photos - and maybe he mentions things to his counsellor but I don't think he's really getting it all out of his system properly. So on Saturday I just let him talk, and I think he talked himself into exhaustion because eventually he started yawning and I told him to try and go back to sleep, which he did. I sat with him for a bit longer, then I went back downstairs.

The phone had rung a few times while we'd been talking but we'd just let it ring - he wasn't interested and I didn't want to leave him on his own. It rang again while I was making a sandwich, so I answered it and it was Dougal. He wouldn't believe me when I said that Jamie was asleep - it was only about half six - so I told him he'd had an upsetting day and Dougal sounded annoyed and said, "What now?" so I told him about the photos and he had a go at me for letting Jamie get them developed! It really annoys me that Dougal treats Jamie like a child, but I kept my cool and pointed out that J's old enough to make his own decisions and I said we'd talked about it and knew it was going to be upsetting but it's something he really wanted to do, and then Dougal said that Jamie 'isn't in his right mind' at the moment and I would be keeping him away from those kind of reminders if I really had any consideration for his feelings.

I said ignoring it won't make it go away and he just huffed at me, but he asked me to please put the photo albums away and then he told me to tell Jamie to ring him this evening, and then he put the phone down on me. Bastard. I just burst into tears I was so upset by the way he spoke to me. He and Jamie may look and sound a bit alike and they even have some of the same mannerisms, but they're so very different. I thought about it afterwards, though, and put the albums on the shelf in the lounge where I'd seen the older one was kept.

Jamie came down just after 8 and he looked dreadful. He had a headache - I'm sure it was because he hadn't had anything to eat or drink, and probably tension too - and he took some ibuprofen with his cup of tea, but he didn't want anything to eat. I told him that Dougal had rung and wanted him to ring back, but I didn't tell him what Dougal had said, and he didn't ask. He sat in the kitchen for about an hour, not really saying much even though I tried to get him talking, and then he went back to bed. I went up around 10 o'clock and he was still awake, so I snuggled into his back with my arm around his waist and he clung onto my hand until he fell asleep.

On Sunday he didn't get up till nearly 12. He'd been awake a lot in the night, so it's no surprise really. I'd been down to the shops and back, and was in the garden when he came downstairs, and I heard him filling the coffee machine so I went in. He looked the same as he had on Saturday (bloody awful) but he attempted a smile and started making us some toast so he must have been feeling better, but he wasn't saying much and I didn't push it.

I was just about to suggest we go for a walk when the phone rang, and he made no move to answer it so I did, and it was Dougal again. He made some comment about me being there again but I didn't say anything, just gave the phone to Jamie and went back into the kitchen. I wasn't paying any attention and couldn't really hear anyway, but then I heard Jamie say, "Fuck off!" quite loudly and there was a crash so I went to have a look and he'd thrown the phone against the mantelpiece, but he was already picking it up.

I've never heard him shout like that before and it was a bit of a shock, and he looked really angry. I just stood in the doorway, wondering what had been said. Jamie put the phone back on the table, and flopped into the armchair, and he looked really, really pissed off. Then he realised I was standing there and he apologised, so I asked him what had happened and he just said Dougal's being over-protective again, so I assume he must have said something about me. I said, "He's worried about you," but Jamie just shook his head and didn't say anything else. He obviously didn't want to talk about it so I suggested we go for a walk and, much to my surprise, he agreed.

It was hot out so we walked slowly. I kept glancing at him to make sure he was okay, and I've noticed that he goes pink really quickly in the sun and yes, I think it's cute. I can't wait to see what he looks like with a tan. I wonder if he'll tan, though, being so pale and with all those freckles? I don't remember noticing a tan on him last year. Anyway we walked down to the river and it was only when we got there that he started talking.

First of all he tried to apologise for the way he'd been on Saturday, and I cut him off and told him I'd been upset too and it was only to be expected, and he nodded. Then he told me that they - him and Helen - had known from very early on that Beth would probably not see her teens, because she had so many problems, and that came as a bit of a shock to me. I mean, I know she had several disabilities but I just hadn't thought that any of them were life-threatening. Jamie said that on the rare occasions when he'd thought about it at all, he'd assumed that Beth's condition would deteriorate at some point and that she'd probably pass away in hospital.

I thought he might get emotional again, so I sat on the wall by the weir and he came and sat next to me, and I just let him talk. I tried not to say much because I felt that he was just verbalising his thoughts and trying to make sense of things, and he didn't really need input from me. And it turns out that it's not so much her death that's been such a shock, since they've been expecting it almost from the day she was born, but the way that she'd died, in the back of his car, and the fact that he hadn't even noticed - that's what's tearing him apart. And he knows - or at least has come to accept - that he couldn't have known that it would happen, and that he probably couldn't have done anything anyway, but he'd always assumed that he'd be there, holding her hand. By that point we were both crying again, so I pulled him into a hug and we just got it out of our system.

We both calmed down at around the same time and by then I was really hot, so we got a cold drink each from the stall by the bridge, and then crossed over to the other side of the river to walk in the shade. Then out of the blue he said he thinks he should start clearing Beth's room, and he asked me what to do with her things - the nice clothes, and the toys and books that were still in good condition - so we talked about that for a bit, and then he said he doesn't think he can bear to sell the house, and asked me if I would move in with him, so of course I said yes. We'd walked down as far as the Rowing Club sheds, and we turned back then, and as we were coming away from the Rowing Club, he took my hand. He doesn't normally do that when we're out, so that was a first, and it made me smile.

When we got back to his house we sat in the kitchen for a while with the door open, because it was the coolest place we could find. Jamie rang Elspeth and was on the phone to her for about ten minutes and I heard him laughing at one point, which really made me feel relieved because I'd been worrying that he might fall back into a dark mood once we got back. He went upstairs then, and then when he came back into the kitchen he stood in the doorway for a bit - I was making a salad dressing for later - and when I looked up to see what he was doing he said, "Will you come to bed with me Tasha?" and I swear my legs wobbled. Talk about 'legs turning to jelly'!

Afterwards we were lying there, him with his arm round me and me with my head on his chest, like we usually do, and he said, "I like this part. This afterwards part when we're all sweaty and sticky and messy and you're ..." he paused. "You're here, you're not rushing off to have a shower." and I got this image of poor Helen running to the bathroom to scrub herself clean, and it just makes me so sad for both of them.

The rest of Sunday was fine, and he was okay - a bit quiet, but okay. He had a lovely long chat with Kelly on Sunday evening, and he said next year he'll definitely go to TRSMT Festival with her, so she's really chuffed about that. Then on Monday he was quiet again because he rang around a couple of the other projects and made arrangements for them to have Beth's things for the kids there, and that night he rang Dougal to apologise for cutting him off on Sunday and they had words again, but Jamie just told him straight to mind his own business. He's still not told me what's going on with the two of them, and I'm dying to ask, but I'll wait until he's ready